Cairo Mon Amour

Cairo Mon Amour

Book One of
The Siranoush Trilogy

Stuart Campbell

Contents

About The Siranoush Trilogy

The Siranoush Trilogy comprises the novels *Cairo Mon Amour, Bury me in Valletta,* and *The Sunset Assassin.* The three stories are stand-alone episodes in the tribulations of reluctant British spies Pierre Farag and his wife Zouzou Faris. The couple are exiled from Cairo to London in 1973, and then to Malta in 1975, ending their quest for freedom and anonymity in the northern Australian tropics in 1978.

Siranoush, meaning 'sweet love', is the stage name of a legendary Armenian actress who began her career in Constantinople, but left Turkey after the banning of Armenian plays. Her acting and operatic career continued in Yerevan, Tiflis and Baku. She died in 1932 and is buried in Cairo. Pierre is Armenian on his mother's side; like Siranoush, he is forced to make a life in exile.

I used Siranoush as the codename of the espionage operation that Pierre and Zouzou are enmeshed in during the 1973 Yom Kippur War. By literary chance, Pierre's great-aunt saw Siranoush perform at the Cairo Opera House in 1928.

The novella *Ash on the Tongue,* is a prequel to the trilogy, introducing the main characters in the run-up to the Yom Kippur War between Israel and Egypt. *Cairo Rations* is a collection of essays that I wrote to jog my memory before embarking on the trilogy.

PART ONE: COUNTDOWN TO A WAR

Chapter 1: A Time to be born, a Time to Die

Thursday 27 September 1973

After drinking a coffee with Madame Serpouhi, Pierre took the Nile river-bus south, got off at Mar Girgis and threaded his way through the dusty alleys to the family mausoleum at Old Cairo. His father stared out from the glass photo-plaque in frozen disappointment. And well he might, given that in 1967 he had been bolting across the runway towards his MiG-21 with a mouthful of breakfast as the Israeli jets swept down on Beni Suef airfield and incinerated him along with half the Egyptian air force. Six years now.

And as he usually did, Pierre stopped on his way home for a second coffee and a Cleopatra at the Suez Café, in sight of the Hanging Church, which his father's people had built into the wall of the Babylon Fortress sixty generations ago.

"Cousin! How's your health?" The man with the tray of glasses was one of the many relatives on his father's side, the Coptic side. This branch of the family had owned the Suez Café since Mohamed Aly was in Abdin

Palace.

"As well as might be expected. The world spins, the days pass. What's the news?" Pierre said.

The cousin called to a boy who was polishing glasses in the corner. "Quick, coffee and an ashtray for our guest!" He sat down close to Pierre and looked around the half empty café before speaking in a hoarse whisper. "Things are getting hot. There are some military fellows—I don't know, captains, officers anyway – who come in looking edgy. I hear things, things that worry me. Time to think about the future. Remember '67? War's no joke."

"Dear God, we don't want to see another '67."

The cousin leaned in closer. "What about your mother's family? Don't you have relatives in California? Clever fellow like you, university education, all the languages you speak. They'd find a nook for you over there, those Armenians . . . find a tasty widow from Texas for you to marry."

The boy appeared at Pierre's shoulder and banged a stained ashtray in front of him. The coffee cup followed shakily and the frothy liquid spilt in the saucer.

"Donkey! Take it back, do it again," the cousin roared, cuffing the boy behind the ear. Pierre watched the ritual; the hand had hardly brushed the boy's head. He tried to remember the lad's name—another Girgis or Boutros, great nephew of someone or other. The whole tribe on his father's side seemed to be composed of Georges and Peters; a family of saints.

"We'll see, we'll see," Pierre said. But he wasn't going to America.

The boy came back with the coffee and the ashtray, now polished with a single Cleopatra resting on the scalloped edge. Pierre had almost conquered smoking;

but, thanks be to God, you could buy a single cigarette when you needed one!

The cousin leaned in again. "Just be careful. It's going to be a difficult time for us if the war blows up."

Sure, he could go to California, Nice, Beirut, even Yerevan if he really wanted to. He had relatives on the Armenian side all over the world, and with patience and guile he could obtain residence papers; it was an Armenian skill long perfected. But Pierre never shared his mother's obsession with getting to America. He'd been born here, not in Turkey like his mother, not a refugee, and anyway his father was a Copt – an original Egyptian. Pierre could be anyone with his pomaded black quiff, his nondescript grey trousers, white cotton shirt and brown sandals: a jeweller, a university lecturer, a bank clerk, Coptic, Muslim, Alexandrian Maltese, Greek. He burrowed unnoticed among the folds and wrinkles of the city, never disturbing its texture, never belonging and yet entirely belonging. If anyone had bothered to ask him, "What are you?" he'd have said *"masri"*, 'Egyptian', and they'd have taken him at his word with perhaps just an afterthought. "His father was probably a Jew," or "I reckon a Syrian mother." But nobody asked. "Forget the Cleopatra," Pierre said. At thirty-five he had a smoker's cough that got worse as the Cairo fumes

thickened in the middle of the day and made the city smell like a burnt sandal. "Keep it for next time."

Pierre said goodbye to his cousin and decided to stop at his office to collect some papers to peruse at home in the afternoon. He waved down a rattling taxi. "Ramses Square please, Professor." The driver, a bovine country boy, steered the car like a bullock cart. Funny, Pierre thought, the more ignorant they are, the more elevated the title.

Of course, he didn't need his cousin to tell him that things would be getting tough soon. He saw it all around, especially among his clients; with the vibrations of war everywhere there were loose ends to tie up, debts to be called in, risky relationships to be severed, high officials to be persuaded to look the other way, money to be made or hidden. Just the evening before he'd met with a matron, the wife of a general, in a car in a shady street among the villas by the Nile in wealthy Ma'adi. "You have a reputation for discretion," she'd said, her face covered with a gauzy scarf.

"My clients have always told me so." Pierre waited. No hurry. Madame would get to the point quickly enough.

"You understand that I have very powerful friends. If you were just the tiniest bit careless—you see my point?" Pierre saw the point. He'd done a month in Tora Farms Prison in 1965, grassed up on a false charge by a disgruntled client. It'd cost him five years' worth of

favours to get out.

"May I ask," Pierre said, "whether this is—a family matter?"

"In a manner of speaking. My husband," – she mentioned a name that wasn't unfamiliar to Pierre—"is a very senior military man."

"Please go on, Madame."

"Yes, of course. Let me put it this way: Like all red-blooded Egyptian men, he has his—amusements."

Pierre waited for a few seconds; this man was a big zucchini. "Is the name of the other party known to you?"

"The other party, as you delicately put it, is Zouzou Paris."

The private investigator's mouth was suddenly as dry as roasted chickpeas. Zouzou Paris's pretty mug was all over Cairo. The giant billboard painters had done her proud—skin like milk, eyes like a panda, chest like the prow of a quinquereme. Nobody believed for a moment she was half French. He rolled his tongue in his mouth and managed to croak, "Indeed, great discretion will be necessary in the case of such a liaison. May I ask the nature of the assignment?"

The woman glared at him through the gauze. "Now listen here. My husband believes—not that he reveals matters of national security to me—that he could find himself on the battlefield one of these days. And who knows whether he would come home?"

The story came out in drips. The husband, she suspected, was feeding the family's cash into Zouzou's bank account, perhaps even paying the rent on a nice little villa on the Giza Road. But what if the esteemed spouse was killed in battle? And then what if the lawyers discovered that he had been keeping the *sharmouta* in luxury all this time? How would she bear the shame?

Zouzou Paris, a 'bitch'? Well, she would say that. Everybody else did.

"And do I understand that you would like to see the arrangement quietly terminated?", Pierre asked gently.

"Exactly."

"And do you have any preference for a particular course of action?"

"Just do the job. Up to you. But I want it fixed properly."

* * *

Pierre's office was in a knot of dusty streets near Ramses Station. He squeezed past the metal security grill and into the grubby beige vestibule leading to the interior of the Italianate building. He smelt the doorkeeper's kerosene stove in the closet under the stairwell, and heard the old *bawwab* coughing along with a Lebanese singer on a tiny transistor radio. Up one flight of cement stairs, through an awkward arched corridor, past the steel door, always locked, with the sign 'Studio Susy', and then his door with the little brass plaque in English, French and Arabic: 'Pierre Farag (Bachelor of Arts) Translator and Private Investigator'.

He opened the door and trod on an envelope that had been pushed under the crack by the *bawwab*. It would contain a phone number. They preferred it this way; there would be a meeting in a hotel bar, a heavily veiled story of suspected infidelity or fingers in the till, a soft handshake on the fee, an address, perhaps a photograph.

He put the envelope in his pocket, found the papers he needed—a translation of a court deposition from French into Arabic that was overdue—and went downstairs.

"What's the news, Professor?" he asked the doorkeeper. The *bawwab* put his hand over his heart and thanked God for his good fortune.

"The gentleman who left this for me. Do you remember him?" Pierre held the envelope under the old fellow's nose. The man's eyes were bleary with trachoma, and he was probably illiterate.

"Sir, yes. A man, a chief engineer, suit and shoes."

"Wearing a hat?"

"Exactly!"

"A foreigner's hat?"

"Exactly!"

"With a woman?"

"Exactly!"

"And a leather bag?"

"By God, yes!"

It was useless, of course. But that was the beauty of it; a client could arrive stark naked with their envelope and who'd be the wiser?

* * *

The driver dropped him at Rue Tala'at Harb, five minutes' walk from Pension Serpouhi where he lived; odd how the French terms hung around, even on the street signs. How long had Napoleon occupied Egypt? Just a few years. Pierre joined the stream of pedestrians shuffling in both directions past the shops that seemed to have less and less to sell. Cash was king with the whiff of impending war, especially US dollars, and it was best stashed away; nobody was buying and nobody was selling.

But why not America? Why not leave, leave his dead father and the two labyrinthine families he was descended from? He'd never been outside Egypt—except in his mind, of course, with travelling companions like Victor Hugo and Charles Dickens. But look at his mother—visited her sister in California five years ago and – pouf, a heart attack. His aunt had sent him a photograph of her grave in the Armenian section of the cemetery in Glendale and begged him to visit to pay his respects. She'd pay the fare, he could stay on for a little holiday, spend some time at the country club, get to know her husband's niece Mary. He'd made excuses: too much work, long flight, give it a few months.

Madame Serpouhi's boarding house was quiet. The six professional gentlemen who occupied six of the eight bedsit rooms were either out at work or snoozing, and Pierre went to his little apartment to work on the translation. As Madame Serpouhi's relative and holder of a small share in the key money, he laid claim to superior accommodation with a tiny private bathroom.

He polished up the Arabic to match the ornate French legalese, typed a clean copy, signed it and pasted a twelve-millieme fiscal stamp at the foot of the paper. He heard Madame Serpouhi's girl moving around in the big dining vestibule and the sound of prayers in the street outside; five times a day, twenty yards of narrow pavement was turned into a *musalla*, an open-air prayer hall.

"Fatima, bring me some tea. And some *basbousa* if there's any left."

The stringy country girl fetched a glass of tea and a little semolina cake, and Pierre opened the envelope he'd collected from his office.

Just a single sheet, with two lines of typing. On the first line, an address in Zamalek and the date October 3, six days hence, just into Ramadan. On the second line, '*Vous êtes prié de vous présenter à 20 heures forte*'.

Polite French, spelt properly: Please attend at 8pm sharp

Pierre knew the street, but couldn't place the building in his mind. He nibbled on the syrupy cake and considered. A trap, a ruse perhaps? Had Zouzou been tipped off that he was sniffing around? Would some thug on the fringe of her circle be hiding at the address with an iron bar? Or perhaps a couple of the green security cops, the tall ones with dark glasses? But it could just as easily be a nervous father willing to pay real banknotes to find out if his son was creaming the cash register at the family jewellery shop to pay for whores and whisky . . .

The Pension was waking up after the hot afternoon. One or two of the professional gents had finished their prayers and were roaming around looking for the servant. Pierre heard Madame Serpouhi coughing and cursing the heat. The lavatory flushed four times in succession.

The girl knocked on his door. "Sir, the lady asks if you will take tea with her." If he happened to be home in the afternoon, Madame Serpouhi, his elderly great aunt, liked to hear him read aloud while she lay propped on her couch in her private quarters, smoking—but not inhaling—a Craven A. She didn't mind much what he read, or in what language. With the tea there was always a tiny glass of *zibeeb*, which Madame Serpouhi poured from a bottle in her wardrobe. He peered along his bookshelf; it wasn't Sunday yet, but why not his French Bible?

"Bedros my boy, something to cheer me up." She never called him Pierre when they spoke in Armenian.

"*Ecclesiastes 3 en français.*" Pierre said. "It's simple to understand. *Il y a un temps pour naître, et un temps pour mourir; un temps pour planter, et un temps pour arracher ce qui est planté.*"

"Ouf. It's so morbid. A time to be born, a time to die. When you are my age you want to forget about time. It's fine for someone of your age to talk about death when it's so far away. There's too much dying going on, and they say there'll be more soon. Drink your *zibeeb.*"

"Thank you, Aunt Serpouhi," Pierre said. The sting of the aniseed liquor shook off the torpor of the afternoon. It was his mother's Armenian blood, of course; he soaked up the languages like a sponge. His father had spoken Arabic and a bit of air force Russian, and used to tease Pierre and his mother when they spoke

Armenian. "Okh okh, bishbosh, you sound like frogs!" But patiently you learned, from your Greek friends, from the rich Coptic families who chose to speak French at the table, Italian from a *New Testament*, English and German at university, Russian at the Soviet Cultural Centre, constantly accreting more words and working out the endings and the beginnings, absorbing the patterns, adding the alphabets.

He'd pondered over Ecclesiastes 3 in half a dozen languages, looking for a key to unlock its enigmatic simplicity. He read further. *'Un temps pour la guerre, et un temps pour la paix.'* Everyone knew it was coming. Hadn't Sadat talked about sacrificing a million Egyptian soldiers to get back what we'd lost in '67?

"*La paix,*" Madame Serpouhi sighed. "Not in my lifetime."

"I wish you would go to California, Aunt Serpouhi."

"Ouf, that's where I should be. That's where Armenians have it good. Look at your aunt—big house, swimming pool, Mercedes, Mexican gardener."

"Go on holiday, just for a month. You can get a tourist visa." Pierre knew about the US dollars sewn into her clothes in the wardrobe.

"But I'd have to come back. How can I get a visa to stay for good? And who'll look after this place? Who'll look after my lodgers?"

Pierre said nothing.

He heard the clang of the birdcage lift and the ring of the doorbell. The girl knocked on the door of the private quarters.

"Sir, Madame, there's an officer at the door." Madame Serpouhi glanced at Pierre with unease.

"For me, I expect," he said and went into the

vestibule.

He heard the voice of his old friend Major Ahmad Fawzi of the Cairo Criminal Investigation Bureau outside the door. Fawzi here? He'd never visited Pierre at home.

And then Major Fawzi filled the frame with his uniform; it must be something serious because he normally wore a baggy linen suit. Fawzi was wringing his fingers and looking everywhere except at Pierre. Behind him was a dim looking junior holding an official document as if it were a crystal vase.

"Fawzi, my dear friend. Welcome. But this must be very important. What's the news?"

"Major Fawzi to you, Mr Farag," his friend said. "This . . ."—the junior passed the document to Pierre— "is a warrant for your arrest."

Chapter 2: The People Advance like the Light

Friday 28 September 1973

Most of the people in the departure area at Heathrow had been British emigrants: carpenters and plumbers, wives brightly dressed to fly, sparkly-eyed children going to Australia via Cairo and Bombay.

Who'd blame them? IRA bombs in department stores, cod wars in Iceland, strikes, beer and cigs up. Bellamy had picked up a well-handled *Daily Express* from the departure lounge floor and smiled at the Giles cartoon: A scraggy housewife tells her portly neighbour that if her husband goes on strike, he'll get no sex; the tubby downtrodden husband has come home early from the factory and is blowing his nose while he parks his bicycle in the rain at the side of the house. I'd go to Australia if I were them, Bellamy thought.

He'd scanned the rest of the departure crowd from the corner of his eye: a handful like himself – European men in business suits – a couple of Egyptian family groups, several Arab men in wide-lapelled tan suits and sunglasses. Everybody smoking with airport nerves. He'd taken off his jacket and tie, turned up his shirt sleeves, tried to blend in with the emigrants, lolled on a seat next to a family, crossed his legs and made a holiday face.

Now, hidden in the window seat of the VC10, he considered the present matter: liaise with the Cairo Crime Investigation Bureau, do it by the book, police officer to police officer, get the Briggs business sorted out, come home. The Foreign Office will assist up to a point but Cairo is edgy; any sign of danger, get your backside up to the Embassy in Garden City and on a plane home. We can't help you if you go native.

The young man next to him tried to strike up a conversation but soon tired of Bellamy's curt replies. He gave up and leaned over the aisle to engage his wife and three small children in a loud debate about how near the beach they would live when they got to Sydney. The wife shot a look at Bellamy and moistened her lower lip. Bellamy pulled an eyeshade over his face. The rumble of the engines masked the conversations around him, and he focused his mind on the stream of random chirps and muted shrieks.

Bellamy felt pressure on his arm, an insistent voice intruding into the random noise. "The lady says, do you want refreshments?" It was the young man again.

Eyeshade off, vision of a soft English face below a nest of backcombed hair, BOAC uniform leaning inwards, swell of breast, polished nails, waft of something from Biba that his ex-wife used to wear.

"Can I offer you a drink, Sir?"

"Whisky and soda please." Bellamy flicked open the ashtray in the armrest, lit a Rothmans King Size and studied the reading light in the bulkhead. It was six years since he'd been in the Middle East, a civilian expert attached to the army in Aden, captain's uniform in his locker so he couldn't be shot as a spy if he were captured. He'd been there in '67 when Britain got out of the Empire business for good.

The young man ordered a vodka martini and took a packet of Players No6 from his shirt pocket. He tapped the little packet of working man's cigarettes but it was empty. He glanced sideways at Bellamy.

"Have one," Bellamy said, flicking the top of the Rothmans packet. Worth a try, he thought. Perhaps he'll enjoy his fag and leave me alone.

"Ta very muchly. Are you going on to Sydney?"

"No, Cairo for me."

"Very exotic," the man said. "Is it for a holiday that you're going, if you don't mind me asking?"

"Good Lord, no. Business."

"We're emigrating. That's my wife over there, the kids as well, the three of them. *'In Australia, I will'* – that's what the posters say, isn't it? My brother's already there, but of course he only paid ten quid. We just missed out, it's costing us seventy-five quid each. Still, can't complain."

The wife looked at Bellamy again. The tongue tip flicked across the lower lip. The drinks arrived, the waft of Biba again.

"And where are you emigrating from?"

"Well, England, but we live, I mean we lived in Hatfield."

The man took a swig of the vodka martini and shuddered.

"Blimey, that's a bit sour. By the way, did you say business? What kind of business would that be, if I'm not being nosey?"

"No, not at all. I'm in textiles, up Cambridge way—

importing, that kind of thing."

"What—cloth and so on?"

"Something like that," Bellamy said.

The man ploughed on.

"Interesting work is it, textiles?"

"Can be. Lot of paperwork." Bellamy stubbed out his cigarette and looked at the seat in front.

"Never fancied Egypt myself," the man said. "The wife's dad was there with Montgomery, well not actually with him, he was a mechanic. Horrible place he said it was. Never knew where you were with the gyppos. One minute it's all smiles and lick your boots, next they're stabbing you in the back. We went to Spain once. Ever been there?"

The wife, in purple hot pants, eased herself out of the middle aisle seat to go to the toilet.

"Sorry, Spain, no never," Bellamy said and finished his drink. "I'd better get some sleep." He pulled on the eyeshade and sank into a state of half wakefulness, his mind flitting from the wife with the wet lip to the briefing in Ealing; and to the fourteen months in Aden in '66 and '67. His thoughts drifted to the hut, stifling hot, heavily guarded; Bellamy and the two silent Americans, headphones clamped to their heads, and their brains full of crackle and Arabic; the whistling as the radio frequencies were squashed and stretched by the shifting atmospheric layers above the junction of the salty Gulf of Aden and the fecund land mass of South Arabia. Writing it all down in English.

* * *

Briggs. Or perhaps it was Blenkinsop or McTavish or Abd El-Qader. The name didn't matter. A man in Cairo bearing a UK passport in the name of Briggs had been found badly beaten up, somewhere he shouldn't have been.

"I'm at liberty to tell you no more than you need to know," the woman had said. *Country Life* type – tweedy, fiftyish, no wedding ring. The meeting took place in a gloomy office at the end of an interminable corridor with walls thickly painted in a custardy gloss. The drizzle made sooty runnels down the window panes. Why Ealing, he'd once asked. Why in an annexe of the Department of Social Security at the end of the District Line?

"And you require what exactly?" he asked the woman. "Bring Mr Briggs home please. Alive, if you don't mind."

"Isn't it a consular matter? Like those people who break their necks skiing at St Moritz? You don't send out a solicitor masquerading as a police officer every time someone gets into a fight on their overseas holiday."

The woman shifted in her tweeds and looked into the fireplace where the gas jet flickered behind a device that contrived to give the effect of glowing coals.

"There are some . . . obstacles as far as the Embassy is concerned. And I don't need to remind you of your former involvement with us, so perhaps you could please drop the disingenuous advice."

"You're dead right that I don't need reminding of my former involvement, thank you. What do you mean by obstacles?"

"Those are not your concern. And please don't ask questions that you know I will not answer. The task is simple. There is a warrant out for Briggs's arrest in the UK, for murder. He is known to be dangerous. You will liaise with the police authorities in Cairo and have him transported to Cairo Airport. You will accompany him back to London."

"With no involvement by the Embassy? Won't that seem odd?"

"Just let us worry about that. I'm going to leave you with this folder. Please read it carefully and leave it on the desk. In one hour somebody will escort you to the exit."

And that was it. Not a 'good luck', 'splendid to have you back' or even 'goodbye'. Just the click as the woman locked the door behind him. The gas jet was losing the struggle against the sepulchral air. He wished he'd brought a scarf.

There wasn't much to the documentation. The name of his contact in Cairo was a Major Ahmad Fawzi: born 1930 in Tanta, an English graduate from Ain Shams University, and a steady climber through the ranks of the Cairo Criminal Investigation Bureau. There had been a secondment to the army in 1966, and a file note mentioned a couple of meetings with a suspected Israeli agent – an Egyptian air force officer. But there was no source and no corroboration. A muddy newspaper photograph of Major Fawzi showed a portly, balding man in uniform pinning a medal on a younger man. There was no address or telephone number for Fawzi; he would contact Bellamy at the Nile Hilton.

Of Briggs there was nothing but a description and a full-face photo. Six feet two, forty-five years old, light brown hair, muscular build, no distinguishing marks. Briggs—or Blenkinsop or McTavish—peered glassily from the photograph. The hair was longish, Brylcreemed back, and curling behind the ears. A fairground-ride operator's face: pugnacious, not too bright.

And for himself there was an envelope containing a passport, a Cambridgeshire Constabulary warrant card, a ticket to Cairo, three-hundred pounds in cash, and a fake letter of introduction from the Chief Constable. He scrabbled through the file looking for a cover story, something to outline the life of Detective Sergeant Clive Rogers. Not our problem, the Country Life woman would have said. You make it up. We don't need to know.

Bellamy sighed and walked to the window. A phalanx of buses waited patiently in the grey drizzle as a squad of office workers in plastic macs crossed at the traffic lights. One bus bore a poster for the *Rocky Horror Show*. Bellamy had seen it at the Royal Court back in June with a woman he came down to visit in London occasionally. He lost focus on the street and thought about that warm night, the nudity on the stage, the transvestite costumes, the raucous Australians in the tiny auditorium, drinks afterwards in the Kings Road and a tipsy walk to her flat in Battersea across Chelsea Bridge . . .

The door clicked. A man in a cardigan came in.

"All done, Sir?"

"All done."

"I'll just get you to sign for the travel documents, if it isn't too much trouble."

Bellamy signed and pocketed the envelope.

"Before you go, Sir, just a couple of tips that my colleague wanted me to pass on, if you wouldn't at all mind."

"Fire away. I need tips."

"Righto. First of all, Cairo is in a bit of a fizz, what with the build-up of arms and so on. If things go," and the man raised his open palms towards the ceiling and clucked his tongue, "there will be very limited help from the Embassy. In the event that you absolutely must obtain their help, the only person you may liaise with— and I stress the only person – is Victoria Patchett. Nobody else will assist you."

"And if I ask you who Victoria Patchett is you'll tell me that she's a librarian in the cultural attaché's office?"

"Yes, I imagine I'd say something like that."

The man carefully checked the documents that Bellamy had left on the desk, slid them into a briefcase and locked it.

"And one more thing before I take you to the exit."

"Yes?"

"Detective Sergeant Clive Rogers doesn't know a word of Arabic."

* * *

Bellamy felt the VC10 begin the descent. He pulled off the eyeshade and looked around. The woman in hot pants was struggling to prise two of her children apart as they fought over a fizzy drink, and the husband was comforting the third, who was crying with earache. Bellamy lit a cigarette and looked out of the window, where scant lights could be seen below. The Delta. They passed over some big towns; Benha, Damanhour, perhaps, Bellamy thought. And then the dots of lights became clumps and the clumps separated into roads, and roads gave way to tarmac, and the VC10 was bumping along the runway with its engines screaming in reverse.

The lines at the immigration barrier were anarchic, with hundreds of people wheedling around the core of each queue. At each desk a forest of arms attached to tragic pleading faces thrust passports towards the immigration officer; the core responded by consolidating and moving forward like a rugby scrum to squeeze out the queue jumpers.

A hand touched Bellamy's shoulder. "Come wiz me. VIP exit." A man in a shirt and tie took Bellamy's wrist and led him to a door. A knock, the door briefly open, the shirt and tie gone, the door slammed shut, two green uniformed officers at a desk in a windowless room.

"Passport please," one of the officers said in English. While they each took turns examining the document, Bellamy took the opportunity to examine the officers. He'd heard about them—an elite police force that handled security matters and serious crime—university graduates, taller and better nourished than the cops who directed traffic.

"Your business in Egypt?"

He handed over the letter of introduction made out to Major Fawzi. The English speaker read the letter and translated it into Arabic for his colleague.

"He's a detective, it says. Here to take someone back to England—a fellow with a UK passport. Someone called Fawzi's meant to help him. It looks official."

"He could be an Israeli, anything at all really. I don't like it. Who's this Fawzi?"

Bellamy looked dumbly from one officer to another.

"Will this take long?" he asked.

"We must make some questions," the English speaker said, and picked up the telephone.

Bellamy stood and smoked while the man tracked down Major Fawzi. He worked his brain hard to catch the rapid Egyptian speech, disciplining himself not to reveal his comprehension. After fifteen minutes of phone calls, the officer was through to Fawzi.

"There's an Englishman here. A detective . . . yes, yes,

Rogeerz, that's his name . . . do what with him? . . . But, Sir, we don't have the authority . . . who? . . . yes, Sir, that's our boss . . . by God, yes, Sir . . . I'll do it . . . thank you . . . yes, right away . . . at your service."

He turned to his colleague and said, "He's trouble. This Fawzi wants to see him right away. I'm to take him to an address in El-Duqqi."

"And who's this Fawzi exactly?"

"One of the clowns from CIB."

Bellamy said nothing as the officer led him into a cubicle where an immigration official stamped his passport, and then into the luggage hall where a handler plucked his travel bag from the carousel. The police officer beckoned to him towards the exit.

"I just need a taxi please," Bellamy said. "To get to the Hilton. That's where I'm staying."

"Of course, of course, I take you in my car."

"I'd prefer a taxi."

The officer ignored him. Bellamy shrugged and followed him outside, where a wall of taxis and buses packed the airport forecourt and the warm night air stank of aviation fuel and smoking engines. A sedan pulled up and the green uniformed officer barked at the driver, "El-Duqqi, quick." He gestured to Bellamy to get in the back with the travel bag, slid into the front seat with the driver and rapped on the dashboard.

Bellamy said nothing, just watched as the dim streetscape flitted past the windows. As they approached the city centre the car stopped at traffic lights and a knot of children with chains of jasmine flowers and paper screws of peanuts tapped on the car windows. Up ahead was a huge hand-painted cinema billboard. Bellamy picked out the name of the black-eyed starlet—Zouzou Paris – and then they were off again, weaving past the Abdin Palace, along Muhammad Mahmoud Street, across Tahrir Square and onto Qasr El-Nil Bridge. The Hilton was left behind on the east bank of the Nile. Time to say something, Bellamy thought.

"Excuse me. I think we've just passed my hotel." No response.

"Look here, I'm a UK citizen. I want to go to my hotel. Please turn around and go back." Still no response.

Bellamy had never been to Cairo before but he'd spent hours converting the big yellow Michelin map into a mental plan and then driving an imaginary car back and forth across the city. They'd cross Zamalek island next, the upmarket green suburb of embassies and film stars, then El-Duqqi.

The car slowed outside an apartment building. On the corner was another billboard—this one with a grinning boy quaffing Sinacola, Egypt's home-grown coke. Somebody had thrown a dollop of something black at one of the boy's eyes.

The police officer brushed off Bellamy's protests and said, "No, leave ze baggage," when he tried to retrieve his travel bag from the back seat. An elevator took them up twelve floors and an apartment door opened. A kowtowing house servant led Bellamy and the officer into an ornate salon, bowed and backed out. A rococo chandelier threw a yellowy light onto the overstuffed sofas and the carved sideboards inlaid with mother-of-pearl. Behind a massive desk of polished black wood sat—true to the press photograph—Major Fawzi.

"Out. Wait in the corridor." The green uniformed officer glared at Fawzi and stiffly retreated.

"Welcome to Cairo," Fawzi said in English. "And

apologies for your method of arrival. I wanted to make it, *ya'ni*, discreet." His eyes were steady, a slight frown on the brow. The Major inhaled an enormous lungful of smoke from a crackling cigarette.

"Please sit – yes, there in front of me."

An Egyptian could speak English for a thousand years, Bellamy thought, but they'd never conquer the *ya'ni* habit. The universal filler gives time to think, softens the edge of hard words, draws the interlocutor in . . .

"Would you like to see my letter of introduction, Major Fawzi?"

The Major raised an eyebrow a fraction and slightly extended the hand that was not holding the cigarette. Bellamy had to lean forward to pass the letter over.

Major Fawzi took another lungful of smoke and perused the letter. Bellamy glanced at the crushed pack of cigarettes; Cleopatra, the Egyptian Queen's silhouette on the gold wrapper. The smoke issued in two perfect jets from the fat man's nostrils, dissipated and melded with the fug surrounding the desk.

"Please – excuse my rudeness." He pushed the pack towards Bellamy, who lit up. His throat burned.

Major Fawzi let the letter flutter to the desk.

"Is everything clear, Sir?"

"Perfectly clear. You are a senior detective from Cambrig-shire."

"Cambridgeshire."

"Apologies. I majored in English but *ya'ni* these English place names are illogical to pronounce."

"Your English is excellent."

"Indeed, perhaps. Now, you have been ordered to take Mr Briggs home—that is your mission?"

"Correct. And are you able to put me in touch with him?"

"Indeed. In fact, I have assigned one of my best officers to work with you." He picked up a telephone and asked for somebody called Zaki to come in. Bellamy played with the foul cigarette. The door opened and the house servant ushered in a fellow who seemed barely out of his teens. He wore a baggy cheap suit and plastic sandals.

"Please let me introduce Mulazim Zaki."

"Pleased to meet you, Mulazim." Bellamy extended a hand but the young man darted an anxious look at Major Fawzi. The Major's stern face remained unchanged. "So sorry, *mulazim* means lieutenant. He is *Lieutenant* Zaki." The Lieutenant slipped his hand into Bellamy's and swiftly withdrew it, so that it almost disappeared into the sleeve of the oversized suit.

"Do you speak English, Lieutenant Zaki?" Again the nervous look at his boss.

Major Fawzi took over.

"He is a top-drawer officer. One hundred per cent. Young but smart. And in English, *ya'ni,* faultless. Your programme begins tomorrow when you will visit Mr Briggs in the hospital with Lieutenant Zaki. Please await him in the Hilton lobby at 8am. Thank you so much. We will now organise transport to your hotel."

The Major stood up and abruptly walked out of the room with the Lieutenant in fretful pursuit. Another door opened and the house servant ushered in the green-uniformed officer from the airport.

* * *

Pierre Farag stood at the window of the apartment's dining room and looked across the Nile. At 11pm Tahrir

Square was seething, and the honking of cars was relentless. He heard Fawzi dismiss somebody.

"The servant will show you out, Zaki. Make sure you're on time for the *khawaga* at the Hilton tomorrow."

The Major came in. He took off his uniform tunic and took a baggy linen jacket from the back of a chair. "It is inexcusable, Pierre my friend. I embarrass you by arresting you in your own home. I drop mysterious hints while I dash from room to room. I leave you here to graze on—" and here Major Fawzi swept a hand in the direction of a spread of stale cakes and wilted salads.

"Ahmad, I haven't been in the least inconvenienced. It was a pleasure to be arrested by an old friend and forced to enjoy these delicious snacks while I gaze at the best view in Cairo for five hours. Now, are you about to enlighten me on why I am so cruelly detained?"

"Pierre, my life has become one of obfuscation and deceit. If I simply ask you to tea, my colleagues will be asking, 'who's this private investigator Fawzi's cosying up to? Doesn't the chump trust his own people?'"

"Go on."

"But if I arrest you, I can say, 'we need to give these private operators a scare now and then, keep them in their place. That one will be keeping his head down for a while'."

"I hope that doesn't mean that I'll be going home with a black eye."

"You'll go home with my blessings, as ever, but it won't hurt my reputation if you say you got a whack, if anyone happens to ask. At any rate, aren't you going to ask me who the apartment belongs to, Pierre?"

"Let me try to guess. The *mukhabarat*, of course, but who specifically?"

"Close enough, Pierre. All you need to know is that one of the big zucchinis makes this place available to the General Intelligence Directorate."

Pierre widened his eyes and made an 'o' with his lips.

"So I'm not here just for the canapés? And if I may be permitted, since when did you work for the GID?"

"I don't work for them. Let's say that I work with them. And indeed, no, you're not here for the canapés or the *basbousa* or the yoghourt salad. Not for me, not for the *mukhabarat*, not for Queen Cleopatra's excellent cigarettes."

"This is a mystery indeed, my brother. Should I be feeling a mite anxious about what you are about to tell me?"

"Anxious? Armenians are never anxious. You just calmly beetle around, getting things done without worrying about anything."

"I'm Egyptian, Ahmad. My father was a Copt. He died for Egypt in 1967."

"You have my deepest respect for your patriotism. Nevertheless, you think like an Armenian. Sideways, upside-down, all the angles."

"You are too generous in your praise, Ahmad, and too modest. You've seen more angles than Pythagoras ever dreamt of."

"Enough! Let's agree that the Egyptian mind is a wondrous organ, the sacred possession of its united people, whether they are Armenians, Muslims, Copts or Greeks . . ."

"Or Jews . . ." Pierre said.

"Or Jews, of course."

"*The people advance like the light, the people stand like mountains and seas . . .*"

"No need to overdo it, Pierre. And don't think I'm impressed because you know the last verse of the National Anthem. Would you mind passing me that bowl of *tabbouleh*?"

"Why am I here, Ahmad?" Pierre said. He gave the soggy *tabbouleh* a turn with a fork and handed it to his friend.

"I need a job done." "Why me?"

"Discretion. Invisibility. There's an issue. A matter. A problem. When I think I've got my finger on it, it slips away. I need someone I can trust, someone who can move independently."

"Independently of whom, of what?"

Major Fawzi pressed his palms to his brow. "Trust is long gone in my profession, my friend. I no longer know if my staff are working for me, for the Syrians, the Americans, the Israelis, for the man on the moon."

"Was it ever different, Ahmad?"

Fawzi sighed and rolled up some *tabbouleh* in a piece of flatbread. The stale bread crumbled and the bits of parsley and grains scattered on his paperwork. He swept the food to one side and lit a Cleopatra.

"Yes, it was different in '52 and '56. It was different, by God! We knew who the enemy was and what we had to do. I can still hear Nasser's voice. Those speeches! Simplicity and grandeur all at once, the way he swelled everyone's hearts with his words. Poetry!"

Pierre said nothing. It hadn't been quite so simple for a half-Armenian half-Copt. The Bedrossians had gone to California in '52, and a whole clutch of Coptic cousins had got out in '56; wealthy optometrists in Sydney now, the lot of them.

"What do you want me to do, Ahmad?"

Major Fawzi slowly shook his head and gazed at his big hands. He looked up at Pierre. "What does Siranoush mean to you?"

"Siranoush. Where on earth did you get that from? It's an Armenian woman's name, of course. A beautiful name. It means 'sweet love'. But this will appeal to your poetic side, my dear friend. The most famous Siranoush was an opera singer—the greatest ever from Armenia. She performed right across Russia and the Caucasus in the last century—Baku, Tiflis, Iran too. She lived here in Cairo in her later years. My mother saw her perform at the Opera House in 1928."

"A dead opera singer, indeed. So why does the old lady's name keep popping up in places it shouldn't?"

"What places?" Pierre asked.

"Informants, snitches, insiders, you know how it works. Was she as sweet as her name, this Siranoush?"

"So my mother said." Pierre waited.

"This is your mission, Pierre, for Egypt. A job for a patriot. A beautiful duty. You will advance like a light, but of course not so brightly that you are observed. You are to find what this Siranoush is all about. Now let me tell you what I know, and believe me, it's precious little."

Chapter 3: School for Spies

Friday 28 September 1973

Lieutenant Zaki was fidgeting on the edge of an armchair in the hotel lobby. The Hilton seemed to be many steps above his salary band. He jumped up to greet Bellamy but seemed unsure how to proceed. The hand shot out and withdrew, and he settled for a type of salute.

"We're going to the hospital?" Bellamy asked.

Zaki nodded and turned, threading his way through the couches where foreign tourists bedecked with camera gear waited for tour guides.

A driver in dark glasses waited by a dusty Mercedes in the forecourt, and they were off, heading northeast but soon squeezing in and out of side streets and alleyways. Bellamy was quickly disoriented. He craned his neck upwards to find a landmark as they turned into a street of auto workshops where small boys, black with grease, lugged gearboxes and bent fenders across the broken pavements, and men in grimy vests bashed oil drums into exhaust pipes. Then they shot out of an alley into a residential area with blocks of peeling flats that sat atop a street of shops and sidewalk vendors and junk dealers.

The car stopped for a crowd watching a band of blind musicians; a small girl in a red dress whirled to the music and her relatives touted among the crowd for change.

The Mercedes began to move slowly as the crowd parted. Leaving the suburb, they hit an arterial road, but Bellamy couldn't read the direction signs fast enough as they gathered speed. After twenty minutes of construction sites, weedy paddocks and roadside stalls, they turned into a large compound of low concrete buildings connected with external walkways, and a car park with rows of ambulances and taxis.

"Is this where I'll be able to see Briggs?"

Zaki looked confused, and Bellamy realised that the man hadn't spoken a word of English so far.

"Briggs. Is he here?"

The young man jumped out of the car, gesturing at Bellamy to stay put. He walked towards a blockhouse and talked to the military guards by the boom gate. The driver of the Mercedes turned to Bellamy and said in English, "Sir, you will see Mr Briggs very soon. Please be patient."

Zaki returned with a sheaf of papers, and Bellamy and the driver followed him into the compound. The military guards at the entrance pointed to one of the larger blocks.

The hospital seemed to have been vacated. Ward after ward stood empty, the doors sealed with paper tape. Zaki led them through endless walkways, speaking to the driver in Arabic. Bellamy made no sign of understanding their speech.

"Is it far?" Bellamy asked, and the driver replied, "Almost there, Sir."

"And why is the hospital empty?"

The driver replied, "Sir, it has been evacuated because of infection."

"What infection?"

"I don't know the word in English." He and Zaki resumed their conversation, and Bellamy heard the word *al-kuzaz* several times.

Bellamy sorted through the stock of Arabic words for diseases; they always confused him. *Al-kuzaz*: Measles? Diphtheria? Rabies? No – it was tetanus! But that didn't make sense; hospital patients didn't infect each other with tetanus.

After what seemed a mile of walkways and empty wards they reached a scene of bustle and efficiency, with a nursing station, a full ward, and doctors quietly working beside patients on metal cots. A female doctor introduced herself as a captain—in excellent English.

"Why is Mr Briggs in a military hospital?" Bellamy asked.

"I should explain, Detective Rogeerz. This is a civilian hospital. The army was brought in to close down many wards for cleaning because of infection."

"And Mr Briggs? Can I please see him and organise his discharge? I have to take him back to London."

The doctor frowned.

"I advise that he is too ill to be moved. You may see him but I cannot let him leave yet."

"And when can he leave?"

"It could be *ya'ni* two or three weeks. I suspect he has brain damage."

The doctor led the party—Bellamy, Zaki and the driver—to the end of a long corridor where a guard stood outside a single door. Inside the room they stood at the bedside of a bandaged and intubated man. Only his nose was visible. Bellamy said to the doctor, "Do you have a tape measure?"

The doctor sent Zaki to the nursing station.

Zaki's footsteps returned along the corridor. He came in and handed a tape to Bellamy, who felt gently for the toes of the person in the bed.

"Please hold it there," he said to the driver, and then laid the tape along the body so that he could read off the measurement at the crown of the head.

"This man is ten centimetres too short. Now can I please be taken back to Major Fawzi for an explanation?"

* * *

Zaki and the driver dropped him at the Hilton and made off at high speed. Bellamy punched the pillows, chucked his shoes at the wall, swore a lot, and then told himself to grow up. He took stock. The feeble Zaki, the enigmatic driver, the empty wards they were so eager for him to see, the bogus Briggs, the lack of any means of contacting Major Fawzi—it added up to absolutely nothing.

Of course there was never any need to know. No need to know how the people in Ealing had learned about Briggs's fate, no need to know whether the source was reliable. Because of the sword that hung over Bellamy's head they could pluck him out of the offices of Freund & Bellamy in Halifax any time they chose, and tell him to get on a plane. Go and buggerise the Vice Nabob of Turdistan? Right away. Shall I kiss his arse on the way out? Spend a week in Tangier interrogating a talking parrot? No problem, I'll go easy on the thumbscrews! That had been the deal. No prosecution under the Official Secrets Act for ten years in exchange for occasional 'consulting' services. "We won't overdo it. We do understand that you have to make a living," they'd said.

He roughed out a plan. Relax during the afternoon heat and study the Michelin. Take a walk later in the day to get his bearings, feel the pulse of the streets and retune his ears to Arabic. When darkness falls, head back to El-Duqqi and find the apartment block near to the one-eyed boy drinking Sinacola.

Lying on the bed with the gritty hum of Cairo drifting through the balcony doors, Bellamy unwound the knots in his shoulders, and the big Michelin slipped from his fingers. He found himself, as he so often did, overlooking Beirut from the terrace at Shemlan. The locals called it the 'spy school', but the Middle East Centre for Arabic Studies took all sorts—business people, diplomats, researchers; you just didn't ask too many questions.

The people at Ealing had picked him out in his last year at London University. Double major in Law and Arabic, stellar marks. You won't have heard of us but Britain can use a person like you. Do your articles first; we can help you find a law firm, and once you're qualified you come to us and we'll put you on our payroll. Just don't get too comfortable, no encumbrances.

He'd ignored their advice and married Angela as soon as they graduated. They'd moved from London to Halifax where he'd spent a year at Freund Associates doing his articles. Of course she'd been stunned when he told her he'd be resigning and going to MECAS for a year.

"You're telling me you have a job that I know nothing about? I came all the way to this nasty northern town so that you could get your law career started. So I'm to sit here saying 'ee bah gum' all day while Lawrence of Arabia is studying the Perfumed Garden in Lebanon?"

"The Perfumed Garden isn't in Arabic—"

"I know that, you bastard. It was the first bloody oriental book I could think of."

"I should have explained."

"What is this job anyway? Are you some kind of spy?"

"I can't talk about it."

And he didn't have to because Angela was gone the next day.

* * *

At the *Asr* call to prayer Pierre rose from his siesta, put on pyjamas over his singlet and undershorts, slipped into *shibshibs*, and went into the empty dining room of Pension Serpouhi. It was the second day of Ramadan, and the professional gentlemen would break their fast at one of the nearby restaurants after the sunset prayers.

"Bring me some hot water, if you please, Fatima." He would make tea in his room. There was *kunafa* and *ishta* in the fridge, and Pierre thought to ask her to bring him a slice of the syrupy golden pastry with a dot of zinc-white buffalo cream. But later; no point in making the girl uncomfortable for the sake of a bit of sticky cake.

It was just a matter of time until one of his informants would be in touch.

"I can't trust my bunglers to keep an eye on the *khawaga*," Fawzi had said. "Pierre, you will be my keen-eyed hawk in this affair. But don't let him see you in the sky."

He returned to his room with the tea, and smoked and worked on some papers for two hours until he heard a tap at the outside door. The *bawwab* held out an envelope containing a brief note. The Englishman was on the move, according to Pierre's distant cousin on the Armenian side, who worked at the Hilton reception desk. Pierre telephoned his relative from Madame Serpouhi's tiny office.

"On foot towards Garden City? Blue shirt and panama hat? Thanks, my boy."

The Ramadan cannon sounded and the *maghrib* prayer washed over the city from a thousand minarets.

Pierre dressed and took a taxi to the intersection of Sa'ad Zaghlul Street and Al-Qasr Al-Aini Street. He started to walk back along the broad avenue towards the parliament building. He soon spotted the English detective, his measured British stride obvious among the Egyptians ambling to get to their evening meal.

He crossed the road so that he and Bellamy would pass one another after about fifty metres. Seconds before they passed, a small boy in a robe jumped out of a doorway and said something to the Englishman, who looked at his watch and made as if to speak to the boy, but then apparently changed his mind and strode past.

Pierre crossed the road and doubled back two hundred metres. The light had almost faded, but he collared another small boy—there were plenty of them lurking in the entrances to buildings and guarding cars.

"Here, see the *khawaga* in the hat? Go and ask him the time and see if he understands. Just walk up to him under the street lamp. Here's three *ta'rifa* for you."

The boy hid the five millieme coins somewhere in his robe and sidled along the railings outside the parliament. A few yards from the Englishman the grubby lad leapt out and said, "*sa'a kam?*", but the man walked on.

Well, Pierre thought, it's inconclusive, but when has anything in this city ever surprised me?

The English detective walked on as far as the bridge

at the north of Zamalek Island. He turned to cross the bridge in the direction of the University at Giza, but evidently changed his mind and walked back towards the Hilton. At Tala'at Harb Square he went into Groppi and found a seat in the far corner of the old-fashioned tea-room, which was packed with well-to-do families.

Despite Pierre's commonplace appearance, he judged that it could be risky to follow; he knew nothing of the Englishman's surveillance skills. To be spotted at this stage would put him at a disadvantage.

There was a delivery entrance in the alley behind Groppi. Pierre entered and made his way to the kitchens.

"Electrician," he said to a pastry chef, and fiddled with a light fitting by the swinging service door until a waitress came in with a tray of dirty dishes.

"Ask Amina to come out here. Tell her it's Pierre."

A plump young woman with a cloudy eye appeared. "It's the *khawaga*, I suppose, Sir?"

"Did you take his order, Amina?"

"Yes."

"What did he say exactly?" Pierre asked.

Amina repeated the order in mauled English, "Tea wiz milk shocolate kek."

"He asked in English?"

"Yes, Sir. I have to go back now."

"Very good, but just one thing. When he asks for the bill, give me a wave. I'll be by the news stand across the street."

He bought two newspapers at the Hachette kiosk—*Al-Ahram* and a ten-day old weekly edition of *Le Monde*—and leaned against the wall so that he was out of the Englishman's line of sight. He watched Amina wait at the tables. She was an ex-call girl, forced out of the business when an unhappy client squirted bleach in her eye. Pierre had fixed her up with new papers and found her a job. Now she provided him with scraps of information and gossip. After half an hour, Amina waved through the window display of French pastries. He knew where the Englishman would go next; the man had no other options. Pierre crossed the road and stationed himself in a doorway thirty metres back from Groppi. The Englishman came out, hailed a taxi and got in. Pierre was in a cab within thirty seconds and gave the driver an address in El-Duqqi. The other taxi was in sight, six cars ahead.

But the gap between the cars quickly increased until the Englishman's taxi was out of sight. And then the traffic locked up and there was a crescendo of horns. Pierre gave the driver some small notes and began to walk around the obstruction. It was a *zabbal*, a rubbish collector from the vast slum in the Moqattam Hills, his donkey laden with baskets of stinking kitchen trash. The creature was gasping on its side, trapped under a van, and the man lay in the muck with a broken leg.

A hundred yards on, the road was clear and Pierre flagged another taxi. By the time Pierre's cab had reached the street in El-Duqqi, night had fallen. He gave the driver some notes and told him to wait for an hour.

"Do you have a watch, Professor?" Pierre said.

"No, Captain."

"Well, if I'm not back soon, you can go."

"At your service, Sir."

Pierre hugged the shadows by the buildings, making his way towards the apartment block a hundred metres away. He passed the building, took the next side street on the left, then left again, intending to emerge where he'd begun. The streets were quiet here; the wealthy residents kept themselves barred in their apartments. He turned left again and completed the square. Nobody. Was it likely that the Englishman had penetrated the apartment block?

He set off again, but instead of walking past the building, turned into its entrance and pressed a bell-push on the polished wooden double doors.

"Yes?"

"Electrician."

"For who?"

"Emergency. There's a fault in the street. Your building's going to lose power."

Something was pressed inside the building and one of the doors swung inward with a loud buzz. Pierre entered and huddled in the angle of a wall, but glancing back he saw somebody slip in just before the door swung closed. It was the Englishmen. Pierre bent down to tie his shoe, and heard the *khawaga* mutter in English, "Thanks, forgot my key." The man brushed past in the direction of the doorway leading to the stairs. The ancient *bawwab* came out of his cubicle and called after the Englishman, "Take the lift, Sir," but he was already halfway up the first flight of stairs.

"Typical *khawaga*. They're always in a hurry. Don't they ever just take it easy? Now, you'll want to see the electricity panel. Your lot were round here yesterday. Nothing works these days, not like when the British Army ran things."

The *bawwab* scratched something inside his *galabiyya* and went back to the football match on his radio in the cubicle, while Pierre hung around the electrical cupboard in an alcove next to the stairwell. After ten minutes he heard the Englishman descend the stairs with Anglo-Saxon purposefulness. Pierre hid his head deep in a switch-box as the man passed him and exited the building. Thirty seconds later he closed the metal cover and opened the front door. There was the Englishman, twenty metres away, striding towards the intersection with the big Sinacola sign. Pierre's taxi was still at the kerb, and the driver got out.

"Just wait," Pierre said to the driver and crouched behind the car.

"Israeli spy!"

Pierre strained to see where the shout had come from.

"Israeli spy!"

He spotted them. A gang of scruffy young men were approaching on the opposite side of the street. The leader yelled again, picked up a piece of broken flagstone and flung it at the Englishman, who turned and ran towards Pierre's taxi. A shower of stones and small rocks was now peppering the man; a larger piece struck him on the back of his head as he reached the car. Blood flowing down his collar, he picked up a piece of rock, squared up and yelled, "Try it again, you bastards!"

Pierre called to him, "Sir, come away. These people are dangerous," and as the Englishman turned to see where his voice had come from, a substantial chunk of broken concrete sailed across the street, hit him on the back of his shoulder and brought him to his knees. Pierre took him under the armpits.

"Open the door!" Pierre shouted at the driver, and lugged the Englishman onto the back seat. He turned to face the gang.

"*Bani sharmouta*. Shame on you!"

The gang looked at each other and shrugged. The leader picked up a bit of rusty steel, but threw it down. He looked around at the other thugs, tossed his head and sauntered away.

"Can you get me to the Hilton?" the Englishman groaned.

"You'll cause a very unpleasant scene if you turn up at the Hilton looking like that," Pierre said. "Let me take you back to somewhere you can clean up. Come on, it's just ten minutes' walk from your hotel."

You'll be my keen-eyed hawk, Fawzi had said. Better the sly fox, Pierre thought.

"Ramses Square, Professor," he said to the driver. "I'll direct you to the place when we get there."

* * *

The Englishman was wearing Pierre's jacket over a string vest and had a square of sticking plaster behind his ear. A pad of bloodstained cotton-wool rested on the tiny sink inside an open cupboard. Pierre unfolded a white short-sleeved shirt from the change of clothing he kept in his desk drawer.

He'd got the taxi driver to drop them directly outside his office doorway. The half-blind *bawwab* greeted them, and Studio Susy was locked as usual.

"Just leave the shirt at the Hilton reception desk and I'll have it picked up. Now have another ten minutes to rest before you go. You're probably a little wobbly on your feet."

"I'm very grateful. You're the man on the sign outside, I gather?"

"Yes, I'm Pierre Farag. Translator."

"That explains your excellent English. And do you do much private investigating?"

"Oh, nothing much—the odd divorce case." Pierre switched to Arabic. "And does Egypt please you?"

The Englishman looked blank.

"So sorry. I'm something of a polyglot and I get my tongues mixed up sometimes. I hope you don't think me rude if I ask you what you are doing in Cairo."

"I'm a detective. Rogers is my name. From England. I'm taking a British suspect back to London."

"A suspect indeed. Has he done something especially reprehensible?"

"Nothing very interesting at all, as far as I know. Look, I'm very appreciative of your help, but I'd better go."

"I'm so sorry, Mr Rogers. Let me turn away while you change."

Pierre looked at the square of filthy stairwell outside the tiny window. Perhaps he'd been too hasty in rescuing the Englishman; so what if he'd been worked over by a gang? The man was well-built and muscled, and might have made his escape; these Cairo street thugs were vicious but they may have been wary of tangling too closely with a foreigner.

But were the gang just a bunch of shiftless nobodies? Was the Englishman a casual target, or were the thugs working for somebody? Fawzi, perhaps? Nothing happened without a reason, especially now the city seethed with plots and counter plots. What had Major Fawzi said about the Englishman? Just a clumsy foreigner.

"Maybe," his late father would have said, "but it's a big maybe."

The one thing Pierre knew was that to survive in this city you needed the kind of information they don't print on the front page of Al-Ahram. He was sure that the Englishman was a much more valuable asset alive than on a slab.

Chapter 4: Does that Cockroach have Clearance?

Sunday 30 September 1973

Bellamy bent towards the bathroom mirror and peeled the sticking plaster from behind his ear. The scalp looked as if it had been worked on with a cheese grater but it was dry and healing. Thank God the shoulder wasn't dislocated, but the flesh at the back of the collarbone was purple.

Today was Sunday; would Major Fawzi and the nincompoop Zaki be at work today? As for the translator, Pierre, Bellamy didn't believe much in coincidences; he'd recognised him as the man with the oiled quiff he'd seen prowling around the apartment block and opening the front door.

He called room service and ordered a large breakfast to set himself up for the day. Better in Ramadan to eat in your room during the fasting hours; that or guiltily stuff your face in the area of the restaurant specially curtained off for the barbaric *kuffar*. He'd rest up, work through the events of the last two days, sort out in his mind who was who and make a plan for tomorrow.

But after breakfast he lay on the bed and blew smoke

rings at the ceiling. Bugger the plan. He'd had enough. He'd sort out the Briggs mess as best he could, get back to England and confront the people at Ealing. Call their bluff. See if the threat of prosecution had any stuffing in it.

He'd never been shown any evidence of the allegations against him, of course. He'd arrived home from Aden in 1967 with two weeks' leave in his pocket before he needed to report back to Ealing. There had been a ring on the doorbell on Saturday morning. Two ex-warrant officer types made it clear that they weren't going to wait to be let in. They settled into his sofa and opened identical black briefcases.

"I am to inform you," one said, "that you are suspended from duty until further notice."

"And," the other said, "I am to inform you that you are under investigation for a breach of the Official Secrets Act."

Bellamy felt queasy. He swallowed hard. His mouth was dry and his tongue stuck to his palate when he found some words. "What am I supposed to have done?"

"All in good time, Mr Bellamy."

The morning proceeded like a grotesque theatre where all but one of the actors knew the script. The security men asked a series of questions about Shemlan. The first set concerned everyday matters: the location of his room, the layout of the MECAS building, the mealtime routines. Sometimes the question sequence backtracked.

"I think I answered that question before."

"Just confirming, Mr Bellamy. We like to be thorough." Another set of questions concerned his fellow students: their names, their employers, their nationalities. After an hour Bellamy said, "Can we cut to the chase?"

The men looked at one another and raised their eyebrows.

"I'm not sure that you appreciate the seriousness of this situation, Mr Bellamy," one said.

"The thing is," the other said, "You're in shit up to your nasty armpits, so just pipe down and listen."

"At any rate, we are about to cut to the chase as you put it," the first man said. "Can you please tell us what your relationship was with a student called Lucy Vickers?"

"We were friends."

"Close friends?"

"Close enough."

"Did you have sexual relations with Lucy Vickers?"

"That's my business."

"No, Mr Bellamy, it's Her Majesty's Government's business."

"You see," the other man said, "when you take the King's shilling, your wick is not yours to dip wherever you wish."

"Spit it out, for God's sake. What have I done?" Bellamy said.

"Let's just take this one step at a time. How many times did you have relations with Miss Vickers?"

"Depends on what you mean by relations."

"Don't muck around with us, Mr Bellamy. I'll rephrase. On how many occasions did you meet with Miss Vickers for the purpose of engaging in sexual relations?"

"Once. We met up in London when we were both on Christmas leave. We spent a weekend at a hotel on

Kingsway."

"And what happened afterwards?"

"We lay back and smoked French cigarettes."

"We could arrest you right now and you'd be smoking very thin roll-ups for the next twenty years. Just answer the question. You've had your fun."

"You obviously know what happened. I went back to Shemlan after the break but she didn't show up."

"Did she tell you who sent her on her course?"

"She worked for a bank," Bellamy said.

"And did you tell her who you worked for?"

"Of course not."

"Are you sure?"

"Yes."

"You see, Mr Bellamy, here's the problem. Lucy Vickers didn't work for a bank at all. And all the evidence points to a serious leak of information."

"Not from me. Christ, where did this all come from? We spent a weekend in bed. That was it."

The men stood up. One of them said, "Somebody will be in touch with the outcome."

* * *

He'd seen Jean-Luc Godard's *Breathless* when he was at university, and she reminded him of Jean Seberg playing Patricia, the American student who sold *The New York Herald Tribune* in the Paris streets: short blonde hair, slim, impetuous. They'd been top students, overtaking the rest of their class at Shemlan. Each day the students took their customary seats, Bellamy on the left towards the middle, Lucy Vickers on the right at the front. They shared glances as they studied, competed for the instructor's praise and smiled across the room at the struggles of the other students to produce a sentence of decent Arabic. A couple of days after the beginning of the course Bellamy asked if he could share her table at lunch.

"You're good. Where did you study?"

"Durham," she said. "And you?"

"London, School of Oriental and African Studies."

She made a low whistle in mock admiration. "Branch Office of the Foreign and Colonial Service, and last refuge for the relics of the Raj!"

"It wasn't quite like that. But you're on the right track. What do you do when you're not here?"

"Accountant. I'm being trained up to go to Bahrain. And you?"

"Government, nothing interesting really. This and that."

"OK, I get it," she said.

They struck up a friendship that was a shade more than professional, meeting at coffee time and lunch, edging towards an intimacy that could attract the wrong kind of attention at the School for Spies. The idea of the Christmas break had come out of nowhere; Bellamy couldn't remember who had suggested it. But it was efficiently and discreetly arranged. They would fly to Heathrow on different days, check into hotels on different sides of London—he at Harrow, she at Richmond—and then meet two days later at Kingsway. It wasn't that Bellamy felt that an affair with a MECAS student was against some regulation or other; rather, he'd learned that you kept your business to yourself in this game.

By the end of the weekend they'd discovered a good deal about one another, at least in their taste for sex, food and alcohol. When she left on a wet and blustery

Sunday evening Bellamy knew nothing about her family, her origins, her work. But he sensed that, like himself, Lucy felt it had been more than a weekend fling. He stayed on at the hotel in order to fly back to Beirut from Heathrow in the morning. She said she'd go back on Tuesday. "There're a couple of people I need to see at the bank before I fly."

After she had left he decided to end the evening with a pint. But his wallet wasn't in his jacket pocket or anywhere else in the hotel room. He broke out in a sweat; the wallet had contained his identification pass for Ealing. The joke in the office was that if you lost it you might as well defect to Cuba—you'd be in less trouble. It was a bland thing: a photo, a serial number and 'Invalid Pensions Review Section' on a square of paper, laminated in a clear plastic sleeve. But it got you past the hawk-eyed security pros and into the custard painted corridors where every sentient being was cleared as Top Secret; one of the office jokes was 'Does that cockroach have clearance?' And of course, his driving licence and three or four other bits of identity were gone; the lost wallet was a do-it-yourself kit for someone to make a fake ID.

He quelled his panic and laid out the possibilities in a kind of mental game of patience. The wallet had dropped out of his pocket at the Indian restaurant they'd been to for lunch the day before; he'd left it in the room this morning when they'd gone for a walk to clear their heads, and a maid had stolen it; his pocket had been picked somewhere. In a futile effort he telephoned the Indian restaurant but the staff hadn't seen it. He sat on the bed and bent his head to his knees. Could it have been Lucy? He thrust the thought from his mind; honey traps were for spy movies.

"Idiot, bloody idiot, bloody, bloody stupid idiot."

His airline ticket, a chequebook and a few pounds in emergency cash were still zipped into an inner pocket in his suitcase; the hotel desk would make a fuss but he'd convince them to take a cheque on Lloyds bank in Halifax.

He called the memorised number for emergencies and within an hour he was with one of Ealing's cardigan brigade in a Wimpy Bar in Fulham.

"Not to worry too much, Sir. These things happen. Could I get some brief details about how the pass was misplaced?"

"I've no idea. It was in my wallet. It doesn't make sense. I've been here all weekend and I either had the wallet in my inside pocket or beside the bed."

"Think carefully, Mr Bellamy."

"All that comes to mind is a pickpocket." He laughed uncomfortably. "But that's a bit far-fetched. Sounds like something from Dickens. I was in a very crowded pub, on the other hand. Somebody could have pinched it."

"And which pub would that be?"

Bellamy mentioned a place in Sloane Square and the man jotted it down.

"Were you with anybody, Sir?"

"I was alone."

"Very good, Sir. That'll be all."

He flew back to Beirut, anxious to gauge Lucy's reaction when he mentioned the wallet. But she didn't turn up on the Tuesday or any other day.

* * *

Bellamy had had four years to reflect on the folly of the decision to lie to the man in the Wimpy Bar about Lucy Vickers. The warrant officer types were right. Someone did contact him a week after their visit, and he found himself in an office in Whitehall facing a straight-backed man in an old-fashioned chalk-striped suit.

"Our investigation has concluded there is sufficient evidence to charge you under the Official Secrets Act."

"All right. I'll put my hands up to lying about Lucy Vickers, or whoever she was, but I'm not some kind of double agent. I haven't sold secrets to anyone. The whole business is preposterous."

"Mr Bellamy, a court may not quite see it that way. Please consider this. You spend a clandestine weekend with a woman who has lied about her job and whose loyalties are, let's say, not to Her Majesty's Government. Coincidentally, your identification pass and other personal documents disappear on the same weekend. You lie to an investigator when questioned about the loss of the pass. And on top of all that, certain information about your work in Aden has been intercepted on a communication channel where it had no business to be."

"You're stitching me up."

"No, Mr Bellamy. I hesitate to use such a vulgar expression, but in this case it is apt; you have stitched yourself up."

"Tell Ealing to get lost. Nobody's been prosecuted under the Official Secrets Act for years."

"And nobody wishes to see a prosecution."

"So what do I do now?"

"What do you do? You do as we say." The man studied a document. "In fact, our employers have seen fit to treat the matter with pragmatism and, I should say, more generosity than you deserve. They have invested large resources in your training, and they prefer to reap a return rather than write you off."

"And the catch?"

"Go back to Halifax, Mr Bellamy, and be a solicitor. Mr Freund will offer you a partnership. It has been arranged."

"It can't be that simple."

"It's very simple indeed."

"And what do you get out of letting me go?"

"It's simple, Mr Bellamy. Ten years. We want ten years."

* * *

Just after midday the call-to-prayer jogged Bellamy from his thoughts. As the prayers ended there was a knock at the door.

"Yes?"

"Service."

A waiter was at the door holding a tray on which there lay a flimsy blue airmail envelope. Bellamy gave the man a couple of coins. Inside the envelope was a postcard of the Pyramids bearing the handwritten words 'Cairo Museum 6pm'. He examined the writing carefully: block capitals, drawn with precision to disguise the idiosyncrasies of a flowing hand. He called the reception desk.

"A letter was just brought to my room. I want to send the person a reply but they didn't write their address."

"Do you happen to know who delivered the letter to the hotel?"

There was a delay while questions were asked in the lobby. Bellamy thought he heard *kan fi walad*, 'there was a boy'.

The receptionist came back on.

"Sir, I am informed that a street urchin handed the letter to the doorman. I hope that you were not inconvenienced."

"Not at all, thank you."

"At your service, Mr Bellamy."

In the six years since he'd agreed to the deal with the man in Whitehall, he'd carried out five assignments, and this had been the pattern: He'd be dispatched to the Middle East with vague instructions and a half-cock cover story, sent from one rendezvous to another, messed around by local contacts who didn't seem to know why he was there. He had no spy craft, as they called it in novels; he'd been originally employed for his language skills. The debriefs when he returned home left him no wiser about the nature of the assignments; the threat of prosecution left him in no position to press for answers about his role in the advancement of Great Britain's interests.

But the Briggs affair wasn't running true to form. There was an edge of menace, a sense of ill intent, a feeling of unease; by sneaking round the empty corridors in the apartment building in El-Duqqi, he'd taken an unnecessary risk; the hospital with the deserted wards had left him unsettled and curious; and who was Pierre Farag, the man who dressed his wound in the seedy office near Ramses Station?

Although he'd never felt in real danger until this assignment, he knew how to look after himself. He'd learned that as the council-estate kid who won a scholarship to the private school in a mock Medieval castle on the hill above the town. He learned the right tricks to merge into the tribe of upper middle-class boys, quickly mimicking the fruity accent and just as easily ditching it when he returned to the Rankin Road Estate after school. He learned to defend himself from enemies on both sides of the dual carriageway that separated the rulers from the ruled. He was 'posh cunt' on the estate; 'scholarship scrounger' behind the battlements. Mark Bellamy fought his class war on two fronts and usually won. When a history teacher wrote on the board, Nietzsche's words, 'That which does not kill us, makes us stronger', he copied the sentence down and inked it into the inside flap of his school satchel.

* * *

At a quarter to six, Pierre Farag stood in the shade of a great palm tree in the Cairo Museum forecourt. It was the fag end of a warm day, and the traffic fumes stuck to his lungs like tar. He reached for the single cigarette in his inside pocket, but then changed his mind; the Ramadan cannon hadn't sounded and it didn't do to smoke before sunset. He amused himself by listening to the sweating tourists plodding in and out of the museum forecourt. A snatch of French here, American English there, and Russian, of course; there were still thousands of Soviet advisors in Egypt despite Sadat's florid announcement that they'd all been kicked out last year; it played well to the populace.

You saw the Russians in Nasr City, big and blonde, buying cabbages. Pierre was here for a rendezvous with one of them—Ivan Maksimovich Zlotnik, who worked at the Soviet Cultural Centre. They'd been meeting there once a week for the last year. Pierre taught Zlotnik Arabic for an hour, and Zlotnik instructed Pierre in Russian over sweet tea and his peculiar *papirosi* cigarettes with the plug of tobacco at the end of a cardboard tube. But a month ago the Russian had suggested they meet in a restaurant. "They are doing building work at the centre, it's too dusty," and they had switched their meetings to lunch at the Estoril, where the head waiter always found them a private booth. It was evident that the centre was being put into mothballs, but Zlotnik still had a job.

Pierre was not naive enough to believe that his Soviet friend came to these meetings merely to brush up his beginner's Arabic; whatever his real job was, it wasn't arranging art exhibitions and looking after the library. And of course Pierre's interest went beyond improving his fumbling Russian. It was no accident that they both reverted to fluent English when the topic of conversation flowed into gossip about who was up to what in the senior ranks of Cairo bureaucracy.

At about ten to six there was a slight commotion on the street outside the museum. An ambulance reversed slowly into the forecourt gates and stopped, blocking the foot traffic. Passers-by stopped and peered through the blacked-out windows; if you saw an ambulance in Cairo the emergency was probably over hours ago, just like the fire service, well-known for turning up when the building had been reduced to ash. Two men in white coats stepped out of the back doors with a stretcher and chased the onlookers away, and then leaned against the vehicle, scanning the crowds.

At five to six Pierre spotted a lone foreigner striding into the forecourt; he was alarmed when he made out the features of the Englishman. The man stopped by the statue of the Sphinx and looked around. Pierre slipped further into the shade and peered down at a paperback, observing the Englishman from under his brow. The man seemed to fit his role as an English policeman, out of his depth in an alien city. With his customary habit of never taking anything at face value, Pierre had considered whether the detective persona was a cover. Perhaps the thugs in El-Duqqi had been half right; even some prominent Egyptians were rumoured to be working for Mossad. But if this man was a covert intelligence officer—Israeli or otherwise—he was either a very good actor or he'd failed basic training.

The English detective walked to the entrance of the museum, still peering left and right, evidently here for a rendezvous. He stood outside the main gate, scanning the forecourt, and dabbed at the sticking plaster behind his ear. There was a tap on Pierre's shoulder, and he turned to greet Zlotnik. They embraced—fraternal kisses on the cheek seemed to traverse their cultures— and greeted one another in a multilingual jumble. When Pierre turned to observe the Englishman again, there was a crowd on the museum steps looking down at a prostrate form.

"Ivan Maksimovich, give me a minute please."

He dashed to the entrance, but was overtaken by two men in white coats. The crowd parted and the stretcher bearers hurtled down the steps with the Englishman, apparently unconscious, swaying between them. The ambulance revved up and sped off.

"Friend of yours?" Zlotnik asked.

"No, no."

"Of course not. I couldn't help noticing how the ambulance service has become so remarkably efficient."

"Perhaps it happened to be passing."

"Yes, probably."

The pair walked briskly across Tahrir Square towards Tala'at Harb. The Ramadan cannon sounded.

"What shall be the topic of our talk this evening, Pierre? Art, science, history?"

"I think it's your turn to propose the topic." In truth, Pierre's mind was elsewhere.

"Opera then," Zlotnik said. "In fact I've been doing

some reading on the opera in Egypt."

"There's Aïda, of course . . ."

"Indeed, but I became very interested the other day when I came across the story of an Armenian opera singer who performed here in Cairo in the twenties."

Pierre was suddenly very interested.

Chapter 5: City of the Dead

Monday 1 October 1973

Pierre arose before the dawn call-to-prayer, after a night of disturbing dreams interlaced with waking moments where he recalled the body of the English detective lolling on the stretcher. His dreams often involved flight from indistinct danger, alternating with blissful relief, the nature of which was too elusive to grasp. He would wake in the early hours trying to disinter from his subconscious the last moments of dreaming, only for them to fall away like grains of sand between his fingertips.

His decision to leave the Englishman to his fate troubled him. But what could he have done? Called the police? He laughed bitterly at the idea. Mentioned it discreetly to Major Fawzi? In fact, he did what he always did. He mulled over the event, considered how knowledge of it might advantage him or endanger him, and placed it carefully in a corner of his mind with all the other events, names, dates and places that made up the tools of his trade. His business was information – other people's information.

And he regretted that impulsive dash towards the

museum steps in plain view. It was impossible that somebody hadn't observed his behaviour, hadn't noted it in a small book, hadn't filed it away for future advantage. He visualised a figure beneath a palm tree swiftly dashing the words down, the loops of the *sīn* and the *shīn* flattened to a mere dash, the dots above the letters just a tickle of ink.

sīn, *shīn* . . . the first and last letters of Siranoush.

Zlotnik had come across the opera singer by accident, he'd said over dinner.

"A charming story, and an obscure but fascinating example of the connection between our countries. I found some references to her in Russian in our library."

The Soviet adviser meandered around the account of the singer's life as they ate fish with *tahina* and fried aubergines in yoghurt. Pierre listened politely, questioning points in the story here and there.

"You say she played Hamlet, Ivan? How extraordinary!" The Russian cleared his throat and gave a coy look.

"Haven't we forgotten something?"

"The patronymic of course. So easy to forget. Ivan Maksimovich—there, much more correct."

Zlotnik smiled approvingly. "Now, where were we? Yes, Siranoush, she did indeed play Hamlet, but it was her Ophelia that was celebrated from Moscow to Baku."

Pierre thought carefully while he served his friend a helping of *fattoush* salad, making sure that the slivers of baked bread remained crisp.

"Don't toss it too much, Ivan Maksimovich. It will go soggy."

"Another Stella, Pierre?"

The waiter brought a bottle of beer. It was flat, and

Zlotnik sent it back.

"A sign of the times, I fear; the alliance between Egypt and the USSR is losing its fizz."

Pierre shrugged. "My friend," he said, "we're both men with—experience of the twists and turns of bureaucracy."

"What do you call bureaucracy in Arabic—*rasmiyat*? Such an apt word, and so hard to translate into English—*officialnesses*, perhaps."

Pierre blinked at the Russian's talented use of English.

"Ivan Maksimovich, *rasmiyat* is *rasmiyat* all around the world. I was thinking more of the hidden corners where men like ourselves might transact affairs best kept out of public view."

"The dark corners of politics, perhaps?" Zlotnik said. "A dark corner where an Armenian opera singer might be discussed over dinner?"

Zlotnik put down his fork and dabbed his fingers on a napkin. "A dark corner where an arrangement might be discussed."

"An arrangement?" Pierre said. "A matter of several parties agreeing on a course of action?"

"Precisely. And I am in need of somebody who I can trust to advance the matter, somebody with discretion."

This wasn't the first time Pierre's discretion had been commented on in recent days.

"And of course I have US dollars at my disposal. Now, we have forgotten our lessons. Shall we start with Arabic or Russian?"

"*Russkii, tovarishch*," Pierre said. "*Ochen khorosho!*"

* * *

Bellamy came to with a jolt. His right cheek stung, then the left as a hand slapped it. Through foggy vision he saw a woman in a white coat bent over him. Widening his view, he saw the dim interior of an ambulance with oxygen bottles and racks of medical equipment. As his senses reengaged he heard the grind of the transmission, smelt hospital alcohol and saw a cannula in the back of his hand.

"Don't move." He recognised the woman as the captain at the hospital. Wriggling, he found he was strapped to the stretcher.

"Fuck you!"

She slapped him again, this time hard enough to rattle his teeth. "You'll speak to an Egyptian officer with respect. I'm not one of your Western whores."

"Where are you taking me?" Bellamy said.

She pulled the cannula from his hand and he winced. "That is not your concern. You'll go where we take you."

The ambulance lurched around a corner, hit several bumps and slowed to a crawl. The windows were tinted, but Bellamy realised that the background noise of hooting cars had stopped.

"I need water."

"Wait. We are almost there."

They stopped and reversed for a short distance, and the ambulance engine was cut. The back doors opened to reveal two of the green-uniformed police. They pulled the stretcher from the ambulance and engaged the gurney wheels. Bellamy looked up at a star-spread sky with a crescent moon. Looking sideways he could pick out the shapes of small buildings in the gloom. He heard a man shout, "Who's there?" somewhere in the black silence, and one of the police yelled, "Get away, son of a bitch, don't come near. We are armed!"

"Who was it?" the doctor asked.

"Thieves, murderers, Ma'am. Who knows in the '*Arafa*?"

The cemetery? Bellamy craned his neck again. The doctor had switched on a portable electric lantern. They were inside the open courtyard of a tiny house with metal grilled windows and haphazard brickwork. The lantern threw enough light to reveal a narrow cobbled street beyond the courtyard entrance. The road was lined with small houses and shrines; a crumbling wall was graffitied with 'long live the 1923 constitution'. He could smell frying food on a waft of warm air, then he heard a dog bark.

In the centre of the courtyard was a large square obelisk carrying the names and dates of deceased people in sweeping Arabic script. It made sense now. He visualised the big yellow Michelin. He had no idea how long he'd been unconscious, but the hooting cars he'd heard a few minutes ago convinced him that they hadn't gone far from the museum. His mind cleared. They were in the 'Arafa, the City of the Dead, the great sprawling cemetery that bounded the southeast corner of the metropolis. He'd read about it. The streets of houses built for the dead, where relatives came to picnic next to the tombs, and where the desperately poor and the outcasts took up residence in a macabre slum.

The doctor unstrapped Bellamy and he sat up on the gurney. His head swirled and he vomited on the trousers of one of the officers, who muttered, "Son of a bitch, I'll punch his teeth in." Bellamy knew he dared not show that he understood the officer's speech. He feigned a cough and braced himself for a blow.

"No, no hitting," the doctor said. "You are meant to be professionals and you'll behave as such under my command."

"Yes, Ma'am, at your service," the officer said in a voice oiled with sarcasm.

"Now help him inside and onto a chair."

A large part of the tiny room beyond the courtyard was occupied by a rectangular stone tomb. In the light of the lantern Bellamy saw three kitchen chairs, a cardboard box of a dozen or so whisky bottles filled with water, and a kerosene lamp. There were a few chipped cups and a brass *kanakah* for making coffee. He looked at the doctor and saw a long black skirt and yellow blouse under the white coat. A sliver of memory came back; the woman tripping on the museum steps, falling against his shoulder, the sting of a syringe in his thigh.

"What did you give me?"

"That's not your concern, but you might feel nausea for a few hours. The cannula in your hand was the antidote. We have a bucket."

"I suppose it would be pointless for me to ask for the British Embassy to be told that I am here?"

The doctor frowned and removed a sphygmomanometer from a bag. She took his blood pressure and said nothing. Turning to the glowering officers, she said in Arabic, "He is fine. I need to go now. You're clear about the instructions? I don't want any mistakes."

The men nodded and the doctor left. Bellamy heard the grind of the ambulance gearbox, and then, again, the barking of a dog in the distance.

One of the officers handcuffed Bellamy's left wrist and attached the empty cuff to a length of chain bolted to a stout iron bracket on the side of the tomb. The officer placed a whisky bottle of water on the floor to one side of the chair and a plastic bucket on the other. The officer made a charade, pointing with his fingers. "Drink—zis one. Shit—zis one."

Short of making off in the dark attached to half a tonne of Ottoman bones, the prospect of escape looked very slim, even if Bellamy whacked one of them with the bottle.

"What's the chance of a cheddar sandwich with a bit of pickle?" he said in English.

The officers looked at one another and shrugged. "I think he wants food," said one in Arabic, and play-acted putting food in his mouth.

"Want eat?"

"Yes, want eat, you idiot."

The other officer pointed at his watch.

"Eat later."

The two men pulled their chairs to the doorway facing the tomb across the street, lit cigarettes and began to chat. Bellamy tuned his hearing to their speech, latching on to phrases, ideas, key words. He was good at this; no, he was a bloody expert, the best in his unit in Aden. The Egyptian accent threw him—*g* instead of *j*, the *sh* jammed onto the end of the negative verbs. But Bellamy's mind filtered the unfamiliar speech patterns into something he could make sense of.

"How's the family?"

"Thanks be to God, my boy's recovered."

"What was it?"

"The doctors weren't sure. Maybe the same thing they've got in the hospitals."

"I heard someone say tetanus, but it can't be true."

"By God, you're right, my brother. It's a cover up— maybe typhus or something and they're keeping it secret."

"Ha! They whine about the breeze around their turbans, but what about the farts in their drawers?" one officer said bitterly.

"And we're the ones sniffing their farts. Anyway, what's this all about with the *khawaga* back there?"

"Don't ask me. Let's just do the job and get home in the morning when Sarkis and Salim take over."

"Hey, move over a bit. Your trousers stink of sick."

"Up your backside, brother."

Bellamy called out, "Hey, food. Eat now."

One of the officers ambled outside. Bellamy saw him turn left into the gloom. There were faint voices, and then the smell of frying again. Bellamy could discern the voices of a young woman and an old man, but the words were too faint to catch. The officer came back and gave Bellamy a lit cigarette.

"Eat soon."

After a few minutes a bent and bearded man in a *galabiyya* entered the courtyard with three tin dishes, his eyes on the ground.

"Leave the food and keep your mouth shut, old man."

Bellamy and the officers silently ate stewed beans and *falafel* in the warm night air. After the meal the men laid a blanket on the ground and pointed.

"Sleep now."

"Need piss!" Bellamy said, and the officers looked away while he used the bucket.

"They say these *khawagas* aren't circumcised," one said.

"You won't catch me looking, you queer," the other said with a chuckle.

Bellamy tucked the chain over his shoulder, found a

hollow in the dirt floor for his hip and closed his eyes.

* * *

He judged it was around 5am when the morning shift took over. He woke, cold, sore and nauseous, to the sound of vehicles parking outside the courtyard, and saw the angled beams of headlights sweeping across the tomb. Two new green uniforms traded banter with the night shift, who went outside. A vehicle did a three-point turn outside the courtyard, and the headlights blinded Bellamy for a few seconds. Blinking, he saw a figure silhouetted against the dazzle. As the vehicle drove away, the figure moved into the circle of yellow light thrown by the battery lantern on the tomb. Bellamy's eyes adjusted to see a thin pale civilian, wearing dark glasses despite the fact that dawn was yet to break. He wore a grey polyester safari suit. The man was in his late fifties and carried an aura of grim authority.

"Get him on the chair and tie him up. Hands and feet! What's been going on here all night?"

"We just arrived, Sir. We weren't here last night."

"Shut up and give me a light. What are your names?"

"Lieutenant Sarkis and Lieutenant Salim, Sir."

Sarkis lit the pale man's cigarette while Salim pulled Bellamy into the chair. The short stretches of wakefulness during the night had given him time to formulate tactics for any eventuality. He'd thought through the scenarios—a bashing or torture of some kind—and decided that he had to give them something. It was a lesson well learnt in his school days, when his contradictory status as scholarship scrounger and posh cunt had led to ambushes on both sides of the bypass.

But he risked at least the overture of a beating if his

captors were to remain ignorant of the fact that he understood most of what they said. He calmed his heart and visualised the second hand of a clock; how long could he last when it started? Twenty, thirty, forty seconds?

Salim opened the proceedings by forcing Bellamy's arms behind the chair and binding them with electrical tape. The officer then taped his ankles to the chair legs so that his unprotected belly and crutch invited a punch.

"Hey, come on. What are you doing? What do you want?"

The pale man inhaled on the cigarette as if it were manna. He leant over Bellamy's face, exhaled a foetid lungful, and called to the officers in Arabic, "Get a rag and water."

Bellamy forced his body to remain still, his face impassive. He'd heard about water torture; the Yanks had banned it in Vietnam. There were the grainy black and white photos—men strapped to a board, their covered faces being filled with water; and horrific variations with tubes and funnels. If he could just endure the first bout, he would give them enough to make them stop.

One of the officers took two whiskey bottles from the box and gave them to the pale-faced man. The other officer shoved the chair backwards and Bellamy's body slammed onto the flagstones. The rag was flipped over his face and he was at once in a writhing, choking hell, screaming through water and vomit. The chair was tilted upright and the pale man put the bottles on the ground.

Bellamy panted and dribbled. His nostrils and throat burned.

"I suppose you think we are barbarians, Detective Rogers." The pale man's English was smooth and barely accented.

"Do you?"

Bellamy said, "I don't give a toss whether you're a barbarian or a bloody baboon. You can't do this to me."

"Baboon, indeed. Do you know how many Algerians died under water torture by the French baboons?" the man asked.

Bellamy hung his head as he struggled to control his heartbeat.

"I'm here to collect some information." He'd give them this much.

"We are talking about espionage then, Detective Rogers?"

"No, we're talking about discretion. I'm here to find out what one of our people was doing. A personal matter." Bellamy visualised the pathways open to him, narrowing with each admission he made.

"Mr Briggs's personal matter?"

"I can't say any more. If you want to kick me out of Egypt, call Victoria Patchett at the Embassy and she'll be pleased to arrange it."

The pale man put his hands in his pockets and walked around the courtyard, poking at pebbles with his shoes. He lit a new cigarette, coughed deeply, and cocked his head at the men gripping the chair. Bellamy was flung backwards forty-five degrees and held rigid. The wet cloth was flicked over his face.

"Just hold him there. No more water for now."

The pale man switched back to English.

"You are an intelligent man, Mr whoever you say you are. You have two choices. I can continue to pour water on you, and you'll eventually tell me the truth. Or you can simply tell me now. You see, I am not a barbarian."

A cascade of ideas from the night before danced in Bellamy's mind; there was no prospect that he could withstand a second dose of the water treatment. He coughed up something sour. An idea was forming; if he knew almost nothing of his mission, then he'd make something up that they'd find hard to check in a hurry. He put his mind into overdrive.

"Briggs used to work at the British Embassy in Benghazi. He had a relationship with the wife of an Egyptian businessman in Libya."

"A relationship? An adulterous relationship? With an Egyptian woman?"

"She isn't Egyptian—she's Italian," Bellamy gasped.

"And?"

"Briggs was becoming unstable, crazy. The staff were worried about him. The woman approached the Embassy—discreetly of course—and told them she was concerned. She flew home to Cairo."

"And your friend followed?"

"Yes, he took a hire car cross-country from Benghazi." They'd be hard pushed to check this in a hurry.

"Why not a plane?"

"I imagine he must have wanted to keep his journey secret."

"An ardent lover, indeed," the pale man said. "And your task is?"

"To persuade him to give up this woman and get him home as soon as possible."

"And this is the job of a detective?"

Briggs said nothing. This naive charade was going nowhere. There were no more pathways left, or at least none that were remotely plausible. The pale man removed his dark glasses and looked into Bellamy's eyes for a few seconds. He said in Arabic, "This is shit."

He put the glasses back on, trained the black lenses on Bellamy for what seemed a full minute, and then said in English, "Well, that's all fine."

He ordered Sarkis and Salim to untie Bellamy. Sarkis pumped up the kerosene stove, spooned powdered coffee and sugar into the *kanakah*, and topped it up with water from the bottle that Bellamy had been spared. It was still dark.

Bellamy rubbed his wrists and wiped the muck off his face with his sleeve. He looked down and saw that he had pissed himself. He accepted a cigarette and a tiny cup of coffee from Sarkis. The pale man drew up a chair and sat opposite him.

"You are a man of courage, Detective Rogers. I admire this quality. You know we modern Egyptians curse the British for their treachery and calumny." He stopped as if to admire his lexical handiwork. "Yes, calumny."

Bellamy dragged on the cigarette.

"But," and here the man waved a finger, "we have admiration for the traits that we Egyptians share with our former colonial masters. Courage, fortitude, resilience."

The pale man stopped to suck the last nourishment from his cigarette. The first ray of dawn light caught the wall behind him and he ground the butt into the floor.

"Detective Rogers. I regret this little—procedure," he said, waving vaguely in the direction of the wet cloth. "But as you will understand, I bear a solemn responsibility to guarantee my nation's security. You entered Egypt with doubtful credentials, but I am satisfied with your explanation. You are free to go."

"Go? Now?" This was making less sense by the second.

"Not quite now, *ya'ni*. We need to complete some formalities—mere paperwork—and my staff will take you to your hotel. We will have Victoria Patchett arrange to visit you there. Perhaps you would sit there for a short while." The pale man indicated the raised tomb.

The three Egyptians went outside—to pray, Bellamy guessed. Sarkis and Salim came back in, packed the chairs and the coffee kit, and carted it outside. As daylight began to flood the courtyard, the colours and textures of the *'Arafa* tomb house emerged: worn sandy-grey stone blocks, the chipped and cracked remains of reddish-brown flagstones on the dirt floor, uneven and misshapen coffee-coloured bricks roughly mortared together.

Soon there was the sound of another car pulling up, and Bellamy saw the pale man enter the courtyard, chatting to a younger man with swarthy skin and an unusually large gold watch. The pale torturer came into the tomb house and said, "You'll be riding with us, Detective Rogers," and beckoned him into the street. Bellamy could now see a stone forest of monuments, domed shrines and miniature houses. Truly a City of the Dead. Three vehicles were parked outside the tomb house.

The pale man instructed the two lieutenants to drive a Jeep and a Peugeot back to A*lqaeda*—the base—and opened the back door of a Mercedes for Bellamy. They set off with the dark man at the wheel and the pale man beside him.

Bellamy's senses were working at a frenzied rate. The passing dusty streetscapes, the loaded goods carts and the robed pedestrians appeared in supersaturated colours; his nostrils were full of his own stink and stale tobacco from the car seats; through the open window came a stream of sound bites—a siren, a hooting truck, a snatch of music from a radio at a sidewalk stall, the shouts of men. But he was suddenly jerked into focus by the men in the front seat speaking in Arabic.

"So it's fixed then?" This was the dark man.

"It's fixed. Third of November, God willing," the pale man replied.

"Where did you get this from exactly?"

"Better you don't know. But just get your affairs in order. There'll be danger, and we'll be involved. Remember '67?"

"You don't have to tell me. Anyway, I know about your little friend in the leader's office."

"Keep your mouth shut. I'm only telling you because you're family. I want my grandsons kept safe. Send them to Beirut for a holiday perhaps," the pale man said. "They're going to announce a special army sports carnival on that day, but you won't be packing your football boots."

"Operation Full Moon—it's been a long time coming. At last we're going to whack the bastards," the dark man said. "What about him in the back? Should we be talking about this?"

"No, he's just a dumb *khawaga*. Doesn't understand a word. Couldn't ask for a fuck in a cat house. But remember, third of November. And not a word to your wife. She might be my daughter but you know how women's tongues wag at that club."

The pale man twisted in his seat and addressed Bellamy in jaunty English. "My British friend, look smartish, we are approaching your hotel."

"Son of a *sharmouta*," he said to his son-in-law and both men laughed as Bellamy shuffled out of the car and through the big glass doors. He pressed the elevator button and a wall of exhaustion slammed into him.

* * *

The bedside phone woke him. It was 2pm. He had a huge thirst—the drugs they had forced into him?

"Yes?"

"There is a Miss Patchett for you, Sir."

He told the desk that he'd be down in ten minutes. "I will ask the lady to wait in the bar."

His clothes from the night before lay in a reeking pile on the bathroom floor.

He had a spare shirt and trousers. He showered, flattened his hair, shaved and cleaned his teeth; all scrubbed up for the Embassy lady and a flight home. He'd tell her that he had information that he had to convey urgently to the Foreign Office in London. He turned it over in his mind as he smoked a cigarette on the balcony; Miss Bloody Patchett could wait another five minutes. It would be a trade; release from his bondage to Ealing in exchange for what he'd heard in the car. He rehearsed the phrases he'd use, considered the way he'd position himself, anticipated the questions that Victoria Patchett would ask him.

In the lift he began to perspire, checked the slight tremble in his hands, the flutter in his chest; what the hell had they injected him with?

The receptionist recognised Bellamy and snapped his fingers at a bellboy in a red fez. "Take the gentleman to table fourteen."

The boy—he was at least forty—beetled through the lounge, which was still crowded with tourists and their vast camera bags, and stopped behind a woman on a couch. She had short blonde hair. Bellamy gave the bellboy a small banknote and walked around the couch to greet her. The woman stood up and looked at him.

"Christ all bloody mighty," Lucy Vickers said.

Chapter 6: Turquoise

Tuesday 2 October 1973

Madame Serpouhi had arranged the outing some months before. "We will go to Saqqara with the Bulgars," she announced.

The 'Bulgars' were only faintly Bulgarian. Madame Serpouhi's niece had married an Alexandrian Greek with a Bulgarian grandmother, and it suited the old lady to associate herself with certain Slavs. She attributed her milky skin to 'White Russian' ancestors, but grew vague when Pierre questioned her on which branch of the family claimed this pearly lineage.

But the real boon was that the Bulgars had a car, a dented Fiat that had been missing a headlamp for as long as Pierre could remember.

"Invite your White Russian friend, Bedros," the old lady said, using Pierre's Armenian name as she habitually did.

When Zlotnik arrived at the pension, she said to him, "You surely haven't seen anything in the Soviet Union as remarkable as Saqqara."

"Certainly not, Madame," the smooth diplomat said without a trace of irony. "My country has nothing to compare with the wonders of Egypt."

Indeed, Pierre knew that Madame Serpouhi had a very dim opinion of the USSR, based squarely on the letters that she still received from a sister who had taken up Stalin's offer in 1950 for émigré Armenians to be 'repatriated' to the Soviet Socialist Republic of Armenia. "They treat us like lepers, and their Armenian is full of Russian words," the sister had written.

Pierre hardly relished the idea of the annual day out to Saqqara. The site of the step pyramids was a mere hour's drive south of Cairo, but the preparations were as if the journey was to take them across the Syrian desert—not that he'd ever mention such a comparison to Madame Serpouhi, whose father had perished fleeing Turkey for Aleppo in 1915. The boot of the Bulgars' car would be stuffed with beer, cold aubergine sandwiches, blankets, soda pop, cigarettes, serviettes, cheese, lamb stew and rice, a kerosene stove, fruit, and matches.

This year Madame Serpouhi sat in the front next to the Greek Bulgarian, with the wife, Pierre and Zlotnik in the back. Each year the language combinations changed according to Pierre's guest, the fault line this year being Zlotnik's weak Arabic and the Greek Bulgarian's wife's poor English. But they spoke a little German, and so the journey sped by as the conversation bounced around the tiny car in three and a half languages.

The step pyramid—much smaller than Cheops— stood bare and worn in the grey desert landscape. They parked the Fiat in the shade behind a snack bar, which was closed for Ramadan. The Greek Bulgarian—or was he a Bulgarian Greek?—brewed tea on the kerosene stove, out of sight of the guardian of the ancient tomb site. After they had eaten and packed away their picnic they found the custodian in *galabiyya* and turban by the tomb entrance and greeted him with "Blessed Ramadan" and "May you be well every year."

"Come on, come inside, ladies and gentlemen."

The party followed the robed man into the step pyramid. Madame Serpouhi deftly negotiated a fee for his services, and the party stood in wonder at the ancient murals of Egyptians with profile faces rowing boats on the Nile, leading lambs through a field and riding in chariots.

Zlotnik took a packet of cigarettes from his pocket, and the tomb guardian gave him a sharp glance.

"Ivan Maksimovich, let's step outside," Pierre said. They returned to the back of the snack bar and lit *papirosi*. Pierre disliked the thin cardboard tubes with a mean plug of tobacco at the business end. What he'd give for a plump Cleopatra!

"The arrangement I mentioned," Zlotnik said. His clothes showed dark sweat stains.

"Go on." They were down to business.

"I have something to trade." The Russian dragged deeply on the cigarette.

Pierre looked out at the utter desolation of the desert. If you forgot the day trippers for a moment, he and Zlotnik could be the only people left on Earth.

"Trade? You are selling something?"

"I'm selling myself, I suppose, Pierre. I am going to defect to Britain."

Pierre stared at his cigarette, took a puff and ground it out in the grey dust; suddenly he didn't want to smoke. Defection? This was new territory. Pierre's turf was personal matters; certainly his clients were often high up the social and political scale, but a Soviet defector? Was

Zlotnik playing some quirky joke?

"You aren't by any chance writing a spy novel, Ivan Maksimovich?"

"I've never been more serious." Zlotnik's normally pale turnip face was flushed deep red.

"And my role in this arrangement?"

"To negotiate the trade and arrange my departure."

"And who will I negotiate with?" Pierre had already anticipated the answer.

"An Englishman here in Cairo right now."

"And what do you know about this Englishman, Ivan Maksimovich?"

"Just that he has been sent here to arrange for a person to be dispatched to London."

"And may I know what you are offering in return?" Pierre asked. He knew nothing of the etiquette of arranging a defection, but it seemed a reasonable question.

"Information, of course," the Russian said.

"There is an infinite quantity of information in the world. What is special about yours?"

"You don't need to know."

"Then forget it."

Madame Serpouhi stepped into the shade from behind the snack bar. Had she been listening? Was her English sharp enough to pick up the gist of their conversation?

"It's Ruth. She has a migraine coming on. We'd better take her home."

Pierre nodded. "Aunt Serpouhi, may I have a minute more with Ivan?"

"Of course. By the way, Mr Ivan, what did you think of Saqqara?" the old lady said.

"I will cherish the memory and, one day, tell my grandchildren about it," he said.

Madame Serpouhi smiled and withdrew.

"Let's go back to Cairo then," Pierre said.

The Russian flicked an insect from his sleeve. He appeared to make up his mind.

"The information is a date, essentially, along with some documents."

"A date? But there are 365 dates in a year. Why is this date more important than all the other dates?"

"That's all I'm saying, Pierre."

"You're the client," Pierre said. In his mind's eye he saw pieces of a puzzle falling into place. The Russian had acquired some piece of valuable intelligence; the British had been alerted to the possibility of a defection through some diplomatic back door; the English detective had been dispatched to escort the defector home.

Zlotnik picked up a sharp rock and drew a figure in the dust with a dollar sign in front of it. Pierre took the rock and added a zero. The Russian shrugged, shook Pierre's hand and walked back towards the Fiat. Pierre noticed the oval of wet on the back of the man's shirt.

He sat alone on a rock. With midday approaching, the pool of shadow had shrunk so that his sandalled toes were almost under the hot rays of the sun. A Kombi van drew up nearby and disgorged six Americans, almost strangled by camera straps.

Pierre had a trick of switching his mind to autopilot, finding a zone somewhere between conscious thought and uncontrolled meandering. He focused his eyes on the horizon until all perspective was lost and his visual sense was of a mere yellowish grey fog, his mind a randomly shifting calculus. And then an idea began to take form—the gossip with his cousin at the Café Suez, the General's veiled wife under the trees at Ma'adi; Fawzi's concern to know the Englishman's business.

It had to be this: Zlotnik knew the date for the invasion of Sinai. Everyone knew it was coming, but when? Pierre wiped his face with a handkerchief. He balled the cloth and turned it over in his hands: long staple cotton, the best in the world, coaxed from the soil of the Delta by the rough hands of Egyptian *fallahin* with their broken bodies, parasites and milky eyes. A fresh sandfly bite had left a drop of blood browning on the white cotton.

He was incredulous that Zlotnik had misjudged the circumstances so egregiously. Could the man be so clumsy as to believe that Pierre would collude in the betrayal of his own country? That, for a fat envelope of US dollars, an Egyptian would aid the Americans and their Israeli friends in a pre-emptive attack on Egypt? He withdrew into the remains of the shade, invisible to the big foreigners with their buzz-saw voices.

He considered what he really knew about the Russian. Zlotnik was a seasoned foreign-service operator, no doubt; he appeared to speak frankly, but gave nothing away. Pierre always ended their meetings with the suspicion that he had learned less from Zlotnik that the Russian had learned from him. There had been mention of Moscow University, family in Leningrad, postings in Jakarta, Damascus, Hanoi—an oriental specialist, perhaps? But the man wove a silky veil of conversation around himself, spinning his words and phrases like a delicate spider, but never committing himself to anything tangible—until today.

For the first time in his life Pierre suspected he was

out of his depth. There were too many unknowns: Major Fawzi with his show of avuncular bumbling; the masquerading Englishman; Ivan Zlotnik's bizarre proposal. He'd been top of his class at mathematics as a schoolboy; he remembered the exhilaration of solving equations with unknown variables, juggling three parts of a problem at once, shaking out the values of a,b,c. What did they call the process for solving simultaneous equations? The elimination method, of course. But here there was nothing to shake out, nothing to eliminate. Nothing linking the variables, but vague talk of a dead Armenian opera singer.

* * *

Bellamy half woke from his torpor and felt Lucy's body cupped against his. She murmured something but he couldn't discern the words. In the wake of their lovemaking, the tang of her skin on his tongue and in his nostrils was as immediate and sharply arousing as it had been ten years ago. The perfume she wore—it was something Spanish, he remembered from the weekend in Kingsway—altered subtly as he'd explored her body—exotically floral where he'd kissed her shoulders, an intoxicating mix of sweetness and astringency between her breasts. They'd made love with complete familiarity; the decade melted away in a tangle of flesh and fragrance, which turned to a heady musk of bruised petals between their moist bodies.

He watched her where a band of light penetrated the curtains. She was still half asleep, the bed sheets pulled down. She'd changed little: a slight fullness where her belly had been flat, tiny stretch marks on her thigh and waist, and the skin of her shoulders freckled from the sun. There was a thrilling glow of maturity about her that he couldn't define. He put a hand over her breast and slid it down to play a fingertip along the horizontal scar above her pubis; he was puzzled, and then he understood. He moved his hand back to her breast and pushed his face gently into her neck. He felt himself becoming aroused again.

"No, Mark, no more—not yet. I can't risk having you here for too long. But it was lovely, more than lovely," she said. The radio was turned up in the next room and the flat was full of sinuous Arab music. She disentangled herself and lay on her back, covering the scar with the corner of a sheet.

Bellamy scanned the room, looking for places where a bug might be hidden. It was hopeless. Every wooden roundel, every silky window sash, every brass-fitting connecting the archaic electrics, a Bakelite telephone—the place could be wired like Battersea power station.

Lucy got up, stepped into a slip and padded into the sitting room, avoiding the patent leather shoes she'd flung to the floor earlier. The flat was in an anonymous but respectable block off Champollion Street. Bellamy had found it easily from the address she'd given him three hours before in the Hilton bar. It had smallish rooms, velvety wallpaper and chipped chandeliers, and there was a vaguely mousy odour from the oriental carpets. Heavy drapes cast a deep gloom over all the rooms. Lucy came back with a bottle of Sinacola and pressed it on the base of his bare stomach. "That's all there was in the fridge. It's cooled you down anyway!"

Bellamy took the bottle, swigged on the oversweet cola, and pressed the cold glass against his bruised shoulder. She hadn't asked about the injury.

For the moment he didn't care why he was in the flat or why Lucy Vickers was calling herself Victoria Patchett, or who the father of her child was. He'd had a decade of casual encounters—on-and-off girlfriends in the north, weekends in London with the woman in Battersea—and others. With his looks and his profession, he'd never had difficulties attracting women. But none of them had captured him in the way that Lucy Vickers had. For ten years the woman with short blonde hair had been the invisible third partner haunting his relationships, sharing his lovemaking, whispering into his ear in moments of intimacy. How many times had he returned to his flat in Halifax after an evening with a new lover, only to torment himself in the early hours with visions of Lucy Vickers?

His heart leapt as the room was filled with a sound like a rasp scraping on bone. The sound stopped abruptly and started again.

"It's that sodding phone," Lucy said, as the ancient instrument burped out a deathly rattle, went silent, and rang again.

Bellamy quelled his heart and stared down the handset, willing it to stop. After six rings it gave up.

"You've gone as white as a sheet," he said.

"Not as white as you when you saw me in the Hilton!" she said, keeping her voice just below the volume of the music. They both laughed.

"And yours! I was expecting Victoria Patchett to be some gorgon in stout walking shoes."

"Brown brogues can be arranged, if that's your thing," she said, slipping on her heels. He looked at her legs and she smiled.

Then she said seriously, "Look, Mark, it doesn't make sense that we're here together in Cairo. Until today I thought I had a straightforward job to do. Now I'm totally confused. No, not just confused, I'm bloody well terrified."

"Who does the flat belong to?"

"Lord knows. I got here two days ago and checked into the Semiramis Hotel. Someone from the Embassy gave me the key and told me to keep out of their way. They treated me like something the cat had dragged in."

Bellamy needed some answers quickly. "You said you had a job to do."

"I'm going to explain, but I'm taking a big risk. I don't really know who you are, despite," she gestured towards the bed, "all that."

"I think we're both at a disadvantage."

They jumped at the sound of shouting in the hallway outside the apartment. Lucy moved quietly to the front door, Bellamy behind her, still naked. Somebody banged on one of the other apartment doors and a male voice said, "*Ir-rayyis mawgud?* Is the boss there?"

"Does that make sense to you? Who's *ir-rayyis?*" Bellamy whispered. Lucy shook her head.

A door opened and another voice—male again—said, "No boss here, you've got the wrong place." The door slammed. Bellamy moved close to Lucy, wrapped his arms around her and pressed his face against her neck, breathing in her warmth. He felt her press back against him. They stood listening for the faintest sound beyond the door—a footfall, a cough. But nothing.

Then a hand rapped four times on the door. "*Ir-rayyis mawgud?*"

Lucy turned and nodded to Bellamy, and he said, "*Laa, mish mawgud!* No, not here." There was a grunt and then silence.

"Look through the peephole, Lucy."

"Nobody there." She turned round, looked him up and down, and said, "Mark, get some clothes on before

I forget what I'm doing here."

While dressing he said, "What happened that weekend in the Kingsway?"

He was hopelessly conflicted; he was in love with a woman who might be his nemesis, might be the sweet jam in some cynical trap devised by the bastards at Ealing.

"Do you want help with that?" she asked, and took the cufflink from his clumsy fingers. She leant slightly to hold the shirt cuff together and push the gold fastener through the buttonholes. When she looked up she slid her hand around the back of his head and brushed his lips with hers. He tasted the tang of sex again.

"All right, I'm going to tell you. They were waiting for me outside the hotel when I left. They took me into a café, told me you were under surveillance, stupid stuff, you had passed SIGINT materials to the Czechs. It sounded like rubbish."

Bellamy stared straight ahead; there was a glimmer of plausibility in what she said.

"Did you tell them to bugger off?"

"I tried that." The radio switched from music to a news broadcast. She got up and changed it to another music programme. It was a deeply sentimental song about Al-Quds—Jerusalem.

"It's Fayrouz," Lucy said. "I fell in love with her voice when one of our lecturers played a record of hers at Durham. It was a filthy day—sleet, cold for weeks, dark at three in the afternoon. When I learned that her name meant 'turquoise' it was like seeing a clear blue sky. It was sublime. I wept."

"What did the bastards threaten you with?"

"Mark, I've loved you since Shemlan. But I don't

know you. Give me a reason why I should stay a moment longer. Why I shouldn't walk out the door and get a taxi to the airport?"

Bellamy said, "Lucy, it's been the same for me." He grasped her wrists, brought his face close to hers and whispered hoarsely, "The same for me!" He saw something change in her. She freed her hands and embraced him tightly.

"It was pathetic, like something from a *Carry On* film," she said. "It wasn't till a few months later, but some Ealing people turned up at my place in raincoats and trilby hats. According to them, some of the top secret briefings I'd written had turned up in Israel. It just wasn't possible. But I was only twenty-five; naive. I didn't want to believe them but I was excited by the situation. Even flattered in a stupid way."

"Flattered?"

"No, it's the wrong word. But you know, we'd been through Profumo and Christine Keeler, and Burgess and Maclean. There was a weird excitement about being part of something dark, something dangerous . . ."

He remembered the volatility that he'd found so irresistible in her at Shemlan. But he needed to focus on the present, on why two former lovers were marooned in a stuffy flat in Cairo.

"Lucy, you mentioned secret briefings. In Shemlan you said you worked for a bank."

"The Bank of England, not handing over ten-bob notes to pensioners in Barclays in Hemel Hempstead. I specialised in investigating clandestine money transfers—funding for hijackers and all that."

"But they said your material had turned up in Israel. Isn't Israel part of the big happy family? I thought we shared everything with them—the Yanks, the Aussies, the Canadians, New Zealand."

"The Israelis had got them from a Syrian source, they said."

It made a ghastly kind of sense. He grasped at a possible truth.

"Let me guess what happened next. They hung the Official Secrets Act over your head. Sent you off to a nice little partnership at an accounting firm in Surrey. Signed you up for occasional jobs for the next ten years."

"More or less." She loosened her embrace and turned to look directly at him. "How do you know that? Christ, not you too?"

"Yes," Bellamy said. "But I thought I was the only one."

Lucy fell silent. He looked at her in profile through the gloom; a stray beam of sunlight penetrated the drapes behind her and her face was silhouetted with silvery motes of dust.

"What are you thinking about?" he asked.

"Apart from finding you again? I'm thinking there might be others," she said.

"Others?"

"Like us."

Bellamy had been turning over the same scenario in his mind. "We're probably part of a special bloody section—B for blackmail."

"B for bloody idiots." Lucy stood up, smoothed her skirt and tousled her hair; Bellamy remembered the gesture from Shemlan.

"I'm so bloody angry, that I want a cigarette," she said.

Bellamy lit two Rothmans and handed her one.

"You realise," she said, "that Ealing's made a mistake. We were never intended to meet."

"Some prat in a cardigan. Those stupid passwords and code names. A mix up."

Bellamy stood up and held her close. He caressed her neck below the short blonde hair, and felt her relax.

"What do you think my code name might be?" he asked her.

She laughed. "A mineral and an animal. That's what they were doing for a while in my office. You know, Sand Otter, Diamond Fish, that kind of thing. You'd be Flint Bear, no, that's no good. What about Quartz Lion?"

"Makes me sound sharp and furry all at once," he said.

"Or like an expensive watch. Maybe there's another one of us called Quartz Action. The one who was supposed to be here instead of you. I wonder what he's like," she said.

"Square jaws, huge shoulders, karate expert, size twelve shoes."

"Ugh, not my type. What would my code word be?"

"Turquoise Gazelle, of course."

"Ha! Very eastern, very poetic, very School of Oriental and African Studies. Have you gone native? They always warned me about that. Fat chance with my blonde hair."

Bellamy said, "If we're right about this, we're finished when those fuckers from Ealing work out that they've put us together."

"How come you talk like a barrow-boy sometimes? I remember that from Shemlan. It's quite a turn on, you know!"

"Classified information. You'll have to pay a very high price to find out," he said.

Any trace of levity dissipated, and she said, "Perhaps they put us together on purpose, and we're finished anyway."

Not a sodding chance, Bellamy thought. He'd let her slip ten years ago and a bunch of cunts in cardigans weren't going to get in the way of this barrow-boy.

They sat for another twenty minutes, speaking softly as Fayrouz's jewelled voice sang of loss and hope.

The facts fell out in a sinister arrangement. Lucy had been called up from the exclusive accounting firm where she was a partner—'all our clients are filthy rich'—and given a sketchy briefing on the Cairo assignment. She was travelling as Victoria Patchett, dispatched to Cairo to organise a film festival for the British Council. Detective Rogers would contact her and deliver an injured British subject to the flat where they now sat.

"Did they say how this Rogers character would contact you?"

"No, it would just happen, and the delivery would be made early in the morning on October 7."

The man would give Lucy some documentation, which she was to leave in a book in the British Council library in El-Duqqi as soon as it opened. She was then to return to the flat to wait with 'Detective Rogers' and the human package. At midday Lucy would go back to the British Council to check that the library book contained the code word for 'Rogers' and his detainee to head for the airport.

"What about travel documents?"

"I've got a passport for him in the name of Briggs. Presumably fake," Lucy said.

"What time am I scheduled to fly out with this person?"

"Six in the evening."

"And when do you get out?" he asked.

"The day after you, October 8. I'm to come down with an illness, cut short my film festival assignment."

"Were you briefed by the same person as me? She looked like my old Latin teacher—tweeds, Brünnhilde haircut and half-moon glasses."

"That's the cow," Lucy said. "I asked her what illness I was supposed to have and she said—"

"—that's your business, not ours."

"Yep. I said, what about dropsy, but she looked right through me."

"Dropsy? What's dropsy?"

"I think it's when you swell up from drinking too much water," she said.

Bellamy looked at her and chuckled. They both exploded with laughter.

When they'd wiped their eyes, he told her about the previous night in the City of the Dead, but not about the conversation he'd overheard; he couldn't see the point in burdening her with more secrets.

"Poor darling. I would have died. The shitty bastards. Here, let me hold you. You must be exhausted," she said. He was utterly drained, but the urgency of the circumstances and the thrill of being reunited with her gave him a charge of determination and energy. He wasn't in a position to be tired. He gently lifted her arm from his shoulder. "I'm fine, really."

The music programme had given way to a didactic talk on agriculture. Lucy raised her head to listen.

"What's *tawil al-tin*?" he asked.

"Long staple. They're on about cotton varieties," she said.

"You must have been an insufferable swot at university."

"And look where it got me," she said. "Holed up with my lover in Cairo, wondering whether we'll get out of this with our lives."

"Lover. That's a word I like. I've never really had a lover. Not a proper one. Have you?"

She took his hand and guided it under her skirt and slip. She moved his fingers above her panties to the scar just along the line of the elastic.

"There's a lot for you to know, Mark."

The evening prayer began to sound, each *muezzin* starting slightly out of synchronisation with the other until the whole city was washed in a tide of entreaty to God.

"What are we going to do?" she asked, letting go of his fingers. The last sliver of light between the drapes glowed red.

He moved his hand downwards. She responded with a shudder, pressed her mound into his fingers. But then she pulled back, removed his hand and kissed his fingertips. "There's no time, Mark. Go. I'll see you tomorrow. I'll leave ten minutes after you."

She was right. It was folly for them to remain there together. They needed to get back to their hotels, to be in public view.

"One last thing," he said. "You mentioned a code word. Perhaps I'd better know it, just in case."

"It's an odd one," Lucy said. "Siranoush."

Chapter 7: Vous cherchez quelqu'un d'autre

Wednesday 3 October 1973

Pierre awoke with the dawn prayer, as always. The street outside was already noisy with people rushing to pray before the long day of Ramadan fasting. He had slept through the racket of the professional gentlemen in the dining vestibule wolfing down their pre-dawn breakfasts, but he could now hear Madame Serpouhi's girl clearing the plates and glasses.

He made a show of fasting during Ramadan for the sake of courtesy to his Muslim neighbours and friends, but excused himself for not trying harder on the grounds that his dual Christian lineage made life complicated enough already. How was a man to keep up? The Coptic year began on September 11; there was the Fast of Ninevah along with innumerable others he could never remember. And while the Copts celebrated Christmas on January 7, the Armenians had it on January 6. Who could be blamed for mixing up the Transfiguration of the Lord on each side of the family? Ninety-eight days after Easter for the Armenians, August 6 for the Copts. No, he wouldn't feel too bad about sneaking a slice of cold chicken and a glass of buffalo milk into his room later in the day while the girl was busy dusting the shutters.

He slipped out of his narrow iron bed and fired up the little spirit burner to heat the *kanakah*. His tiny room overlooked Huda Sha'rawi Street and a grocery shop. The Filfila Restaurant was on the other side of the street to the right and the Liver and Rice Shop to the left. He opened the window and leaned out. A boy in a *galabiyya* was sweeping the dust from the steps of the shop one storey below.

"Tssssst!"

The boy looked up. "Morning of goodness to you, Sir."

"Morning of jasmine to you, my boy. Send up the newspapers, if you don't mind." He folded a small banknote and lowered it into the boy's hands in a small basket on a rope. He wondered why he'd used 'jasmine' today, and not the usual 'morning of light'? And 'if you don't mind'? An excess of graciousness! The froth of the boiling coffee threatened to bubble over the rim of the *kanakah* just as he flipped it into a tiny cup.

He was, he supposed, feeling optimistic, to the extent that he experienced that particular emotion. If anybody had asked him—and nobody would—he would describe himself as a man 'turned in on himself'. His quiet courtesy was the external manifestation of some dimension of the interior man, but his true nature was his business and his alone. Nobody but he knew about his deepest beliefs, his moral scaffold, his aspirations, his human impetuses, and his emotions. He permitted himself feelings that were measured, circumscribed. And on this morning of jasmine he permitted himself to feel hopeful that the day would end with several strands of his current untidy dilemmas neatly tied up.

The note lay on his desk. *'Vous êtes prié de vous présenter à 20 heures forte'*. He allowed himself a hint of *frisson* at the elegant words with their pretty accent marks. What obstacles would be set against him tonight? What dangers might he face, and how might he use his superior intelligence to counter them. 'Superior?' Yes, he admitted to himself, he was smarter, sharper, more far-seeing than his clients and his network of professional contacts. But he briskly tucked the notion away. It was time to check his gun.

He'd been given the Beretta in part payment for a job two years ago.

"I'd prefer cash," he told the brute who'd passed the loathsome thing under the café table where they'd met to the settle the account. The client—the word was hardly apt for this ape-faced thug—had engaged Pierre to spy on his teenage daughter. As far as Pierre could ascertain, the man was a drug dealer with a sideline in pimping; he had a paranoid suspicion that his demure daughter was having an affair with a hooligan he occasionally did business with. The poor girl had an uncorrected strabismus and wore a *niqab*.

"It's a .22 calibre model 70," he grunted. "Israeli military issue. Good quality. Liberated from the enemy. Probably used to shoot some poor Egyptian fucker. Haha!"

"Take it back," Pierre hissed.

"Too late, brother, it's in your hands," the monster said, springing to his feet and leaving Pierre to stuff the horrible thing into his pocket. He walked home with a shopping bag of onions pressed to his side, unsure whether the gun might go off and shoot his kneecap off, even though the safety was on. When he got to Pension

Serpouhi he carefully pulled it from his pocket and placed it on his bedside table without injuring himself. He'd seen one like it before: the Egyptian Maadi pistol his father had owned, a locally manufactured Beretta copy, except this one was stamped in Italian. '*Smontaggio*' was etched under the disassembly lever. It had no ammunition. Thank the Lord there was no Hebrew lettering on it.

What a world, he'd thought as he made a hiding place behind a loose piece of wainscoting; Arabs and Jews killing each other with Italian guns.

Pierre pushed the image of the thug from his mind and finished his coffee. He scraped away the seam of plaster that disguised the loose edge of the wainscoting, and prised the wood back. The gun lay in the recess, wrapped in a two-year old copy of *Al-Ahram*. He hesitated for a few seconds. It wouldn't shoot, but it might buy him the few seconds he needed to think himself out of a dangerous spot. He left it untouched for now, pushed the wood back and smeared a damp sponge over the plaster seam.

A cloud passed over his mood of cautious hope. Major Fawzi. It had been four days since the Major had briefed him in the apartment in El-Duqqi, and Pierre couldn't delay giving a progress report. The dilemma was, what counted as 'progress'? The notion suggested moving forward to a resolution, being a step further forward than where one was yesterday. There had been some steps, no doubt, but they were mostly sideways.

He was disturbed by a commotion in the street below. He leaned on the window sill and watched a small crowd pointing to a window high up on one of the shabby Italianate buildings opposite.

"Tsss. What's happening?"

The boy looked up. "It's Umm Karim. She's yelling about Israeli spies."

The poor woman was deranged. She had spent years in the room high above the street, yelling incoherently whenever the barred window was opened. Where had she got the notion of spies into her head?

Pierre leaned out to see the woman being pulled inside and the window slammed shut. Her face was pressed to the glass, her mouth working like a catfish. Two dim-faced cops in black berets chivvied the crowd away. It had been the third or fourth such incident in a week. People were feeling edgy, the sniff of war was in the air, rumours swirling.

But, Pierre wondered, what was to be done about Fawzi? What was Pierre to report to him? He had known the older man for a dozen or so years, and was indeed in his debt. Fawzi had been a friend of his father and had referred work to Pierre when he set up his translation business after graduating. First it had been routine stuff—translating personal documents found in the possession of suspects, interpreting police interviews on the odd occasion when a foreigner got into trouble. But gradually Major Fawzi introduced less straightforward tasks—"I can't trust my own people on this one"—and Pierre found himself involved in shadier jobs where the line between the legal and the criminal was hard to discern. While the money was good, Pierre tucked the moral questions into a secret compartment in his mind, along with the details of the characters he encountered in the twilight world that Fawzi preferred to inhabit by proxy. But the young man began to take on his own clients and Fawzi's hold loosened; they reached a stage of mutual, if wary, respect and affection.

I'll talk to him tomorrow, Pierre thought. I'll think of

something.

He examined the big paper calendar on the wall, with the Muslim, Western and Coptic calendars crammed into a crazy design of panels and tables and swirls. Today was the first Monday of the Western month, marked, as was the third Monday, with a tiny red-inked cross. Unmarried, and with no desire for a partner in life, Pierre took a rational view of his needs as a man; he had a fortnightly arrangement with a lady of uncertain age in Shoubra. She wasn't, she insisted, a whore; just a lady with special men friends. He wasn't, he insisted to himself, a whore's customer; just a gentleman helping the lady to manage her difficult circumstances. Sentiment didn't come into it, he told himself, even when later in his room he sometimes let his thoughts wander to some hazy scene where he and the lady might walk on the beach at Ras El-Bar and he might offer her a piece of jewellery from Beirut. But could he fit in seeing the lady from Shoubra immediately after the rendezvous with the author of the note? It could be a squeeze.

But thoughts of Fawzi wouldn't leave him alone. He rehearsed the next meeting with the plump Major, sifting out what might be reported and what might not. Should he mention that he had met the Englishman in person? And what of his doubts about the man's real identity? And his abduction at the museum? But surely Fawzi would know all of this; perhaps the thugs in El-Duqqi were linked at a long arm's length with Fawzi? Perhaps Fawzi and Zlotnik were cronies? And then there were Fawzi's links with the General Intelligence Directorate; Pierre suspected they were deeper than the Major chose to reveal.

Pierre spent the rest of the day translating a brace of

commercial documents, half his mind on the humdrum language work, half on autopilot shuffling the fragments of the Siranoush affair into an infinite array of unsatisfactory solutions. At sunset he walked to the Filfila where the locals were breaking their fast. He enjoyed the unhurried, gentle camaraderie of the first meal after sunset during Ramadan; it brought out the best among his neighbours.

At the very last moment he baulked at the idea of shoving the Israeli Beretta in his pocket. He set off, giving himself half an hour to walk to Zamalek, not that it was very far, but his preference was always for the lesser streets, the darker alleys.

He reached the building and walked past it a couple of times, head down, hands behind his back, picking up what he could with his peripheral vision. It was a smart apartment block with an impressively modern front entrance. On his third pass, two big men fell into step with him, one on each side, and shepherded him into an alley. He flinched, but they politely emptied his pockets, examined his identity card and carefully put his belongings back into his pockets. One of them said, "You're OK, brother. Come with us."

Pierre was led like a child between two uncles into the lobby, where one of the men called out to the *bawwab*, "Look away, old man." Into a gilded lift, a whoosh up the core of the building, and they were in a corridor with plush pastel-green carpet and framed sepia prints of Ottoman palaces. A knock on a pair of double doors, a slippered servant in a silk robe and fez, a large vestibule that boasted of too much money and too little taste, and a heaviness of rosewater and cooked lamb in the stuffy air.

"Wait here, brother."

Pierre sat on a silk padded bench beside one of the large men, who winked at him in a comradely way and tapped his knee. The other man left through an internal door, to return after a minute.

"Madame is expecting you."

Madame? So far so good, Pierre thought. I haven't been stabbed in the guts and I'm to have an audience with a lady.

He was ushered into an antechamber and then into a spacious salon decorated with garish modern paintings, risqué statues and more silk covered furniture. The large men melted away.

"Approach." The voice came from a cluster of furniture at the end of the large room. On one of the settees sat, in all her full-figured pulchritude, Zouzou Paris. She was a magnificent woman, Pierre thought, barely able to suppress his awe: the glistening emerald dress with a panel of delicate net barely concealing a generous cleavage, smooth china-white legs exposed from the calf down, and feet encased in delicate silk pumps. She was daringly bare-armed. Her face was an unblemished powdered white, the eyes swimming in black pools, the eyelashes like fans, the lips like ripe purple grapes. The entire assemblage was topped with a crown of dramatically swirled hair, which, it appeared to Pierre, threatened to take off like a black cheetah.

"When did you start calling yourself Pierre?" she asked, with a singsong Lebanese tinge to her Arabic.

"Excuse me, Madame?"

"Yes, I thought it was you, Boutros."

"Surely you are mistaken, Miss Paris. *Vous cherchez quelqu'un d'autre.*"

"*Vous?* It was *tu* when we last spoke, Boutros." The vision that was Zouzou Paris raised her hands and levered the large wig from her hair to reveal a demure bun. Pierre goggled.

"Now how about this?" she said, peeling off her false eyelashes one by one. Pierre continued to gape, but an improbable idea was forming in his mind.

Next, the woman took a tissue and a jar of cream, and wiped off the lipstick.

"By God, it can't be," Pierre said.

"Can't it, Boutros?"

"You're Zouzou Faris. You used to play with my sister and me at the chalets!"

"Well, Aziza Faris really, but people call me Zouzou these days."

"And how did Faris become Paris? What on earth happened to you? How did you become—"

"How did I become what? The brazen actress? The national bitch?"

Pierre looked at her shyly. It must have been, what— '47 or '48 when his mother started taking Pierre and his sister to Alexandria for the holidays, his father joining them when he could get away from work for a few days. Zouzou's family rented the beach chalet at Agami next to Pierre's family for four or five summers. Pierre remembered her mother, who fondly called him 'Pasha' and teased him, "One day you'll be a businessman with a Mercedes and you'll marry my Zouzou." Their fathers often came up to Agami at the same time, and the families joined together on the beach at night to barbecue lamb brochettes and eat potato salad. Pierre loved to sit outside the ring of firelight and watch the adults, the men laughing over their bottles of beer, hairy arms against white cotton shirts, his mother dark-haired, Zouzou's mother blonde. Zouzou told him her grand-mother had been Cherkess, descended from a Circassian woman enslaved by the Ottomans in Syria.

"The good old days are not the days of today, Zouzou."

"You still haven't told me, Boutros. Why 'Pierre' now?"

"And why 'Paris'?"

They laughed, not comfortably.

"And your family?" Zouzou said.

"My parents and sister dead."

"God bless them," Zouzou said. She eased off the tight silk pumps and Pierre saw the little creases in the pale flesh. He looked away quickly when she saw where his gaze lay.

"And your family, Zouzou?"

"Gone too. This is my family." She flourished a hand to indicate the apartment.

"These ugly paintings and statues, those men outside who protect me, the wolves who run the film industry, him." She wagged a contemptuous finger at a framed photograph of the General.

Pierre feigned ignorance of Zouzou's connection with the big zucchini.

"You mean that the General and yourself are— connected?"

"I'm his mistress, Boutros."

"The men outside. Will they tell him I'm here?"

"No. I gave his monkeys the night off. These two work for me."

Pierre gathered himself. A teenage crush was all it had been. She might be in the top three or four film stars in Egypt, but he was here to do a job. He put on his professional frown.

"Miss Paris — " "Zouzou."

"Zouzou then. What service can I render you?"

There was little trace of the sweet girl who'd flashed shy glances at him as she played beach tennis with his sister. This one had grown hard as a brass *kanakah*, tough as a sheep's ear. She swivelled a wily eye on Pierre. "They tell me you can be trusted. I did my checking, of course, and now I've confirmed who you are I feel confident that I can tell you a few things about my situation. You were always such a proper boy—you kept secrets, played things straight. You had a thing for me, of course, didn't you?"

Pierre cleared his throat.

"All right, Boutros—or Pierre, if you like," she went on. "You're as prim as you were all those years ago. At any rate, listen to what I have to say." She folded her arms.

"The General here, well, things have been getting odd in recent times. Not his usual self is the way I'd put it."

"And may I ask what is 'his usual self'?"

"I'll take the risk of shocking you Pierre. The General and I have an arrangement that entails me paying off a kind of debt. When my parents died he took me to Beirut—he was a friend of my father—and set me up with some movie characters. I couldn't act, but I could—let's say—give him the kind of companionship he needed. So with the help of his movie cronies the owl became an actress, as the old saying goes."

"You're known as a fine actress, hardly an owl."

"You obviously haven't seen any of my films. I might be famous but I don't do much on screen except breathe deeply and flutter these." She pointed at the false eyelashes lying like dead centipedes in an ashtray. "My part in the whole charade is to be Egypt's favourite *sharmouta*, and they love it."

"And the arrangement with the General is—continuing?"

"To the extent that the gent can keep up with his own expectations, yes, you could say that it continues. He's a month shy of seventy and he smokes like a slaughterhouse bonfire. My worry is that the arrangement is coming to a nasty end. I wasn't sure until last week, but I think my time's up."

"Can you be a little clearer?"

For a brief moment he saw again in her expression a trace of the sweet girl from the Agami days.

"He means to have me killed this coming Saturday," she said.

Chapter 8: An Old Rolex

Thursday 4 October 1973

Bellamy hadn't risked going back to the apartment where he and Lucy had met two days ago. In the absence of any clear information about the whereabouts of 'Briggs', they agreed that he would wait at the Hilton to be contacted. In the last minutes before they parted, they discussed the need to plan for an escape in case their worst fear was realised: that Ealing had deployed them together on purpose, to be used and then trashed in a back alley. Neither came up with a clear plan, but they had at least arranged a simple rendezvous protocol.

"Find the Filfila Restaurant in Huda Sha'rawi Street," Bellamy said. "A hundred yards in the direction of the market there's a *kushari* stall next to an ironing shop. Let's both approach the stall at 10am, 2pm and 6pm. Two missed meetings means it's gone arse-up and we look after ourselves."

She nodded. "As long as I don't have to eat that horrible *kushari* stuff. If I have to make a run for it I don't want a belly full of lentils and macaroni. Kiss me before you go."

They had liaised on two of the three occasions

yesterday, passing close enough for each to make a slight shake of the head.

The Englishman ordered a coffee '*Américain*' in his room and considered the dilemmas confronting him. At the front of his mind were the conversations he'd overheard at the City of the Dead—rumours of hospitals being infected, Operation Full Moon starting on the third of November. It didn't take much to put it all together. It was a military operation, Sadat's long promised reclamation of Sinai. But he was torn; was it a staggering coincidence that he, a foreign SIGINT expert, had been in exactly the right spot when a loose-tongued intelligence officer was tipping off his son-in-law? On the other hand, had he convinced them that he was no more than an English suburban detective? He was confident that he had been correct in not revealing to Lucy what he'd heard.

On the matter of Briggs, the most logical explanation of the current mess was that the individual being prepared for transfer to Britain was not yet in place, hence Fawzi's delaying stunt with the bandaged short-arse. But a murderer on a British arrest warrant? Not a chance. There was a political angle to this, and again it was too much of a coincidence to think that 'Briggs' was unconnected with Operation Full Moon; the charade in the empty hospital wards was the clincher. Somebody had to be got out of Egypt, for whatever reason.

But all of this was, in the end, insignificant if he and Lucy Vickers were dispensable. The absolute priority was to find a way to get himself and Lucy out of Egypt at short notice. But he knew nobody in Cairo who he could trust. Fawzi? Zaki? Bollocks. The Embassy? They'd tell him to get lost.

He drank the milky coffee and slipped a Rothmans

from the slim white pack with the navy blue stripe, turning the problem this way and that, subjecting it to a lawyer's scrutiny. The tobacco smoke hit the back of his throat and the nicotine charged his brain with clarity. The question, he told himself, was not who he trusted in Cairo, but who did he distrust the least? There was only one answer.

* * *

He was fairly certain that he could retrace the route to Pierre Farag's office. The day was already warm and he set out on foot in shirt sleeves, across Tahrir Square, along Muhammad Mahmoud Street, past the Rio open-air cinema. He stopped to look at the hand-painted posters. They were showing a war epic about the biggest tank battle ever fought. Bellamy guessed this would be a Soviet film subtitled in Arabic. He glanced upwards, alerted by a bleat; a sheep was peering from behind the balustrade of an apartment balcony, awaiting its fate. You and me, my friend, he said to himself.

He cut through a lane running north that he guessed would bring him out at the *kushari* stall; it was closed until sunset, but the ironing shop next door was in full steamy swing with flat irons heating on a charcoal brazier. He slowed to watch the sweating man swig a mouthful of of water and spray it through his lips over a shirt before attacking the garment with a sizzling iron.

Pierre Farag's office, he remembered, was in a narrow street, marked by a tiny watchmaker's shop squeezed between two shuttered premises. He found the entrance and knocked. The steel rod securing the door slid back and a *bawwab* peered out. The man had milky eyes.

"*Na'am?*" the old man said.

Bellamy weighed his fate, made his decision, and asked in Arabic, "Is Professor Pierre here?"

105

"Not here, Sir."

"Does he come every day?"

"Yes, Captain, every day!"

"Has he been here today?"

"No, Sir. Do you want to leave him a *gawab*?" the old man said.

A *gawab*, an 'answer'? It was the local word for a letter, Bellamy realised.

"No, no answer. Just tell him the *khawaga* was here."

"The *khawaga*?" The old man looked doubtful. Bellamy noticed that his palm was open and he pressed a banknote into it.

"At your service, Sir!"

It was three minutes before ten when he reached the *kushari* stand.

"Keep walking." It was Lucy behind him. He walked on until he met a big traffic intersection and waited for a chance to cross. She was beside him in a headscarf and dark glasses.

"Anything?"

"Maybe today. Can't guarantee two o'clock," he said to the back of the head of a man in front of him.

"I'm passing something to you. Open the fingers of your right hand," she said. When he turned she was gone and he was holding Briggs's fake passport.

* * *

Pierre looked at the big Rolex he had inherited from his father, who had an unshakable belief that he should never wear it on a flying mission; they'd found it in his locker after his charred remains were gathered from near the burnt-out MiG.

The watch said nine. A hot morning. Another clandestine meeting with Fawzi, another apartment, this time arranged by way of a note delivered to Pension Serpouhi just after Pierre had returned from his assignation with the lady in Shoubra the night before. When he left she had commented that he seemed distracted.

"You're growing tired of me, I suppose?" The real problem was that, despite the lady's professional efforts, he hadn't been able to chase the visions of Zouzou Paris from his mind.

At least Fawzi hadn't found it necessary to arrange another fake arrest, but with an eye to discretion Pierre spiralled his way through the back alleys to reach the characterless block near the synagogue on Adly Street.

The two men sat at a dining table with a vase of plastic flowers between them. "Almost nothing at all to report, you say, Pierre?" Major Fawzi fiddled with the packet of Cleopatras, but left it unopened. He dabbed his brow with a creased handkerchief.

"Are you unwell, my friend?"

"I'm a big fellow and fasting hangs heavily on me. That's just between you and me, of course. You're a *nasrani* but you understand these things."

"We are all people of the Book." Pierre knew that he couldn't evade Fawzi's questions once they'd got past the polite formalities.

"Yes, yes, of course, of course, people of the Book. But what of the matter we discussed last week? There has been no progress? The Englishman, this Siranoush nonsense?"

Pierre needed to divine what the portly man in the crumpled jacket might know. Yesterday's mood of buoyancy was fast turning to unease as he found himself caught in a vortex of misplaced faith in his ability and integrity. What was it about him that made people trust him? Fawzi, Zlotnik, the General's wife, Zouzou Paris—they'd each burdened him with conflicting confidences. Perhaps he should have got out to California when he had the chance. Or, better, he should have been a priest and made a profession of being a confidant.

Trust for him was a commercial matter. Trust me to get the job done, pay my fee, and we're done till next time. This was all too unsettling.

"My sources have given me some reports of the Englishman," Pierre said.

"Tell me."

"Apparently he went to the apartment in El-Duqqi on Thursday evening and was assaulted outside by a street gang."

"By God!" Fawzi looked stunned. "Was he injured?"

"Slightly, I'm told. A Good Samaritan helped him away and I'm told that he returned to the Hilton later."

Major Fawzi excused himself and went into the next room to make a phone call. He pushed the door shut, but Pierre could hear his raised voice. When he came back his brow was spotted with perspiration.

"Bunglers, amateurs. What I'd give to retire from all this and play backgammon in a café in Alexandria. What else?"

"I've learned that this Siranoush affair might have a connection with the Russians."

"Indeed?" Fawzi's plump eyebrow flicked up a millimetre. "Russians, you say?"

"Yes, but my source was vague, too vague to make very much sense at all."

Fawzi screwed his features into a conspiratorial smirk. "You wouldn't, of course, be able to extract a little more detail from your sources? Could I offer a bit of muscle to help you persuade them?"

Pierre tipped up his chin and tutted a 'no'.

"But I have one more thing for you—a name."

"A name, Pierre?"

"A big name. Possibly involved with the Siranoush matter."

"Write it down." Fawzi passed a scrap of paper and a pen to Pierre, who wrote down the name of the big zucchini, the General.

Fawzi glanced at the paper. He looked up at Pierre, then stared at the paper. He pressed his palm to his chest. His face went a blotchy purple.

"Fetch me a glass of water, Pierre, *habibi*. Quickly."

"But are you not fasting, my friend?"

"Please, fetch it. Acid stomach." He scrabbled in a pocket and found a bottle of pills.

Pierre brought the water, led him to a sofa and placed an arm across his shoulder. The big man slipped a tablet under his tongue, groaned and coughed a little, and let his shoulders slump, his elbows on his fat thighs.

"Better my friend?" Pierre asked. The label on the pill bottle said 'Nitro-glycerine'.

"The water now please, Pierre. Stay with me for a little while. Just leave your arm there, yes, across my shoulder. It is comforting. This silly ailment leaves me feeling apprehensive."

Pierre sat for five minutes or so holding the Major's shoulder. The man smelt of sweat and stale cigarettes; Pierre guessed that he smoked half a pack in the hour before dawn each day of Ramadan.

"It's a matter of trust, Pierre," he said when his body had calmed.

"What is? What's a matter of trust?"

"Your methods, your sources. I know how you work, my friend. Your father was like you, a man who would bide his time, didn't blurt out everything, said what needed to be said, no more and no less. He was my guide, my elder brother in a manner of speaking, the man who taught me the virtue of patience."

"Go on," Pierre said.

We are patriots, Pierre, Egyptian patriots. We have the same aim, we—how does the verse go?—*we advance like the light.* I understand that you have good reason to hold back what you know about all of this. You'll tell me everything when you are ready. Go now. I'm well."

Pierre walked swiftly away from the building, his head down. He unfolded a large white handkerchief and wiped tears of shame from his eyes. His dead father's disciple was a sick man; how could Pierre string Fawzi along, knowing that he might die ignorant of this unpardonable betrayal of trust? He glanced at his Baba's Rolex. 10.30am. Time to call in at the office.

* * *

It was the same bellboy in the red fez. "Your taxi is outside, Sir."

Bellamy carefully placed his magazine on the coffee table and took his time to get out of the lounge chair. He hadn't ordered a taxi, but as far as the watching eyes in the Hilton lounge were concerned, he had. The bellboy wove a path through the lounge, glancing back to check that his gratuity was in tow. The man opened the taxi door wide, and Bellamy saw him make sure he got a good eyeful of the driver and a slightly-built man in the back seat.

"Where to, Sir?" the bellboy asked as Bellamy paid him his *baqsheesh* and slid into the back seat next to

Pierre Farag. The driver looked over his shoulder at Pierre, who said, "Drive."

They ground into the thick traffic, neither Bellamy nor Pierre speaking. This, Bellamy thought, was akin to madness. His cover was in shreds, his life was in peril, the woman he was crazy about had been swallowed up in this rambling junkyard of a city.

"Take the Giza Road; we're going to the Pyramids," Pierre told the driver, who swung the taxi in the path of a looming truck that barely missed crushing the car's flank. My last sight on this blessed Earth, Bellamy thought: a rusted Leyland badge on a radiator grille.

"Ever been to the Pyramids?" Pierre asked in Arabic, calmly.

"*La, abadan*—no, never," Bellamy said. Pierre nodded his approval and gestured faintly at the back of the driver's head. The message was clear: No foreign talk in the cab. There are informers everywhere.

"Have you ridden a horse?"

"Once or twice," Bellamy said. A bloody horse. What next?

Approaching the Pyramids, Pierre gave directions to a stables compound where tourists were being helped onto half-asleep nags. A young man in a dazzling white robe greeted Pierre warmly but ignored Bellamy. The taxi driver was told to wait for two hours.

The young man led out two ponies and helped Bellamy and Pierre mount. He passed each man a folded red-checked k*ufiyya*.

"So we're to be *falasteeni*?" Pierre said.

"The tourists like them. They can pretend to be Bedouins."

They wrapped their heads to protect against the early

afternoon sun, and Pierre led the way through the stable gates and into a dusty lane at the end of which could be seen the improbable dun mass of Cheops, half a mile away. He set a course across the landscape that would take them well clear of the Pyramids. Once they had left behind the taxis, buses, and camel-riding tourists Bellamy urged his pony forward so that he was riding alongside Pierre.

"If you don't mind, we'll speak in English," Pierre said. "It is most unusual to encounter a *khawaga* who knows Arabic, but you speak so correctly that you'll give me a headache. You sound like a man who has swallowed a dictionary and eaten a grammar book for dessert."

Bellamy laughed, for the first time in days. He liked the man's arcane wit. "Fine with me. Where are we going?"

"Oh, we are already there, my friend. We are in the only spot in the whole of Cairo where two men can have a private conversation. There are only scorpions and beetles and hawks to hear us."

Bellamy looked around. The stables were just a smudge behind them. There was a puff of dust ahead of them—half a mile, five miles? The desert swallowed up all clues of distance. He should, he thought, feel deep apprehension. But there was something about Pierre Farag that communicated a sense of trust, of integrity. He seems, Bellamy thought without full understanding, a *whole* man, a whole man who knows himself.

"Why did you come to me?" Pierre asked.

"I had nobody else."

"Of course. And what do you need from me?"

"I need to get out of Egypt discreetly. Myself and a companion."

"And what makes you think that I can help you leave Egypt? You don't know me. All you know is what is written on the plaque on my office door. I might just choose to shoot you here and now, or hand you in to the *mukhabarat*."

"I'm a good judge of character."

"Or," Pierre said, adjusting the *kufiyah* against the sun, "you are clutching at blades of grass."

"A bit of both, I suppose. If you want proof that I'm throwing myself on your mercy, I have nothing to trade. Some currency, but not enough to buy what I need."

"The currency I deal in is more elusive. Should I continue to call you Detective Rogers, by the way?"

"You can call me Bellamy."

"Bellamy." The Egyptian rolled the name in his mouth two or three times until he appeared satisfied that it was apposite.

"What do you mean by currency?" Bellamy said. "You mean information, I suppose."

"You know, Mr Bellamy, I think I like you. And I think I can help you. It's most likely that you can find a way to repay me for helping you and your—companion, a lady, I expect?"

"Yes, a lady. How did you know?" Bellamy asked.

"You're that kind of man, Mr Bellamy; I'm also a good judge of character."

The Egyptian's eyes twinkled. "Just think, you a British gentleman, me an Egyptian gentleman of sorts, and so much in common. I've always wanted to go to England, you know."

"Look me up one of these days and I'll buy you a pint of bitter." Bellamy saw that the puff of smoke on the horizon seemed bigger.

"In an English public house! Is it true that a pub is just like a drawing room and that complete strangers converse like old friends?"

"Can we get to the point please?"

"Yes, we can. Here's the point. You haven't come to Egypt to take a criminal home. You're here to extract a Soviet defector."

Both men stopped their horses.

"And," Bellamy said, "You know who the defector is. Fucking hell."

"My friend, I have never learnt to use your blunt English curses properly, but yes, fucking hell sums it up beautifully."

Bellamy's mount had shuffled around so that its rump was against the puff of smoke. He saw Pierre look over his shoulder. Three or four sounds rang out like sheets of glass cracking.

"Mr Bellamy, do you know how to gallop?" shouted Pierre.

"Sort of."

"Well, sort of gallop like fucking hell. We're being shot at."

They arrived at the stable, dark with perspiration, the ponies with heaving flanks and foaming mouths. The white robed man was furious, taking Pierre into a shaded corner where they argued in loud whispers. Bellamy hung around, just in earshot, hearing snatches.

"You went too near! It's a military zone."

"It wasn't last week."

The matter seemed to be settled with Pierre peeling off a wad of notes.

"You didn't take us there by accident," Bellamy said as they walked to the taxi. Pierre said nothing.

* * *

Bellamy had missed the 2pm rendezvous with Lucy. He spent an anxious couple of hours in the hotel room reading a paperback and playing with some indifferent food sent up from the kitchens. With the end of the day's fasting just hours away, the hotel staff were listless and glassy eyed. Porters and maids leaned against door frames to ease sore feet, and the desk staff nodded over the massive varnished reception desk.

At 5.30pm he set off for the *kushari* stand. He was familiar enough with the city centre by now to navigate a crab-wise route in the hope that whoever was following him—he had no doubt that they were— would not be able to divine his intentions. On his previous trips he had included four or five common landmarks before and after the *kushari* stall.

Making his first pass of the stall at a minute before six, he saw no sign of Lucy. He kept walking and made a circuit that brought him back five minutes later. Again, no Lucy. But this time one of the green uniformed police was picking up shirts at the ironing shop. The man turned and glanced at Bellamy; the sharp-eyed ironing man must have pointed out the *khawaga*. Bellamy slowed his walk to a Cairene amble, but he knew it was no use. A voice behind him said, "'*Andak kibrit?*' It was the cop with an unlit cigarette in his mouth asking for a light. Bellamy struck a match and the man took a deep drag. He looked at Bellamy and asked in Arabic, "Are you with us?"

"Of course," Bellamy said without the slightest understanding of the intent of the question.

"Peace be on you," the officer said, and Bellamy had barely returned the conventional reply, "And on you be peace," when the man walked away.

He couldn't risk another circuit. It had gone arse-up.

He remembered that Lucy was at the Semiramis. He hailed a cab to Garden City and had the driver drop him a hundred yards from the hotel. Walking casually through the evening crowds he weighed up the risks. But surely they were beyond risk; surely their fate was in the hands of invisible players, invisible watchers. Surely they were being borne on an unstoppable tide towards an unknowable destiny. As he reached the hotel his mind was made up—he'd ask for her at the desk.

But the man at the Semiramis reception desk had never heard of Victoria Patchett or Lucy Vickers. Bellamy described her short blonde hair.

"Ah yes," the clerk said, "there was such a lady. She left—" He consulted the register. The head receptionist approached and glared at the clerk, who scuttled away.

"Sir, our guest register is confidential."

"But I need to speak to her. She's my—" He groped for a word. The head receptionist beckoned to a tall, heavy-set man who was undoubtedly the house detective. The man gripped Bellamy's arm and steered him to the exit. He took a cab to Champollion Street, found the building and studied the balconies until he was sure that he had identified the flat where they had made love. It was dusk and the lights were on in the sitting room. The drapes were pulled open, and a man was visible, back to the window, hands busy with some task. The angle of view prevented Bellamy seeing what he was doing; the only clue to the man's appearance was a head of thinning grey hair and the shoulders of a creased tan jacket. Major Fawzi? He couldn't be sure. The lights were snapped off and the drapes closed. Bellamy eased into a doorway unlit by the street lamps, and a minute later saw the front door open.

The pale-faced interrogator from the City of the Dead stepped out and glanced left and right. A Mercedes drew up beside him and he got into the back seat.

Chapter 9: Calamity Remembered

Friday 5 October 1973

Pierre blinked awake. It had been another night of flight from some vague horror, and he felt sour and giddy. The nightmares were becoming more frequent. The thought of America nagged at him more often.

He had spent most of the previous evening consulting his *shabkah*, as Fawzi called it; well, you could call it a 'network' if the word adequately described the troupe of misfits, malcontents, blackmailers, and square pegs in round holes who fed him scraps of information, shreds of rumour and dollops of sheer spite. He returned home late after visiting coffee shops, alleys, *bawwabs*, high-class brothels, and dark lanes behind military buildings. His bladder ached and his heart fluttered from too many cups of gritty coffee.

Sifting through the detritus of half-truths, lies and revenge, Pierre found enough solid evidence to know that it was time to talk to Madame Serpouhi. It was after 11pm but he knew that she would be reading old copies of Paris *Match* and drinking warm milk in her room. He knocked on her door.

"Aunt, it's me."

"Ouf, it's so late, my boy. You missed dinner. I sent out a dish of lamb and potatoes for the baker to cook, and there's some left. I can wake the girl. She will warm it for you."

"No, really, Aunt, I'm not hungry." He looked at her plump hands resting on the magazine, open at a story about Jackie Onassis. The pictures showed handsome men in tennis shirts and women wearing swimsuits. Everybody wore sunglasses and held long cigarettes.

"Aunt, I want to ask you a great favour. I need a place for some private business, a flat or a room somewhere."

Madame Serpouhi looked down at her magazine. "Cairo was like Paris then. Parties, wonderful dinners at the casinos. The streets were swept. Everyone knew their place." She glanced towards heaven with a resigned expression. "What can we do?" she asked.

Pierre knew this mood; he didn't have the time for lengthy reminiscing about the golden days when the British looked after Egypt so nicely.

"I wouldn't ask you if it weren't absolutely necessary, Aunt."

"It's the war, isn't it, Bedros? Won't they ever leave us alone?"

"Yes, Aunt. It's to do with the war, I suppose."

She lit a Craven A, took a mouthful of smoke with a flourish of her hand, and blew it out without inhaling. Pierre knew her ways. After five or six more puffs she crushed the cigarette into an ashtray shaped like Nefertiti, with a plunger that whirled the dog-end into a hidden container in the base.

"I'll talk to him first thing in the morning," she said, and patted his hand.

* * *

"The lady went out early," Madame Serpouhi's girl said. "She asked you to meet Mr Kebabjian at his apartment."

She'd done as he'd asked, and not without risk to herself. But as his aunt had told him a dozen times, she had Poghos Kebabjian on a string. The old skinflint had been asking for her hand for ten years, and the fact that they'd both been born in 1903 hadn't dampened his ardour. He was rich as a Pharaoh and uglier than a dung beetle. One of his sidelines was managing properties, and Pierre knew that if anyone could discreetly acquire a short-let apartment in Cairo, it was Kebabjian.

An underfed servant girl in a faded dress let Pierre into the big apartment. He hadn't visited Kebabjian for some years, and the flat was even more derelict than before. The carpets were hardly more than threads, and the seats of the leather sofas looked as if they had been excavated. Madame Serpouhi and Poghos Kebabjian sat on hard chairs with tarnished gold paint. The old man stared at her with the expression of a love-struck schoolboy while she held a cracked plate with one hand and a stale looking almond biscuit with the other. Pierre tried not to look at the large skin-tag on Kebabjian's eyelid that flapped when he blinked.

They seemed to have concluded their business because Madame Serpouhi stood up and allowed Kebabjian to stoop and brush his lips on the back of her hand. She glanced at Pierre with a grimace.

Kebabjian called the servant. "*Ya Fatima.*" Nameless country girls, they were always called Fatima, whoever they were.

"Show the *sitti hanim* out," he said with what he seemed to think was panache. Pierre winced at the archaic Ottoman title.

When Madame Serpouhi had gone, Kebabjian switched off the charm. He took a sheet of paper from a drawer and growled, "Sign this." The document referred to an address on the Giza Road.

"A lease?" Pierre asked.

"Where's your brain, man?" he said. "This is a private agreement, not a lease. You sign and it goes in my pocket."

Pierre looked at the total payable for two weeks. It was extortion.

"Cash up front. Discount for US dollars. It's a woman, I suppose. Not that it's my business. Are you going to sign or not?"

Pierre took a roll of Egyptian pounds from an inside pocket. He signed the paper and handed over the cash to Kebabjian, who blinked as he counted the notes, the flap of skin bobbing up and down. He gave Pierre a key, and said, "That's it then," and turned away. But as an afterthought he muttered, "Your aunt, have I a chance, do you think?"

"The eye of the sun cannot be hidden," Pierre said. There was a gleam of pathetic gratitude in Kebabjian's squint as he tried to divine the intent of the old Arabic proverb.

Pierre pocketed the key and took the lift to the street. The meeting with Kebabjian had taken his mind off the Siranoush affair for a few minutes, and he found that somehow his thoughts had clarified all on their own. He needed to see Major Fawzi quickly.

* * *

As dawn broke, Bellamy read the note for the hundredth time. It had been waiting when he had returned from Champollion Street the night before. The pink envelope had been arranged among a bouquet of flowers. No florist's name, no point in asking the desk who had delivered them.

'Get out now, L' it read in careful block letters. He realised that he wasn't familiar with Lucy's handwriting. A phrase kept popping up in his mind, something to with neat handwriting and the illiterate. Orwell, he thought, and bloody useless in the circumstances. But he peered again, and concluded that Lucy wasn't a woman who'd write in neat squares. He pictured her writing in sweeping Italic with green ink, with art nouveau curves like a Parisian Metro sign, or with the dramatic spikes of a Dali signature. Anything but a kid's wooden-block letters.

He tore the bouquet to bits, and the smell of crushed flowers clung to his hands. He recalled the afternoon with Lucy, but the bitter undernote of ripped green leaves nauseated him. Rational thought had entirely evaporated. He was running on instinct, on raw impulse. One scenario after another flashed through his mind: Lucy at the hands of the pale man, Lucy in a ditch, Lucy forced to write the note.

The telephone rang. The desk clerk said, "Your bill has been settled, Mr Rogers. We have ordered a taxi to the airport at 11am."

Bellamy opened his mouth to ask who had settled the bill and ordered a taxi, but stopped. He hoped beyond hope that it was Pierre Farag. He had nowhere else to go. Another gamble.

He threw his few belongings into a holdall, stopped, and looked at his watch. There were two and a half hours until the taxi came. He forced his brain to stop racing and went onto the balcony to smoke a cigarette. At this time of the morning, the Cairo air still clung to the cool freshness of night, before it was overwhelmed by the day's fumes. His eyes scanned the endless blocks of dun brickwork pierced by grey minarets and dusty palm trees. Where was she? He ranted silently, watching the city heat up, the buses cram into streets throttled by sidewalk stalls and milling pedestrians. He couldn't just stand and watch; he knew it was futile but he could at least try the 10am rendezvous by the *kushari* stand.

By 10.30 he was back. It had been fruitless, the same ironing man spraying shirts with his mouth, the *kushari* stand boarded up till evening. No Lucy. Nobody to trust except Pierre Farag. He smoked the last of the Rothmans, crushed the pack and chucked it into a corner of the room. On the balcony the roar of the city rose up like a menacing animal. He looked down on Cairo and loathed it.

The telephone rang again. The taxi was there. The bellboy in the red fez met him by the lift and led him to the entrance where a black and white cab waited. Bellamy hesitated. Get in or run? He took the holdall from the bellboy and got in. The figure in the back seat turned towards him. He'd got it wrong. It was a stranger. "Good morning, Detective Rogers," the man said in English, and rapped on the side window with his ring as the bellboy slammed the door. While the taxi lurched into the traffic Bellamy calculated his odds. The drive to the airport—if that was where they were going—would be mostly a crawl; he could likely jump out at a dozen intersections and grab another cab. But to where? Pierre Farag's office? The flat in Champollion Street? The British Embassy? Was the man armed? Would there be a carload of goons following them?

"It will be a very short journey, Detective Rogers," the man said. "Indeed, very short. Would you please prepare to get out very quickly when I tell you?"

"Who are you? What the hell's going on?"

"Just do as I say please." They were travelling south, away from the airport, towards Bab El-Luq market. The man told the driver to slow down by a motor repair shop on Muhammad Mahmoud Street.

"You see the alleyway. Jump out and run into it as fast as you can," he said. "Now!"

Bellamy threw open the door of the moving car at the throat of the dark alley. He considered for a second running along the street to the right or left, but his way was blocked by a barrow of flatbread on one side and a man carrying a sheep's carcass on the other. He barrelled into the alleyway, slinging the holdall over his shoulders, weaving left and right to avoid the bullets he was sure would come. He slipped once on some muck, got up, looked behind and saw nothing but daylight and passing figures at the far end of the alley. Looking ahead he could see a figure at the exit beckoning. A car pulled up, the back door was opened, and the figure got in, still beckoning. For a second he recalled those descriptions of passing from life to death—the distant light, the beckoning spirits. In the last five yards before the alley turned into the street, Bellamy saw that it was Pierre Farag in a small, dented, square-looking car. He threw himself in, and before Pierre shoved him to the floor he glimpsed the back of the driver's head and a pair of dark hands on a scratched and faded FIAT steering wheel.

* * *

Bellamy lay back on a leather armchair holding a towel filled with ice against his swollen knee, which had taken the impact when he'd slipped in the alley. Time had slowed down. It was the hour for reason, not anger, not instinct.

"We know where she is," Pierre said, "and we think

we know who she's with." The man in the white short-sleeved shirt was perched on a wicker chair under a big ceiling fan that swept the spacious sitting room with great draughts of air that had the smell of cool stone. A sunny garden of palms was visible through the halfopen shutters of the villa on the Giza Road.

"We?" Bellamy asked. He stubbed out a Cleopatra. "Who does 'we' include?"

"I hope you don't think me insolent if I say that your manner of questioning will not elicit the kinds of answers you seek," Pierre said.

Bellamy was irritated by the Egyptian's punctiliousness and finicky speech. But he pulled himself together; he was utterly in Pierre Farag's power. No profit in getting agitated. "I apologise. Tell me what we can do to get her back."

"I have, perhaps—how do you put it in English?—got ahead of myself. My colleague will be here shortly to explain for himself."

Bellamy stared at Pierre, willing him to say more. The two men sat in a column of silence. At last Pierre said, "Cairo is not a place for you, Mr Bellamy. You English like to see life in neat slices, like a sandwich on a nice white plate. We're not like that here. My life is not like that."

He sat primly on the edge of the chair for a long minute, and then, without looking at Bellamy directly, said, "Can you guess what I am, Mr Bellamy, what sort of Egyptian I am?"

Bellamy hadn't thought about it. He'd assumed from his name that the man was a Christian of some kind, although he wore no cross. He shrugged. If Pierre Farag wanted to make riddles, let him get on with it.

"My mother was Armenian and my father was a

Copt—an original Egyptian. My mother was born in Turkey in 1905. Her parents were good Ottoman citizens and they expected to live out their lives in the suburbs of Istanbul. My dear grandfather was a jeweller and my grandmother—she was a woman of refinement and erudition—taught English in a school for young ladies." Pierre stopped and looked at Bellamy, forcing him to meet his gaze. The man's expression was unreadable, emotionless.

He went on, "Do you know, Mr Bellamy, what happened in 1915?"

Bellamy nodded. He'd read about the pogroms, seen some photographs of crucified Armenian refugees. He remembered something about Hitler studying the methods of the Armenian genocide. Pierre's words had pricked his curiosity.

"Go on."

"Thank you. One day, my grandparents became enemies of the state. Just like that. Can you imagine? Of course, they should have seen the signs, seen it coming. My grandfather disappeared on April 24, 1915, and was never seen again—rounded up, you see, along with the entire high echelon of the Armenian community. Can you possibly imagine, Mr Bellamy, such a thing in England?"

"Why are you telling me this?"

"Let me finish. The remains of my family arrived in Athens in 1916. There were American missionaries in Greece who helped them reach Cairo a year later. By then my mother was thirteen. My grandmother was befriended by a kind Coptic family, who helped her establish herself as an English teacher here. I imagine she had managed to keep some valuables—gold, jewellery—to sustain herself. Five years later, my mother married one of the sons of the Coptic family. What's the expression you use? Happy ever after."

Bellamy wasn't certain whether to wait for more or to make some response. But the Egyptian seemed to have finished. Bellamy asked whether his parents were alive. "My father was a fighter pilot. Killed in '67. My mother passed away on holiday in California." Pierre's face momentarily darkened.

"God bless them," Bellamy said in Arabic. Then, in English, "You still haven't said why you are telling me this, Pierre."

"Perhaps it's to do with trust; you deserve to know a little about the man who holds your fate in his hands. But I think there is a lesson for you in my story. And I think you are a man who can learn lessons. Do you know French, by the way? I'm sure you do. You must be familiar with this. *Il y a un temps pour naître, et un temps pour mourir; un temps pour planter, et un temps pour arracher ce qui est planté.*"

Bellamy completed the stanza in English. "A time for peace, a time for war. It's from a song. The Byrds. *Turn! Turn! Turn!*"

"Singing birds? Turning? Indeed. Excuse me, I think our visitor is here."

He went out to the vestibule and returned with Major Fawzi.

"You!" Bellamy said, raising himself from the chair.

"It is a surprise, I am sure," Fawzi chuckled. He bowed slightly, offered his plump hand, and sat on a sofa.

Bellamy looked from Fawzi to Pierre and back again, and asked, "Is somebody going to explain?"

Fawzi spoke first. "I think we can dispense with the

Detective Rogers nonsense, Mr Bellamy."

"Go on."

"I'll be frank, Mr Bellamy. We—you and I—have interests in common."

"Indeed?" Bellamy had ceased to be alarmed by the ground shifting beneath his feet.

The fat man fingered his worry beads and arranged his features into a semblance of sincerity.

"My dear friend Pierre Farag," he began, "has persuaded me that your situation presents opportunities for all of us to profit. We have *ya'ni* put our noggins together in your absence."

"Noggins?" Bellamy wasn't sure whether Fawzi's quaint English was part of a sophisticated act or simply the result of a diet of Noel Coward and P.G. Wodehouse; he remembered from the briefing notes that Fawzi was an English graduate from Ain Shams University. Was he a buffoon or a highly skilled detective?

Pierre cut in. "Major Fawzi and I can help you, if you can help us." He looked to Fawzi to continue.

Fawzi settled into the sofa as if he was at a tea party, but the rapid fingering of his beads betrayed a mind in turmoil.

"Let me try to explain. My country is *ya'ni* at a point of turning, you might say. War is coming. Nobody knows who will be the victors, and who our friends will be. Indeed, we patriotic Egyptians are unsure of who among us are trustworthy, and who are traitors."

"What the hell has this got to do with me? I want to know how to get—" He stopped. How to get his lover back? How to get his girlfriend back? How to get his colleague back? What was Lucy to him?

Fawzi came to his rescue. "Please do not worry. Your fiancée is in the keeping of the same man who detained you in the City of the Dead."

Bellamy must have blanched because Fawzi wiggled his fingers and said, "We are monitoring everything. She is safe for now. We can extricate her without too much difficulty. Let me continue."

"Just get to the bloody point, man." Bellamy's mouth was dry, his chest pounding. He snatched a packet of Cleopatras from a coffee table, lit one and let the blessed nicotine clear his fogged brain.

Fawzi said, "You were kidnapped last Saturday by a member of the General Intelligence Directorate. The man who interrogated you is a senior officer, and he is involved in a plan, a project, a stratagem, that is widely ranging and closely concealed *ya'ni* behind walls of secrecy. It involves many parties, including your good self and your young lady."

"And what's your connection with this man? And the woman doctor who jabbed me full of God knows what? Are these the people who are—what was the word you used?—untrustworthy?"

"Mr Bellamy, you are remarkably perspicacious," Fawzi said, obviously savouring all four syllables of the word.

"You're still not getting to the point."

"The point, Mr Bellamy, is that I can obtain the young lady's release. Tonight. But I'll be blunt *ya'ni* in the English manner; there is a price."

There's always a price, Bellamy thought. The price of his scholarship education, paid out in punches and kicks on the council estate. The price of falling in love with Lucy Vickers; ten years of passionless liaisons with women who barely interested him. The price of a stupid lie in a Wimpy Bar; ten years in Ealing's clutches. Was this Pierre's oblique lesson? That our lives are mere accidents of fate, where free choice comes at a cost?

"Name the price, Major Fawzi."

"A debriefing of yourself and the young lady. After we have her released."

"A debriefing?"

"Everything about your mission in Cairo. Why you are masquerading as an English detective, what you aim to achieve. Who you work for. The names of your superiors. The young lady's part in your mission. All of these things are of interest to me."

Bellamy looked at Pierre, who was studying his fingernails. If Pierre and Fawzi were in this together, wouldn't Pierre have told him everything he knew? Wouldn't Fawzi already know about the defection of the Russian? He needed to probe, to judge how much Pierre was holding back.

"You think I'm some sort of James Bond, Major Fawzi? Soviet defectors, invisible ink, poison fountain pens, all that kind of thing?" He glanced at Pierre, who caught his eye and shook his head almost indiscernibly.

Fawzi put on an expression of mock amazement. "Is it snowing? Is there a red star on the top of the Sphinx? Are we in Moscow?"

"Of course not. But I think you know a good deal already. The man in the City of the Dead, the stratagem that you say the lady and I are involved in. But yes, I'll give you a debriefing if that's what it takes."

Bellamy looked again at Pierre, who had resumed observing his fingernails. He looked back at Fawzi. The man was still working the worry beads. There were damp patches under his armpits despite the cool of the room. Something else was in play here. Something linking the two men. Something in the past. He recalled the briefing notes he'd studied on that rainy day at Ealing in the building with custard coloured paint.

"Major Fawzi. Tell me about 1966. The Israeli business."

Fawzi gaped. His right hand went to his shoulder and then to his pocket. He took out a bottle and slipped a pill under his tongue. Pierre had stopped looking at his nails, and was glaring at Bellamy.

Bellamy knew an impending angina attack when he saw one. He stifled his instinct for compassion and pressed on.

"You met with an Egyptian Air Force officer. Tell me what happened."

The swish of the ceiling fan marked the seconds of silence until Fawzi whispered, "Tell him, Pierre."

Pierre writhed almost imperceptibly. Bellamy knew by now that he was a master of composure, but the strained cords in his neck and the white knuckles pointed to a profound mental struggle.

"Tell him. He's part of it now," Fawzi said. His hand now rested in his lap, and his breathing was calm.

"Very well." Pierre offered cigarettes and all three men lit up. "The man in the City of the Dead—his name is Dimashqi—used to work with an army intelligence unit that reported directly to a general. Major Fawzi was seconded to the unit in 1966. There was—what's the expression?—a falling out between the Major and Dimashqi."

Pierre stopped, as if finished with the story.

"That's it? A falling out?"

Major Fawzi swept his hand back and forth at Pierre, as if urging a horse to cross the road.

Pierre resumed. "There was a personal matter, a grave matter."

Again, Fawzi waved him on.

"Major Fawzi invited Dimashqi to his home. My father was also there. Dimashqi took an excessively bold interest in Major Fawzi's wife."

At this point the horse dug its hooves in: Pierre was prepared to go no further.

Major Fawzi took over in a slow monotone, all traces of buffoonery gone.

"Later he proposed a *safqa*—a bargain; I would gain promotion if I made my wife available to him from time to time."

The fat Major paused and sucked hard on the Cleopatra. His face was grey.

"You appear shocked, Mr Bellamy. But these things are commonplace in Egypt."

"Bastard!" Bellamy said. The water torture in the City of the Dead was still a raw memory. He was desperate to question Fawzi on how they were to extract Lucy from the pale-faced Dimashqi, but he had to hear Pierre and Fawzi out. He needed to know precisely what his place was in the events to come.

"So," Major Fawzi said, "I refused the *safqa* and reported the matter to my superior. Dimashqi then circulated a rumour that Pierre's father was an Israeli agent. By implication, I was also under suspicion."

"Why implicate Pierre's father?"

"Who knows?" the Major said. "There had perhaps been some falling out in the past, to use your very apt expression, and Dimashqi saw a chance to kill two chickens with one stone."

So there it was. The two men were joined in revenge

against the pale torturer, and Fawzi planned to use Lucy's rescue to bring their enemy down. But there remained the question, how much did Fawzi know of Pierre's plans?

Fawzi took his leave, but not before insisting that all three men 'synchronised chronometers'. It was 5pm, and Fawzi promised to return at 2am the next morning. Pierre suggested to Bellamy that they sleep, in preparation for whatever the night might bring.

Chapter 10 : A Candy-Striped Hat Box

Saturday 6 October 1973

Pierre arose from the couch in the front bedroom, from which he could observe the street frontage on the Giza Road. He was aware that he had napped briefly once or twice, woken each time by visions of crucified figures with formless faces. It was 2am, and a car was approaching. He squinted through the shutters; it was Fawzi's Mercedes.

While the Major parked the Mercedes under the dark shapes of the palm trees, Pierre's mind flowed back to the beach at Agami, to his parents in the ring of firelight, to Zouzou Faris's coy glances.

He got up to let in the Major, who was accompanied by a skinny young man in an over-large suit.

Bellamy was in the sitting room, barefoot in a vest and crumpled suit pants. His face was a wreck of anxiety. There was no point in Pierre asking the Englishman whether he had slept.

The young man stepped forward and shook Bellamy's hand briskly. His English was thickly accented but precise. "Lieutenant Zaki. We met at the hospital. Very pleased to see you again. I am sorry that I had to act the donkey on that occasion."

Fawzi cackled and put a hand on Zaki's shoulder. "My nephew, you see. He was a ruddy champ at amateur dramatics."

"I didn't find it funny at the time," the Englishman said.

"It was not a joke," Fawzi said, the fat man's face now stern. He took Zaki's hand in his and raised it like a trophy. "My nephew is my liaison officer with the General Intelligence Directorate. You have already met these people. We don't make jokes about dealing with them."

Pierre hid his surprise. How had he missed this link between the bumbling Cairo Criminal Investigation Bureau and the shady corridors of the General Intelligence Directorate? He felt a nudge of anxiety at finding a loose brick in the foundations of his profession. But one thing was certain: He thanked God that he had no part in Zaki's mission tonight; he had his own duties to fulfil.

Pierre indicated the coffee table, where there were glasses and bottles of Sinacola. Zaki unpacked cold aubergine sandwiches made from rough pocket bread. "My mother insisted, what with Ramadan." The four men sat. Pierre watched Bellamy wolf down the food, as if he was glad to divert his attention from his woman's plight.

Fawzi began to outline the plan. "She is, we believe, at the hospital where Zaki took you on our wild chicken chase . . ."

"Goose, not chicken," Pierre said.

"Goose, Indian duck, pigeon, *ma'alesh*. Our sources tell us *ya'ni* that Dimashqi is at a briefing with the

General at Helwan between 4am and 5am. Now, while Miss Lucy is under a substantial guard, there are no high-ranking officers in the hospital at the moment. We have drawn up a set of orders to release her into the custody of the Cairo Criminal Investigation Bureau. I will present the orders myself."

"And why would they just give her up?"

"Because the order is authorised by Dimashqi."

"You mean he signed it?" Pierre asked. This plan looked like a half-cooked *falafel*.

"Not exactly, but it will look authentic enough to the people at the hospital."

"Surely they will ring Dimashqi for confirmation?"

"Indeed, they most likely will." Fawzi looked smugly confident.

Pierre's eyes were gritty, and he struggled to concentrate on the Major's explanation.

"Let me continue. We have arranged for a technician to attend to a fault at a telephone junction box three hundred yards from the hospital. Not a real fault, of course. One of our own making."

"To what end?" Pierre asked.

"The technician is, of course, Zaki. He has rigged the box so that he will intercept the call for authorisation from the hospital. When the call comes, he will impersonate Dimashqi."

"Is he such a convincing actor?" Pierre asked.

"Without doubt. And he will provide to the caller some details that are on the order that I will have in my own hand in the hospital."

It was lunatic, but just plausible.

"I'll come with you," the Englishman quietly said to Fawzi.

"Completely impossible," Pierre said. "What do you think the guards will say when Major Fawzi turns up with an English gentleman in the middle of the night? Will they offer him a cup of Darjeeling and a cucumber sandwich? It's ridiculous."

"And do you think she'll just walk out with a couple of strangers? From the frying pan into a bloody furnace?" Bellamy said, his voice rising.

He had a point, Pierre thought. But the Englishman was utterly out of his depth. Fawzi's plan was preposterous, even for Cairo; Bellamy's presence would turn it into farce. But perhaps there was a way.

"What about a talisman?" he said.

Fawzi frowned; he didn't know the English word. Pierre explained in Arabic. "Something private or special that will convince her that you come with the Englishman's authority."

"Tell her," Bellamy said in English, "You came from the *barrow boy*." Pierre saw that the Englishman was struggling to stay in control of his emotions.

Fawzi raised his eyebrows. "Ah yes, a *barrow boy*. Very mysterious. Excellent. I will say it." He turned to his nephew. "Zaki, chop chop. We have work ahead tonight."

As Fawzi got up, Bellamy said to him, "What happens to Lucy and me afterwards? How do I know that you won't just shoot us and dump our bodies in the Nile?"

Pierre sighed. How did these people conquer the East? People for whom everything had to be black or white? But perhaps that was the answer. There were no shades of grey for them. Things were right or wrong, left or right, known or unknown, East or West.

"Mr Bellamy, you have my solemn and binding guarantee that your lives will not be sacrificed," Fawzi said. But the Englishman still looked doubtful.

Bellamy suddenly leapt up and blocked the door of the sitting room.

"Fuck the talisman. I'm coming."

Fawzi made to protest, and then seemed to deflate.

He looked to his friend for help. Pierre shrugged. "*Yalla*, Englishman, come, but you will stay in the car."

The Mercedes pulled away, taking Fawzi, Zaki and Bellamy to whatever fate might bring at the hospital. With the villa empty, Pierre sat quietly watching a chit-chat stalking a spider on the ceiling. A dim bulb on the outside wall of the villa threw bars of yellowish light through the shutter. The creature's body flattened against the smooth stone, half in light, half in shade.

There was a gramophone in the corner of the room, and a small stack of records next to it, perhaps left behind by some former tenant. Pierre nudged apart the disks in their soft paper sleeves. They were mostly frothy dance numbers—he recognised Bob Azzam's silly *Ya Mustafa*. It had been played day and night one summer at Agami, and he remembered his and Zouzou's fathers serenading their wives in chorus. How did it go? 'Darling, I adore you, my tomato sauce . . .'

But the last record in the stack was Umm Kulthoum's *The Ruins*. He put the record on and let the exquisite Classical Arabic stanzas caress his wary heart, almost against his will. The words told of the capriciousness of fate, the powerlessness of the lover's heart to follow its destiny. The song—the performance was half an hour long—ended on an ambiguous note, somewhere between hope and resignation.

Pierre straightened himself in his chair, at once exhausted and yet elated. He was surprised to notice that his cheeks were wet. His thoughts were five kilometres away at Zamalek at the overdecorated apartment where a woman waited. He looked at his watch. Almost four. There was a gleam of car headlights outside and the sound of an engine running rough. He opened the shutter and saw the old Fiat reverse up to the front door.

* * *

For the second time in two days Bellamy lay on the rear floor of a car, this time looking at Zaki's shoes. The Mercedes lurched around curves and bashed through potholes; Bellamy guessed that Fawzi was unused to driving himself. The streets were almost empty, as far as he could make out from the floor. Once there was a deep grinding roar and he glimpsed a tall military transport vehicle looming alongside the car, its rubber tyres higher than the Mercedes' roof. The car eventually slowed and then stopped under a street lamp that cast a beige light. Bellamy sat up and opened the back door. They were in a slip road behind some sickly trees. Fawzi and Zaki got out and picked their way to a gloomy rubble-strewn patch of ground where barriers had been erected around a metal cabinet. Bellamy followed, ignoring Fawzi's hand waving him back. Zaki sat on a crate and lay a torch on a pile of loose bricks beside him. In the cone of torchlight, a spaghetti of wires spilled out of the door of the cabinet. A telephone was connected with crocodile clips to two bared strands.

"Ready to intercept?" Fawzi asked. His nephew nodded, and moved the crocodile clips to another set of wires.

The three men jumped as the phone rang. Zaki looked at Fawzi, who said, "Answer!"

"Hello. Yes. Uncle Wisam, you say? Heliopolis? No, you've got through to the exchange. There must be a fault." Zaki detached one of the clips. "He's gone now."

"Did he suspect anything?" Fawzi asked.

"No, I reckon it was a private call and he got off in a hurry when Uncle Wisam didn't reply."

"Good lad. Now listen. Once we've got the lady I'll pass by this way and pick you up. We'll drop the *ingleezi* and the *ingleeziyya* at the Giza Road, and you and I will have time to get a dish of *ful medames* and eggs before daybreak, if God wills."

"If God wills, uncle."

"Englishman, back in the car, and keep your head down."

Fawzi started the car and drove the last few hundred yards to the hospital compound. He parked outside the boom gate, leaving the keys in the ignition. Bellamy found a patch of gloom in the back corner of the car from which he was sure he could not be seen. He watched Fawzi flourish some papers at the guard, who went into his box and made a telephone call. The Major stood, fidgeting, in the floodlight until the guard returned and gestured towards the hospital entrance. The fat man entered, and the guard returned to his box.

Ten minutes passed. Bellamy's stomach was a pit of acid.

Another ten minutes and nothing had changed: the floodlight that cast a magnesium pool around the guard's box, the gloom of the buildings, the smell of old sweat from the car seats.

But then a knot of men tumbled from the hospital entrance, and the guard raced out of his box clutching a rifle. Fawzi was struggling to free himself from two tall officers, who had his arms clamped in their hands. The fat man appeared to drop like a sack of chickpeas, and the officers bent to support him. He slumped to his knees. Bellamy saw his right arm clutch his left shoulder.

The edge of the floodlight caught his agonised expression as he rolled to one side, the officers springing back to watch his contortions. They called to the guard, who pointed at the Mercedes and turned back to shout something to them.

Bellamy threw himself into the front seat, started the big car and gunned it out of the car park. He found the headlight switch just as he reached the telephone cabinet where Zaki was waving his arms. The nephew flung himself into the car and Bellamy pressed the accelerator to the floor.

"She's not there. She's not there," he yelled at Bellamy.

"What do you mean, she's not there?" Bellamy shouted back, wresting the wheel. He had taken a wrong turn, and was heading back towards the hospital.

"They knew we were coming. We were tricked . . ."

But there were no more words. The windscreen dissolved with a deafening crack and Zaki's head slammed into the seat restraint. Bellamy was splattered with warm stickiness and broken glass. Had he been shot? Didn't they say that you didn't feel the pain straight away? He punched the brake, skidded to a stop, and ran his hands over his upper body. Nothing, nothing but—Zaki's blood and brains.

The kneeling guard aimed the rifle for a second shot. Bellamy declutched, banged the gear stick into first and stamped on the accelerator again, wrenching the wheel hard to the left. The big Mercedes slewed in a ninety-degree arc, slamming Zaki's lolling body into the right-hand window. The nephew's head took a second bullet, and Bellamy was showered with more warm muck. He tried to change up to second, but the gear stick was slimy. He wiped his gory fingers on his shirt, tried again, upshifted, and trod on the gas.

* * *

Pierre asked the Bulgar to stop a hundred yards short of the Champollion Street building where he knew Lucy Vickers' safe house was located. He took a shopping bag from the back seat and padded through the shadows, avoiding the street lights. At the entrance he pressed the bell once, waited, and then slipped inside as the *bawwab* checked the street.

"Up you go, Sir," the man said, rubbing the sleep from his eyes. Pierre trotted up the staircase, ascending through the floors until he was at the corridor that Bellamy had described. There was a garbage chute cover in a small cupboard by the apartment door. Pierre took a tight bundle of rags from the shopping bag, wedged it in the mouth of the garbage chute, and held a lit match to the rags until they began to smoulder. He used two clothes pegs to hold the chute cover and the cupboard door open, to induce a draught. As he ran down the stairs, the smell of smoke was already strong enough to sting his throat.

"Wait for ten minutes and call the fire brigade," he told the *bawwab*. Get the residents out into the street. Don't worry—nothing will catch fire."

And with the building crawling with police and firemen, Zlotnik won't come near the place, he thought. He climbed into the car and the Bulgar drove slowly away.

The Fiat reached Zamalek just as dawn was breaking. Pierre loved this time of day. The light had the texture of honey, and the air was at its freshest. She was already outside, wrapped in a dark robe. A pink suitcase and a candy-striped hat box rested on the doorstep. The Bulgar opened the back door and handed the luggage after her. She quietly thanked him, leaned back and covered her face with the corner of the robe. From the front seat of the car Pierre could smell her perfume. He shuddered ever so slightly.

The car began to move, and Pierre watched the waking streets lit by the apricot glow of dawn, as if in a bubble of bliss. The guttering of the Fiat's motor smoothed to a soothing hum; the grubby buildings appeared as if made of fine marble; and the faces of the passers-by seemed wreathed in happiness.

The sun was up when the Fiat pulled into the driveway of the villa on the Giza Road. The Bulgar pulled up close to the door so that Zouzou could enter the house unnoticed. Pierre unlocked the door, and she slipped inside. He turned to the Bulgar and said, "Go now." The battered car pulled away.

Just as Pierre pushed the front door open, there was a scream from inside the house. He stumbled into the sitting room to find Zouzou standing rigid and white faced in front of the Englishman, who was covered in blood, and profusely apologising.

"Fucking hell!" said Pierre.

* * *

Being a man 'turned in on himself', Pierre suppressed his anguish when Bellamy recounted the story of the pathetically inept rescue mission. He was not, perhaps, surprised; he might even have mentally prepared himself. Major Fawzi had seemed more and more like a man doomed by his past and the spite of his enemies. His old friend, he was now certain, had been played for a fool by Dimashqi all along. Pierre would grieve in his own time, in a way of his choosing. The days ahead would bring enough unhappiness.

Zouzou sat with her hat box on her lap, listening to

the Englishman's story. She only spoke once, to spit like a snake, "I met Dimashqi once and wished him dead."

"Where's Fawzi's car?" Pierre asked. "In the Nile," Bellamy said.

* * *

At around 8pm Pierre started up the motorbike he had parked at the side of the villa, and set off for Pension Serpouhi.

Zouzou and Bellamy had come to some kind of reckoning with the events of the night, and had installed themselves in their separate quarters in the villa. Pierre had begged them to be patient, saying, "You are in the safest place you can be. Preserve your strength for what tomorrow brings. It will not be an ordinary day."

As he rode the clattering Triumph 500cc, he pondered on the Englishman. He felt a curious affinity with the man, although they were so unlike. He'd met other English people on occasion, but these had been slight, casual encounters from which he'd learned nothing of their essence, their ways of thinking, or at least nothing beyond the frozen pictures of Englishness painted by the authors he'd read—Dickens, Hardy, Maugham and the rest. But he'd known Bellamy under dreadful stress, when a man's authentic spirit was forced into the light. He admired what he'd seen.

An idea had been sparking faintly in his consciousness. He had no stomach for America; he would be smothered by cloying cousins. It all looked too fast, too pressed. If his time in Egypt was coming to an end—something he'd faced as a reality in the last day—England would surely suit. He had an Armenian cousin in a place called Shepherd's Bush, who worked as a translator. He and Zouzou could discreetly settle in this rustic corner. There would be oak trees, a public house, and sheep on the greensward.

And he could turn his link with Bellamy to advantage in this regard.

A pothole almost threw him from the bike, and he corrected a dangerous wobble. He focused his mind on the streets of Cairo, which were unusually empty given that the fast had broken. It was as if a portentous aura had draped the city.

* * *

A hasty meal had apparently been prepared and the fast quickly broken at Pension Serpouhi. The girl was listlessly finishing the washing up. Madame Serpouhi was in her room, and several of the professional gentlemen were sitting silently at the big oilcloth dining table, fingering their beads, sharpening pencils or leafing through *Al-Ahram*; by this time of evening they would normally have retired. There was the smell of kerosene as the girl filled the Primus stove to boil water for tea. Pierre went to his tiny room to pack a few clothes and to get the Israeli Beretta; his instinct told him that it would be better to have the vile instrument on his person than behind the wainscoting in his room.

But when he knelt before the hiding place, it was evident that somebody had tampered with it. The piece of moulded wood had been wedged in at an oblique angle so that an unpainted edge stood proud of the adjacent piece. Pierre knelt back, stifled his rising alarm and listed the possible explanations. None of them fit the facts. Madame Serpouhi's girl getting too nosey during her cleaning duties? An unseen housebreaker? One of Major Fawzi's clodhopping juniors doing a spot of extramural investigation? He leaned over and prised back the wainscoting. The Beretta was gone.

There was nothing to be done. Things happened in

Cairo for obvious or obscure reasons, and each had consequences that might be equally obvious or obscure. The theft of his Israeli gun was a link in a chain of fate that had begun years ago when the gangster had won it in a dirty deal, and later turned his suspicions to his boss-eyed daughter's virtue. The chain extended, unbroken, into the cloudy future. Let it be. What could he do? Pierre pushed the wainscoting back, changed into a pair of pyjamas, and lay on his bed with a Cleopatra.

At about 10pm he dressed and went back into the dining vestibule. The birdcage lift clanged and a uniformed man let himself into the premises. Pierre saw that it was one of Madame Serphouhi's long-term residents, Mr Abd El-Aziz. But in an officer's uniform? He then remembered. The uniformed man was a journalist for an army magazine. He must hold a military rank. The other professional gentleman came out of their rooms, and everybody gathered around Mr Abd El-Aziz. He opened a holdall and took out a piece of grey painted wood with Hebrew lettering on it. It looked like the side of an ammunition box.

Madame Serpouhi and the servant girl came into the room. The piece of wood was passed from hand to hand. It was clear from everybody's face that they knew its significance. Pierre watched as the professional gentlemen wavered between elation and dread, beseeching God that it not be like 1967.

"It's from Sinai. I've just returned. The glorious Egyptian armed forces crossed over at four o'clock this afternoon, thanks be to God," Mr Abd El-Aziz said.

It was as I guessed, Pierre thought: 6 October. But what a difference a week had made. His friend Fawzi dead; the vile Dimashqi and his stooges lurking in every dark corner. Had he deluded himself with his Egyptian patriotism? 'The people advance like the light,' the anthem went. Would the half-educated boys on the battlefield 'advance like the light' as they fell in blood soaked swathes? Would their fathers in the Delta with their trachoma-blighted eyes 'advance like the light' towards their sons' coffins? Would a half-Armenian private detective 'advance like the light' towards betrayal and imprisonment at the hands of a Dimashqi?

He considered the women in his tangled life, reflecting that he had no male friends now that Fawzi was dead.

Aunt Serpouhi would surely leave for California soon, despite her protestations. As for the lady in Shoubra, he must discreetly leave her an ample gift. Bellamy's girl must be found; he needed them as a pair. And Zouzou; he and she would start again, an English couple in Shepherds Bush.

He looked at his father's Rolex. There was one more call to make before he returned to the villa on the Giza Road.

He realised then that he had forgotten the woman who'd started all of this: the dead opera singer, Siranoush.

Stuart Campbell

PART TWO: DEAD SOULS

Chapter 11: Men who'd Seen it All

Thursday 4 October 1973

When Lucy slipped Briggs's passport into Mark Bellamy's hand at the crowded street crossing, she fought the urge to turn her head and look at him. Instead, she slid into the river of humanity flowing in the direction of Champollion Street, in a swirl of conflicting feelings: the ache of desire to be with him again; deep apprehension about the mission she'd been charged to fulfil; guilt for what she hadn't told him about his role in the defection plan; and a creeping intuition that she herself was the subject of a heinous betrayal.

But for now she could do nothing but keep moving through the steps of the plan: wait for the defector to make contact, move him to the safe house with Mark Bellamy, confirm the bona fides, and hand him over to Mark to be conveyed to Britain as Mr Briggs. And if something went wrong, be prepared to change tack.

And in three hours there was the 2pm rendezvous with Mark, when, like coy sweethearts, they would briefly peep at one another from different sides of the street near the *kushari* stall to confirm that each was safe, and then part until the next rendezvous at six.

She had divided her luggage between her hotel and the Champollion Street apartment, and before returning to the hotel she told herself she needed to collect some personal items from the safe house. In truth, she had two reasons to visit the apartment. She had an irresistible compulsion to lie on the bed where she and Mark had made love, to bury her face in the pillows and breathe in the enthralling scent of a ten-year-old affair so deliciously reprised yesterday afternoon. At the same time, her professional instincts told her that she must check the safe house for evidence of intruders. In this Janus-like state, Lucy, cool intelligence operative and passionate lover, pressed the bell on the apartment building.

"Yes, Madame?" The *bawwab*—robed, turbanned, leather-faced—asked in Arabic. Lucy's blonde hair was covered with a flowered headscarf.

"Apartment 36, *law samaht*—'if you please'."

"Madame's name, *law samahti*?"

She remembered the upside-down style of addressing these doormen.

"You know me, Professor. I was here yesterday."

The man put his palm on his chest and made a face of resignation to the will of God.

"Your face is not familiar, Madame. I cannot allow you to enter. The owner of the building would be displeased."

Lucy produced an Egyptian pound note, and the *bawwab* let her in after checking the street. She took the lift to the third floor. But the key would not work. She looked closely and saw that the brass barrel of the lock was shiny and new. Lucy stared at the ornate door and resisted the urge to kick it. The creeping intuition of betrayal by the smug civil servants at Ealing forced itself out of the murk of her subconscious. The smoggy midday heat clung to her skin. There was a fiery blister on her heel from the patent leather shoes. She was perspiring in her European skirt and jacket, but she marshalled her professional *sang froid* to fight the looming panic.

"Madame, you had better leave this place." The *bawwab* had followed her to the third floor. "Others are involved in this matter. I am a simple man, but, by God, this is not a place for a lady like yourself."

It was, as Mark would put it, going arse-up.

Outside in the street she was almost paralysed with unease and indecision. There were two ways forward: the Semiramis Hotel, where she could sit and pretend that she was safe, surrounded by people in suits and dresses doing ordinary things; or the Nile Hilton, where she and Mark would throw Ealing's defection plan in the rubbish where it belonged, and thrash out a plan to save their lives. Only the Nile Hilton made sense.

But the stickiness of her clothing reminded her that she'd need to retrieve the rest of her things. Worse still, her passport and travellers cheques were in the Semiramis Hotel safe. She'd stop there briefly before fleeing to the Hilton.

* * *

"Madame, we have no record of your registration at the hotel."

"That's rubbish. Room 624, Victoria Patchett. I had breakfast here this morning."

Lucy removed the head-scarf. "Look at this hair. Don't tell me you don't know who I am."

The familiar gesture, the palm over the heart, the eyes imploring God for merciful release from this dilemma.

"This is ridiculous. How can you treat me in this way? I want to get into my room. I want my property. And please get my valuables from your safety box!"

The desk clerk spread his hands in submission and tutted; Lucy recognised the Egyptian gesture for 'no'.

"Can I please make a phone call at least?"

The clerk gestured to a row of glass-fronted phone cabinets to the side of the foyer. A row of clocks above the cabinets showed the time in ten cities around the world. It was 9am in London, and she imagined walking across the frosty lawn of her parents' house in Brighton. The callers behind the glass windows were silently gesticulating into telephones. There was one empty booth. She picked up the receiver and asked the operator for the memorised number.

It rang for half a minute and then answered. "British Embassy."

"I was given this number for emergencies."

"Your name?"

"Victoria Patchett."

"Please wait."

Lucy studied a framed sepia picture on the wall of the booth for a full five minutes. It was a photograph of a bearded peasant by a palm-ringed *wadi* in the oasis, inscribed in the corner with *Lehnert & Landrock Bookshop, 44 Sherif St.* Willing her mind to be calm, she focused on the fine lines of the palm leaves and the languid reflections in the water. The telephone line clicked and burbled. At last, the voice returned.

"Sorry, no record of that name, Miss"

"Are you sure? Please check again." The line clicked

off.

Lucy jiggled the phone cradle and the operator came back on.

"Nile Hilton, please."

But the Nile Hilton had no record of anybody by the name of Rogers.

"You're sure? An Englishman, brown hair, thirties."

"I am sorry, Madame."

She went back to the desk.

"Sixty piastres please."

"What for?"

"The telephone calls."

Lucy switched to Arabic, hissing quietly, "Get me the manager straight away if you value your job in this hotel."

The clerk's face hardened. He looked over Lucy's shoulder and nodded to somebody behind her. She turned. A tall European man with a broad face sat casually in an armchair. He wore a baggy tan suit. The immediate impression was of a man with an untidy body—limbs too long, paunch too plump, straggly hair swept back behind the ears.

The man looked at her and tapped the seat next to his. She knew this face. It belonged to Briggs, the face on the passport she had slipped into Mark's hand at the traffic intersection.

Lucy had no choice. She walked robotically towards him and sat down. He exuded cologne and stale tobacco. Her heel hurt. Her head swam. She felt nauseous.

"Let's avoid any unpleasant scenes. Please understand that the fellow at the desk is under my instruction. He released your luggage and valuables to me an hour ago, and removed your details from the register." The man spoke with deliberation in American-accented English with an overlay of Russian.

Despite the shock of his frank admission, Lucy maintained her calm breathing and studied the man dispassionately. She had no doubt that she was completely in his control—or almost completely. He was a type of man she'd seen before among diplomats and international agency functionaries: effortlessly multilingual, cynical and world-weary, neither at home nor abroad wherever they found themselves; men who lived half their lives in aeroplane seats and hotel rooms; the type of men who'd seen it all.

He locked his gaze on hers, apparently waiting for her reaction to the trap. She stared back, marvelling at her composure; was it borne out of sheer terror? She'd think about that later. For now her priority was to try to set the rules of the game that was to follow.

"I'm going to call you Briggs. That's the name on the passport you will enter the UK with."

"Briggs? Thank you. I'd better get used to it. I suppose there is no point in asking where this passport can be found?"

"No point at all," Lucy said. "You'll be given it at a safe house on Saturday after your bona fides have been verified." She watched him carefully. There was no indication that he knew about the apartment in Champollion Street or that it had been compromised. But then, men like these could sit flint-faced while watching their grandmothers being boiled in acid.

"And there's no point in asking where my own passport is located?" Lucy asked.

"No point at all," he said. "You'll be given it when I am given Mr Briggs's passport."

"And my luggage?" It was too late to bite back the words. She'd exposed her amateurism. The tiny smirk around the man's mouth showed that he had won a point. Sod the bloody suitcase with thirty quids' worth of stuff in it.

Lucy had to regain just a slim edge of control. She examined him again. Was this the face of a prude, perhaps?

"I presume you searched my things. Did you enjoy looking at my underwear?"

"I beg your pardon?"

"My panties, my brassieres? Did you play with them, imagine things?"

The man glared at her and said something in Russian that she didn't like the sound of. Well, she'd got under his skin; something to save for later if need be.

She pressed on. "So, Mr Briggs, you have appointed yourself my travel agent for the next two days. What have you got planned for me?"

"Take this and get changed in the lavatory next to the bar. Go out the rear entrance and wait for my car." He handed her a plastic bag and walked away.

Lucy put on the black robe and looked into the bathroom mirror. She'd worn an *abaya* in Syria and knew how it magically made a woman invisible. But the short blonde hair marked her like a Belisha beacon. She tied the headscarf securely so that her head was completely covered.

The Arab driver replied to Briggs's directions in rough-sounding Russian. The car—a black, heavy, dome-fronted model she didn't recognise—took them through the suburbs until they reached an area of respectable apartment blocks and street markets.

"That building, you see, with the buses outside. I will drop you one hundred metres further on, and you will walk back and come up to the fifth floor. The name on the door is Zlotnik. It is in Cyrillic but you can decipher it quite easily. We are nearly there. Please prepare yourself to get out."

Lucy walked back the hundred yards with a feeling of detachment from the world. Nobody in the crowded street paid her a glance. If she'd fallen dead on the spot, nobody would know her name. She had no money, no map, no identity, no plan.

Lucy was surprised to see that the corridors of the apartment block were choked with Russian women and children, all evidently on the move. The lift had been commandeered for luggage, with a squad of Egyptian youths in vests humping cheap fibre suitcases onto the buses parked outside. Lucy forced herself up the staircases against a stream of mothers and toddlers stumbling downstairs with handbags, school satchels and teddy bears in their arms. One Russian woman stopped Lucy and gave her a key, saying to her in kitchen Arabic, "Give to cleaner for Apartment 421."

An Arab woman hefted a trunk through the doorway of one of the apartments next to the staircase on the third floor. "Where are they going?" Lucy asked in Arabic. The sweating servant looked up and said, "Home to Russia, along with my job."

The fifth floor appeared to have been mostly vacated, and she quickly located the door bearing a plastic strip inscribed with ЗЛОТНИК. It was unlocked, and she entered. She glanced at her watch. Half past one, too late to make the two o'clock rendezvous. If she missed six o'clock, the whole affair would have truly gone arse-up.

"Hello." No answer. No Zlotnik.

The apartment was jerry-built, with floor tiles that ended an inch short of the lumpy stucco wall. The front door had an array of levers, bars and bolts to secure it, all unlocked.

Lucy kicked off her shoes, and took off the *'abaya* and headscarf, dumping everything in the hallway. She went into a lounge room with a kitchen alcove at the end. It was a man's room, spartan and apparently barely used; a large glass ashtray sat on the plywood coffee table next to half a dozen Soviet magazines with their dull matt covers. She had done a crash course in Russian five years ago and remembered enough to recognise the title— *Ogonyok*; it was a famous current affairs magazine. She picked up a copy and opened it at a photo essay that seemed to be about a factory that turned out left-handed gloves. A small bookcase contained books in Russian, English and French: Pushkin, Lermontov, Tolstoy, Shakespeare, Victor Hugo, Stendhal, Zola. There was a sofa covered with brown plastic fabric, textured like a skin rash. A movie poster was sticky taped to the wall; the Russian title said *Solyaris*. Tarkovsky's *Solaris*—Lucy had seen it in Kensington last year.

She stood looking at the poster in a frozen sliver of time; here, now, nowhere, linked to a Russian called Zlotnik by a film about a man searching for his dead wife on a distant planet.

The outer door banged shut. Lucy ran to the kitchen alcove. She flung open a drawer and palmed the only knife—a cheap plastic-handled thing a few inches long. Zlotnik suddenly filled the entrance to the lounge. He charged across the small room and wrenched her to the floor. His hands were everywhere, sliding under elastic, efficient, fast, across flesh, approaching her private places but not touching them, his knees pinning her to the floor. This wasn't for sex; this was a body search.

The hand holding the fruit knife was momentarily free and she lunged without aim till it struck meat. The Russian sat up and looked with puzzlement at the flimsy blade protruding from his shoulder. With Lucy still pinned by his knees he gently pulled it from his shoulder. There was an ooze of blood on his jacket. A single drop fell from the knife onto Lucy's brow. She cringed.

He released her, stooped and gave her his other hand as if to help her to her feet. "I am very sorry," he said. "I had no choice. I am not a barbarian. I have never laid violent hands on a woman before."

"You bloody swine. I told you I don't have the passport." Her heart pummelled. Her stomach and thighs crawled as if worms were inside her clothes. The man's smell was on her skin. He stank of fear.

The Russian looked at his hands. "I play the cello, you know," he said.

Lucy picked herself up, stripped of dignity, her blouse yanked free of her waistband and skirt rucked around her thighs. Her clothes were creased and grubby, her underwear unfresh and invaded. She snatched a teacloth from the kitchen bench and scrubbed the blood from her brow, outraged at the man's violation of her flesh.

But her rational self told her she'd acted like a foolish amateur. What if she'd stuck the fruit knife in his eye, or hit an artery? What if her one set of clothes had been soaked in blood, with the Russian screaming in pain? Shouldn't she have just grit her jaw as he pawed her? And what was this cello business, the hang-dog face, the ludicrous curtsey and the proffered hand?

Zlotnik left the room and returned swiftly with iodine, cotton wool and sticking plasters. He stripped to his vest and dressed the place where the knife had pierced the muscle. His paunch and spindly arms were pathetic, his trembling fingers peeling the sticking plaster.

"Please give me the iodine," Lucy said. He passed the bottle and a pad of cotton wool. She sat on the sofa and leaned over to dab her raw heel; the last thing she needed was blood poisoning. Zlotnik knelt and handed her an unwrapped plaster. She winced at his sour odour. It occurred to her now that they were joined in a grotesque partnership, she and this desperate Russian. And despite his assault on her, his squirming contrition gave her a slim advantage for now. She extended her foot, even if her mind recoiled at the thought of his touch.

"Put the sticking plaster on for me."

He fumbled over the plaster, and when he had dressed her foot, Zlotnik said, "I have to go to the Embassy. You must stay here. There's a bathroom, food in the cupboard."

"Don't lock me in."

"But I must."

"What if there were a fire? I'd die," Lucy said.

"There won't be."

"When will you be back?"

"Seven, eight. We will talk about our plan then."

"My plan, not our plan," she said. "It's me who will get you out of Egypt."

The Russian smirked. "By parting the Red Sea? We both know that your plan is in ruins."

He opened a door from the lounge and Lucy glimpsed a bed made with military neatness. Zlotnik went inside and a wardrobe door banged. He came out wearing a checked Viyella shirt and yellow wool tie under a sports jacket. Like an estate agent from Dorking, she thought. One who plays the cello and violates women.

"Why were all those Russians leaving today?" she asked. "What does it mean?"

Zlotnik lit a cigarette but said nothing.

"Speak to me."

"I will be missed if I do not leave now," he said. He left the room. There was the triple click of a deadlock and he was gone.

Nothing mattered but to wash the man's stink from her body, to scrub the spot on her brow. In the bathroom Lucy fumbled with the Vesuvius boiler on the wall. It lit with a woof, and fragments of scorched cockroaches blew out of the vent onto the stained enamel of the bath. She stood under the bronchitic shower head until she was sure that Zlotnik's fear-stink and his blood spot had washed off her skin.

There were grey towels in a cupboard, laundered, sun-dried and rough as rope, smelling of hard soap. Lucy dried herself and sat on the couch. She allowed herself to weep a churning tumult of tears: for the sorrow of ten lost years of Mark; for fury at the cardigan-wearing mandarins at Ealing; for disgust at Zlotnik.

With her ration of tears exhausted, she spoke aloud to the empty room. This was a private habit she often practised in times of turmoil, staging a dialogue with herself. She'd done it the morning after the weekend with Mark at the hotel in Kingsway ten years ago; she'd persuaded her better self to do what Ealing asked of her and regretted it ever since.

The seedy flat and the street noise of honking cars and shouting market vendors provided the backdrop to the drama.

"Listen girl, you've got no papers and no money and

you don't know where you are. Mark's left his hotel. You don't have any choice but to stick with this Russian."

"*Silly cow. You dumped Mark once and look what happened. Go after him. You've got a robe, you speak the language. Get out there and find him. You've got nothing to lose.*"

"Nothing to lose? Is that right? How about my life? I could end up in the City of the Dead with a hose pipe down my throat."

"*Your life isn't worth a stale pork pie without Mark. You're supposed to be smart—it's time you worked that out. Get back to the city and find him.*"

Her mind was made up; get herself by wit and guile to the Nile Hilton, where she'd kick up such a stink that someone would tell her where Mark was.

She went into the hallway to put on the '*abaya*, the headscarf and the shoes. They were gone. The bloody bastard had taken them with him. She couldn't hobble to central Cairo dressed like a barefoot Miss Moneypenny.

But then she remembered, her handbag. She'd slipped it behind the sofa when she'd arrived. Zlotnik hadn't thought to look for it. Why should he? He was a man. Lucy rummaged through the make-up and cigarettes and packets of traveller's tissues. She unzipped the inner pocket and there it was. The key to Apartment 421.

The front door was deadlocked; it would take the Corps of Royal Engineers to get her out. There was nothing of use to her in the flat. Zlotnik's wardrobe contained only four tan suits and two pairs of very large shoes, complemented by a basket of soiled shirts and Y-fronts. The kitchen cupboard contained tins of meat that looked like spam, bottles of Polish pickled cucumbers, and vodka. Of documents, money, keys, there was nothing. The telephone was fitted with a lock on the dial. She picked up the receiver; there was a dial tone, but no means of calling a number. The hopelessness of the situation only firmed her resolve. This was Lucy Vickers, she told herself—a woman of imagination, intellect, strength; not the kind of drip who'd sit and wilt while she waited for a man to rescue her.

She patrolled the apartment and discovered a door in the bedroom, closed with a long sliding bolt. The bolt slid back easily and the door swung outwards onto a tiny wrought-iron balcony. A waist-high padlocked gate led from the balcony to an elaborate system of fire escape ladders around an internal courtyard. Scanning the backs of the apartment, Lucy saw nobody. A couple of windows and doors had been left open, presumably by the Russian families in their haste to leave. She swung over the gate and ran barefoot down the iron steps to the fourth floor.

Chapter 12: Comrade Boss

Thursday 4 October 1973

Zlotnik's embassy driver was in a talkative mood, if you
could call it talking. A throaty mess of half-digested
Russian phrases drifted back over the Egyptian's
shoulder to the back seat, where Zlotnik made a show
of calmly shuffling papers. The man probably reported
back to Dimashqi. Half of Cairo seemed to report back
to Dimashqi.

"Comrade boss. Why Russian lady all go home?"

Good question, he thought. "Shut up and drive."

Zlotnik was perspiring heavily. The Viyella shirt
itched like sandpaper. The woman's shoes and
headscarf were bundled up in the *'abaya* on the seat next
to him. What he'd done to her was unspeakable. He
cringed—not just at the way he'd pawed her, but at the
state of panic that had driven him to it. He despised the
use of violence. It was uncouth and unnecessary for a
man like himself to physically force himself on another
person, let alone a woman; he was well-read, an
accomplished musician, a cultured polyglot. Violence
was for the trained specialists, the dead-eyed men he'd
encountered now and again in the grey zone where

Soviet diplomacy, espionage and special operations rubbed shoulders.

Why hadn't he followed the plan, waited for Pierre to arrange the rendezvous? He'd paid half up front to the Egyptian private detective—in US dollars. Pierre had told him it would be an English woman with short blonde hair. There was a safe house, he had said, in Champollion Street. "You'll be moved there with the woman the day before so that you can be briefed on the transfer." His Egyptian friend seemed sanguine, almost casual, about the arrangements. Zlotnik was, for once, ignorant of the procedure; he could write the handbook on covert diplomatic operations, but defection?

And then he'd tried to be too clever, to get one jump ahead of Pierre, to play by his own rules. It had taken just a couple of calls to track down a newly arrived English woman with short blonde hair. But now he had a hole in his shoulder and the skinny yellow-haired cat planning to greet him with God knows what when he returned home. And no UK passport.

"Comrade boss, many, many car. Maybe accident."

They were locked in a hell's kitchen of flats, market stalls and honking gridlocked vehicles. Zlotnik looked at his watch. It was late, and on such a day.

* * *

The normal calm running of the Embassy had suddenly been ruptured yesterday lunchtime. The Ambassador issued the evacuation order without any explanation: 'Wives and children to be sent home on the 4th and 5th of October'—nothing more. Whole sections of the Embassy staff were assigned to the logistics of the evacuation, struggling to get a couple of thousand people notified, packed and transferred in readiness for planes that were already taking off in the USSR. At the same time, an unusually large stream of military intelligence began flowing in from Syria. Zlotnik was assigned to assisting with logging and analysing the material—not his usual kind of work. Gathered for a tea break in the afternoon, frazzled colleagues had come together to discreetly speculate on the events of the day. Was Sadat's invasion of Sinai about to begin? Would there be two fronts—in Sinai and the Golan? No, was the consensus; there had been plenty of false alarms. And anyway, the Egyptians weren't ready, let alone the Syrians.

Somebody mentioned a story he'd heard. "A friend of mine, a military trainer, he was at an exercise in the desert a month ago. According to him, they get the Egyptian soldiers to run up a sand hill holding these metal suitcases. The gyppos fling themselves prone and open up their cases. Out come these finned *Malyutka* rockets, wicked looking little bastards, with a gunsight and a joystick. My friend says the thing shoots off like a demented toy, with the Egyptian controlling it on wires. It's supposed to put a hole in a tank three kilometres away."

"I saw it in Vietnam. It's a terrifying thing when it roars off, the *Malyutka*," somebody else said. "The Viet Cong knocked off Patton tanks with it."

"Yeah, but my friend was doubtful. He says the Egyptians don't have the will. They're undisciplined, he says. They're not ready for war, not against Israel."

"Who wants the Third World War anyway?" somebody else said.

Zlotnik hung back as the workers left their empty tea glasses and went back to their cubicles. His old classmate Irina had caught his eye during the chitchat, and she also lingered by the tea urn. They'd graduated from MGIMO in the same year, and had remained firm friends, and even on occasions, confidants. Neither of them had joined in the gossip.

"What's your take on all this, Irina Andreyevna?"

"In a nutshell, I'm confused," she said quietly.

"Confused?"

"The word is that Brezhnev doesn't want Egypt to go to war. It makes sense when you think about it. As the comrade said just now—nobody wants World War Three. On the other hand, Sadat's pushing us hard for more weapons and support. Let's face it—there's been a low-level war going on since 1967. They might be better prepared than our loose-mouthed friend thinks. And there's all this stuff coming in from Syria; what if they're preparing to attack on two fronts?"

"But Sadat can't win, surely, Irina Andreyevna?"

"Maybe he doesn't want to. Maybe he's putting on a show for Nixon and Kissinger."

Zlotnik nodded. Yes, he could see it. "You mean he launches the attack, and gets his troops across the canal in the hope that the Yanks will intervene before the Israelis force them back?"

"Could be. Then we and the Americans cosy up and agree that we don't want it to escalate, and Sadat negotiates some sort of agreement that keeps the canal in his possession."

"That's one scenario," Zlotnik said. "But there could be a dozen others."

"As I said, Ivan Maksimovich, I'm confused." Irina stubbed out a cigarette.

"Better get back to my desk."

As the afternoon ground on, Zlotnik, swamped in documents—radio intercepts, transport movements, air traffic data—began to sense in his guts a cold burrowing worm of doubt: doubt about his trust in Dimashqi; doubt that the defection plan was tight; doubt that the invasion of Sinai was to be launched a month from now; doubt that he would ever join his exile compatriots in London; doubt that he would live another week.

* * *

He was jerked back to the present by the driver's dirty Russian.

"Comrade boss. Not moving."

Zlotnik checked his watch; they'd been stationary for ten minutes and the fumes in the car were as thick as his grandmother's buckwheat porridge.

"How far to the Embassy?"

"Half kilometre."

"I'll walk."

Zlotnik got out and pressed through the seething pedestrians. At a big intersection the cause of the traffic jam was clear: a taxi, a bus and a tram had collided. Injured children—they had probably been riding the roof and bumpers of the tram—screamed in the gutters. There were no ambulances, no police, just civilians doing their amateurish best with whatever there was to hand—towels and whiskey bottles of water. Fight a war against Israel? These people? For God's sake!

He skirted the accident—the last thing he needed was to get involved in an altercation with some hothead looking for a foreigner to blame. And as he negotiated the broken pavements and the knots of pedestrians, Zlotnik's thoughts turned back—as they had many times in the last twenty-four hours—to Dimashqi.

He had cultivated the sinister intelligence chief for a year; that was his job, after all, to build clandestine networks loyal to the USSR. Obscure hints were exchanged that opened the possibility that Dimashqi could be turned. The Egyptian began to pass on a dribble of secret material—mostly fluff, easily verifiable and of no practical use. But here and there were gems of intelligence that began to convince Zlotnik that the man was prepared to betray his country. The Egyptian's motive was trickier to discern. He shrugged off money, almost as if it were an insult. At one meeting the man made some obscure remarks about a new order in Egypt. This was around the time that Dimashqi revealed to Zlotnik that a junior Soviet diplomat was feeding military intelligence to the Israelis. Zlotnik arranged for the man to be recalled to Russia. The double agent attempted suicide, but was got onto the Moscow plane more or less alive.

Then the tease began: the hints about a special date, the request for assurances of Dimashqi's anonymity, the promise of an intelligence breach that could change history, the veiled remarks about their 'common aim'. And then a discreet meeting in Khan Khalili market when he told Zlotnik that Operation Full Moon would be launched on November 3.

But today was October 4. The Syrians were mobilising, the Soviet advisers' families were being shipped home in haste. And he was supposed to move to the safe house tomorrow in preparation for his defection the next day.

Zlotnik forced the unthinkable from his mind and looked for a shortcut he knew—a street that ran past a small museum, a former palace, now closed. But as he passed the building the iron gate creaked and a tall green-uniformed officer stepped out. Zlotnik recognised the garb of the security police. A second officer came out and said in English, "Your papers, please."

"I'm a diplomat. Please let me pass." Zlotnik showed his diplomatic passport.

"Why are you walking in the street?"

"There was a traffic jam."

"It is dangerous for you to be in the street."

"I request that you let me pass. I have to get to the Embassy of the USSR. This is an official request."

The English-speaking officer nonchalantly snatched the passport and went inside the iron gates. He beckoned to Zlotnik, and opened the door of what appeared to be an old ticket office. The first officer dialled a number on a telephone of such antiquity that Zlotnik wondered if it was a museum exhibit. The devil take these amateurs! Let them make their phone call and give me back my damned passport!

There was a rapid exchange of Arabic, which Zlotnik could not follow, other than the spelling out loud of his name from where it was printed in Roman characters in the passport. The officer put the phone down, placed the passport on a shelf behind himself, and deliberately ran his hand over his buffed pistol holster.

"Wait now."

Zlotnik seethed. Three or four minutes passed. The phone rang and the officer passed it to him.

"Hello."

"Mr Zlotnik. How are you?"

It was Dimashqi

"I am very well. However, I am being detained by your staff in breach of diplomatic protocols."

Dimashqi chuckled. "Mr Zlotnik, you are not detained. You are merely under the protection of the

General Intelligence Directorate. My officers have orders to drive you to the Embassy immediately."

"Thank you." Zlotnik hesitated. He had to glean some clue about the date that Dimashqi had entrusted him with.

He asked, "By the way, did you check that date we discussed?"

"Date of what?"

"November fourth. The cocktail party at the Cultural Centre."

"Yes indeed, absolutely. It is in my diary." Dimashqi rang off.

A Jeep appeared from an alley. Zlotnik got in the back. The vehicle sped through a tangle of back alleys while he grasped the metal frame of the canopy to prevent being thrown out. Fifteen minutes brought them to the Embassy gates where Zlotnik, legs like jelly, stepped onto firm ground. Checking his pockets for his passport, wallet, keys and fountain pen—they were all there—he suddenly realised that he'd left the bundled *'abaya* in the Embassy car. He looked around the parked vehicles to see if his driver had got back before him. He spotted the car—it had a distinctive dent—and walked to it as quickly as he could without provoking the interest of the rubbernecks who hung around the Embassy. The driver was gone and the back seat was empty.

With his legs barely under his control, Zlotnik walked to the concrete blast wall that had recently been built in front of the gates. A gang of workers were filling sand-bags, the first few of which had been stacked at the base of the wall. He showed his passport to the guard and was admitted to the compound.

* * *

At seven in the evening he left the Embassy for what he hoped would be the last time. Although it was dark, the heat of the day still lingered, but the stink of traffic fumes had lost its acrid edge. He knew that, despite his folly in deviating from the plan, Pierre Farag would contact him tonight or tomorrow.

In the morning he would telephone and plead sickness; frequent gastric complaints kept a proportion of the staff off work on any given day, despite the fact that everyone boiled the Cairo tap water assiduously. He'd have to make it convincing under the circumstances; the Embassy was on high alert, the evidence pointing to war within days. But he couldn't be sure; Zlotnik's position in the hierarchy, like Irina's, placed him one rung below those who would have definitive knowledge—those who liaised with the most senior of Sadat's people.

Exiting around the blast gate, he bumped into Irina coming around the opposite side; she must have been just behind him as he walked across the front courtyard, so engrossed was he in his thoughts.

"You look thirsty, Ivan Maksimovich."

"No thanks, Irina Andreyevna; tomorrow perhaps." They sometimes had a beer or two before leaving for home.

"Tomorrow? Always an optimist. This time tomorrow these Egyptian *duraki* might have landed a SAM 6 missile on our roof by mistake."

"Fools, Irina Andreyevna? I don't know who the fools are any more."

The woman threw a cigarette butt on the ground and sighed.

"Ivan Maksimovich, we're old pals. I used to see that expression at MGIMO. You look unsettled, not your breezy self."

They'd been fellow students at the Moscow Institute of International Studies, he the American-speaking scion of a diplomatic family, she the daughter of a man who'd died in the Gulag. MGIMO erased the differences; nobody could take away a degree from the Moscow Institute of International Studies. Well, that was the theory. He hesitated on the cracked kerb. What harm was there in it? Would it matter if he had to deal with the scrawny English cat an hour or two later? The urge for alcohol—it had haunted him for years—bent his will. At the same time he had an irresistible yearning to be close to somebody, not in the way of the contrived joviality he practised with Pierre Farag and the parade of informers and quislings who skulked through his professional life. And Irina—she was a woman you could talk to openly, up to a point. He'd often wondered if she shared his feeling of unstuckness, of almost unbearable duplicity?

"You're a pal all right, Irina Andreyevna. Just one or two Stellas. Let me give my driver his instructions."

The man was leaning on the roof of his car, apparently speaking to somebody on the road side of the vehicle. As Zlotnik approached, the driver turned to face him and the person on the other side slipped away, but not before his face was caught in a street lamp. Was it Pierre Farag? Zlotnik couldn't be certain. He lit a cigarette. Get a hold of yourself, man; it was just two drivers having a chat. Pulling the smoke deep into his lungs, Zlotnik felt that moment of clarity and invigoration as the nicotine lit up his brain. Idiot! You're getting paranoid. Focus!

"How was your afternoon, Commissar Mamdouh?" he asked the driver.

"I rest. My friend Abdullah take car to airport."

Inconclusive. Perhaps his driver, Mamdouh, had seen the *'abaya*, perhaps not. Perhaps the other driver found it and took it home to his wife. Perhaps Dimashqi was poring over it, squinting as cigarette smoke wreathed his face. Or perhaps Zlotnik's department head had secreted it in a drawer, waiting for a break in the workload to consider how to exploit the existence of a pair of Bally patent leather shoes, a Liberty of London headscarf and a black Arab robe in his deputy's car.

"Wait for me till eight o'clock."

"*Ochen khorosho*, comrade boss."

Zlotnik and Irina walked a hundred metres to a 'casino' with tables overlooking the Nile. Cold bottles of Stella arrived with tiny plates of roasted chickpeas.

"Bring two whiskies too," Zlotnik said to the waiter.

"What's troubling you?" Irina said. She was dark, slim, angular. Another Armenian, or at least she had an Armenian mother. You found these half-and-halves throughout the diplomatic service; staunchly loyal but with a streak of Armenian individuality and foreignness that the party meat grinder could not strip out.

The whiskies were brought. Zlotnik pushed one towards Irina, but she pushed it back.

"No troubles, Irina Andreyevna. Just exhausted, worn out with this lousy country. I need a posting to a place where things go in straight lines, where 'yes' means 'yes' and 'no' means 'no'."

"Like Switzerland? New Zealand? You'd be bored stiff. What about the US? Can you use your connections to swing a comfy billet there?"

Not a chance, Zlotnik thought, taking a long swig of the yellow beer. He'd been to high school in

Washington DC, where his father had been a diplomat. He knew the West as an insider; he knew instinctively how the West *felt*. And this, he knew, made him dangerous, more susceptible to blandishments from beyond the Iron Curtain, more prone to accusations of disloyalty, a man to be carefully watched. They'd never post him there.

"Ha! Another year and a half, comrade, and I'll be gone to some other oriental paradise. Let's get a couple more Stellas." The whisky chaser on top of the first beer had hit his empty stomach and the alcohol was surging through his blood. Behind his brow his head fizzed; he felt a recklessness in his heart. He slugged back the second whisky.

"Do you ever wonder," he asked Irina, "if life could be different somehow?"

"I don't follow."

"If—let's be hypothetical—events had taken a different turn in 1917? A different kind of Russia?"

"Different in what way?"

"In lots of ways," Zlotnik said.

Irina frowned and looked around the bar. She leaned forward. "Check yourself, my friend."

They swigged more beer and looked at their hands. Then she said, "Of course I wonder. Everyone does. But it's pointless, stupid. Why not wonder what would have happened if we hadn't turned back Hitler. You and I might not be here to talk about it."

He felt himself blush. Irina might not have survived Hitler, but he would have. He'd sat out the Great Patriotic War in Papa's apartment in capitalist America while his fellow citizens froze their *yaytsa* off and lived on black bread crusts.

"I'm sorry. I embarrassed you," Irina said. She'd caught his blush. He was the American-speaking Russian who'd never known hardship.

The bar was emptying. Irina leaned back in her chair and narrowed her eyes.

"It's not just you. You don't have a monopoly on being out of place."

"That's a curious expression, 'out of place'. What do you mean?"

"I think you know. You started this conversation," Irina said.

"I've often sensed that you don't really fit," he said, watching her carefully.

"Forget I said it, Ivan Maksimovich. We've both had too much of this diabolical beer."

"No, really. It's the fact that you're only half Russian. The other half—it's as if you have a secret place in your heart. Somewhere you can be somebody else who's you, but a different you."

"What you see is me, no more," Irina said, locking her eyes on his. "The handmaiden of *homo sovieticus*."

He held her stare. Surely he was right about her!

"I want to tell you something, Irina Andreyevna. Something terrible."

"Don't!" She leaned over and placed a hand over his lips. "Say nothing!" He took her fingers in his hand and kissed them. "This might be the last time we sit like this, as friends," she said. "Let's get out of here."

Zlotnik pressed his knee against hers under the table, and she pressed back.

She lived two buildings along from Zlotnik's apartment block. They sat quietly in the back of the car as his driver assaulted the Russian language in the front.

Irina's hand snaked between their bodies and rested on his thigh. They had done this before on occasions, tacitly, no need for discussion, an itch to be scratched, a need to be fulfilled. At Irina's building, Zlotnik said, "We'll both get out here. I'll walk the rest of the way."

The driver leered. It'll be noted, Zlotnik thought: *Comrade boss go lady comrade house.*

Irina undressed and lay on her narrow bed. In the dim light of a desk lamp she was white as bone, thin, taut, almost bisected by the triangle of black pubic hair. Zlotnik was bashful of his paunchy body, but she got up and helped pull off his baggy clothes. Free of the cloying Viyella, his skin tingled in the humid night air. They embraced and fondled each other, hands sticky, hot and urgent. Irina lay back and they coupled wordlessly, overlooked by a row of *matryoshki* on a shelf, the dumb peasant smile repeated on each of the hollow wooden dolls. Zlotnik's mind found a plane where ecstasy and memory were intermingled; the woman below him was all the women he'd bedded, from the first to the last.

All at once he was spent. "Sorry," he grunted. He looked down at her face and saw that she seemed unconcerned at his shame, staring wide-eyed at the *matryoshki*. She caught his glance, smiled, said, "Let me do this, you clumsy bear," and eased him upwards so that she could press her hand to the triangle. He watched as she deftly finished herself, oblivious in her private task, joined to him but not joined, shuddering and pulling him closer at the moment of release. "That's OK now," she said.

Afterwards, she said, "Go now, quickly, my good friend. Please be careful tonight."

In the street Zlotnik wrenched himself back to the here and now. He'd rehearsed how he would deal with the English woman. Charm. In normal circumstances he had enough of it to grease a T-62 tank. He'd open the door an inch or two, call out to her, promise her no harm and speak of their shared fate. He'd apologise— genuinely—for his unforgivable behaviour. Softened, she'd warily let him in. He'd sit down in a submissive posture and ask her what she required of him.

He pushed the key into the deadlock and jiggled it to alert her. He coughed loudly, waited a few seconds, listened, jiggled again. No response. The woman probably had the cast iron frypan raised to brain him as he walked in. He unlocked the door, stepped back, and pushed it open with his shoe. There was nobody in the hallway. Stepping warily into the lounge he looked into the bedroom and saw the open door leading to the fire escape.

"Where's that fuck-your-mother Englishwoman gone?" Zlotnik rarely cursed. It had all unravelled, all gone to shit. He sank into the sofa.

There was vodka in the cupboard. He opened a bottle and drank steadily and deliberately, considering his 'unravelling' life. He thought of the early years of hope and prospect and privilege, when all you did made a kind of sense, and the bits that didn't could be explained away. He thought of the years when you could reconcile the *doublethink*—where had he learned that English word?—by never daring to admit that Soviet power was not impregnable; when you pledged to uphold the might of the USSR, while not actually having to live there; when you reasoned away the sick in your gut when Hungarians and Poles were crushed for daring to defy Soviet rule. *Proletarii vsekh stran, soyedinyaytes'!* it said under the golden wheatsheaf on the USSR state emblem. 'Workers of the world unite!'

The bottle was empty. He tottered to the open window and shouted to the black Cairo night, "*Proletarii vsekh stran, soyedinyaytes'*!" Somebody yelled back, "Blessed Ramadan."

He bumped into the bookshelf on the way to the kitchen cabinet where he remembered there was half a bottle of Armenian *konyak*. A pile of books had fallen out. Clutching the bottle, he scrabbled to pick them up, but was distracted by a back cover photo of Solzhenitsyn with his bloodhound eyes and priest's beard. He took the book back to the sofa and leafed through it with clumsy fingers. It was *One Day in the Life of Ivan Denisovich*, with '1962' scribbled on the inside cover. Sixty shitting two, when all their lives had shifted off balance with Krushchev's thaw. When you could suddenly buy Solzhenitsyn in the Moscow bookshops.

Doublethink, doublethink. Of course, it was Orwell, the clever bastard, who'd planted the word in his brain at school in DC in 1949, or was it 1984? No, that was eleven years in the future. Who gave a damn? He'd spent the past eleven years with his mind unstuck, split, out of kilter. Only copious alcohol could force him back into s*inglethink. Singlethink*? Where did that come from? From the great mind of *durak* Ivan Maksimovich Zlotnik, the intelligence expert who fucked up his own defection. Pitiful.

His lolling eye slid to the *konyak* bottle. Ararat brand, it said in honest Cyrillic script. He turned the bottle round and peered at the square-sloped Armenian lettering on the back; he'd learned the rudiments of the script years ago. There was the 's' letter, like 'u' in English, and there was 'sh', shaped like a figure 2. 'Siranoush', perhaps? He didn't give a damn. The dead opera singer could go to hell, if she wasn't already there.

Ararat! He'd been in Yerevan in 1962, the day they pulled down Stalin's statue and stuck Mother Armenia in its place. Oh, the jubilation when the Georgian pig was lowered to the ground!

Ararat! He remembered swigging a bottle of Ararat *konyak* that night on a hotel balcony, drinking in the balm of spicy air that blew across the slopes clad with grape vines and citrus. The mountain was fifty kilometres to the south, inside Turkish territory, invisible but palpably sacred in the dark.

* * *

Cairo's night-time traffic noise played like an endless tape. The snow-capped mountain on the label was the last thing Zlotnik saw before he passed out.

It was 1am when he woke with a filthy headache and a mouth like a tortoise's backside. The empty vodka and brandy bottles lay on the floor next to an open jar of *ogorki*. There was a smear of mucousy vomit on the Viyella shirt.

A low rumble, a visceral sensation rather than a sound, filled the air. The rumble grew to a bass roar, and the furniture shook. Zlotnik stumbled to the window and looked into the shard of inky sky above. The dark blue was blotted out by the vast lumbering fuselage and wings of an Antonov cargo aircraft. Full of fuck-your-mother T-62s and *Malyutkas*.

He turned away from the window. A muffled step, the creak of a shoe. Somebody was moving around in the apartment.

Chapter 13: Israeli Spy!

Friday 5 October 1973

Apartment 421 had a working telephone and a fridge containing some unedifying leftovers, half a chocolate cake and two bottles of beer. Lucy badly needed a cigarette, but there were none; however, her search of cupboards and drawers turned up an old electricity bill that bore the address of the apartment—in Nasr City, about half an hour's drive from central Cairo. The phone directory was in Arabic. With her training in cryptanalysis, Lucy had easily found the telephone number of the British Council Library. She had gone to bed with a grim supper, but the makings of a plan.

In the early hours there had been a tremendous rumbling in the walls and floors. Half awake, she wondered if there had been an earthquake, but then she recognised the sound of gigantic lumbering aircraft. Around the same time, she'd flinched at the sound of shouts and scuffling nearby in the building. Then she'd sunk into a wretched half-sleep, squirming on the bare mattress, creating and replaying improbable scenarios by which she would get back into contact with Mark Bellamy.

She'd been momentarily dreaming when the noise of banging pots and voices woke her. The windows of the tall apartment block on the opposite side of the street were visible from the bed. Lights were going on as the devout made their last meal before the day of fasting.

Her parents had been in the dream, in a frenetic scene where they sat side by side writing in unison with fountain pens, before being swept into a maelstrom of robed figures from which Mark Bellamy appeared and disappeared like a drowning man. Yesterday's news, she thought, put through a blender. She'd never been one for interpreting dreams.

Her father would have liked Mark. He was a dealer in old books and manuscripts, an erudite man with a nimble sense of humour that concealed mordant depth. He had read classics at Cambridge, and worked for some highly secret department during the war, a topic he refused to discuss in even the most general terms. The antiquarian bookshop had passed to him on the death of an uncle.

From when she was a little girl, Lucy spent her school holidays in the shop at Brighton, and by the time she was a teenager she knew her way around the oriental manuscripts that her father specialised in.

Lying on the seedy mattress, she smiled at the memory of her first antiquarian triumph around her seventeenth birthday. A man had brought in a locked metal briefcase and placed it on the glass counter. "You serve this chap," her father said.

"I've acquired a manuscript, and I'd like a valuation." The man carefully unlocked the case, put on a pair of white cotton gloves, and drew a single illuminated page from a folder.

Lucy leaned over the paper. It was obviously

Stuart Campbell

worthless. She took a large magnifying glass and examined the sheet in detail—really quite unnecessarily, but she was rehearsing how to break the news.

"It's the kind of item that would make a lovely display above a small mantelpiece."

"Oh, I don't think so. I've been keeping it at my bank," the man said.

She could almost feel her father egging her on.

"Can you see here where it has been glued? You've got a page that's been removed from a Persian book— I think it's on a religious topic, with a hand-painted picture glued onto it."

"It's old then?" the man said.

"Oldish."

"Oldish?" he asked.

"The painting is nineteen-thirties perhaps. The Persian page might be nineteenth century. A lot of these were done in India for the tourist market. It's really a very interesting curio. No real value, but lovely."

"Do you mind me asking if there is somebody here who can give me a second opinion?" he asked.

Lucy called her father. He leaned over the manuscript, making little whistling noises through his teeth and the occasional *aha*.

"Twenty pounds tops for a good example," he said, "and as my daughter suggested, this one's a beauty. I've got a couple over in the corner, far inferior articles. Care to have a look?"

The man took a long look at the manuscript. "It's the mantelpiece then," he said with brittle civility.

"Nicely handled, Lucy. The poor sod's been robbed," her father said after the man had left. His retelling of the story had been honed to dramatic perfection over the years. She pictured him regaling Mark with it over pints in the Bird in Hand.

The tang of cigarette smoke drifted through the open window: somebody on a nearby balcony having a last gasp before the sun rose. How she craved a cigarette!

As the first smudge of light heralded the dawn prayer, she forced her thoughts away from Mark and recalled her instructions. She was to leave Zlotnik's documentation in a book in the British Council Library, and to come back later to retrieve a note in the same book giving her the go-ahead, assuming that the Russian's bona fides were confirmed.

It was a long shot, but a call to the library might provoke a reaction.

She waited till 9.05 before dialling. She knew something about libraries, but didn't actually know any librarians; she imagined that they'd get settled with tea and a biscuit before answering the phone. They were in for a shock.

"Donald Waters, British Council Library." Then, in Knightsbridge-accented Arabic, "Donald Waters, *maktabat al-majlis al-britani.*"

"Mr Waters, this is Lucy Vickers. I'm a spy. I work for the British Government. I need to speak to the Ambassador. If you won't help me, I'll call the BBC."

There was coughing on the other end. Then, "Tell me where you are and get off the phone."

She told him and Donald Waters clicked off.

* * *

Here he was, half an hour later, in Apartment 421, sweating and pink in his elegant tropical-weight suit.

"You've got some nerve. Bloody nerve, I'd call it. I don't know why I don't take you outside, point at you and yell *gasus isra'ili*."

"Perhaps I *am* an Israeli spy, Don. Walk out the door and give it a try." Lucy said. She looked at him wringing his hands, perched on a hard chair. She wished Donald Waters would stop crossing and uncrossing his legs. He appeared to be in a dreadful flap, and his fidgeting was making her feel worse. He smelt of tobacco. Would he offer her a cigarette?

"It's Donald, not Don."

"Noted, Donald." She thought he might be a homosexual. People didn't say *queer* anymore, she remembered.

"Do you have any idea what danger you've put me in? You realise that most of the residents of this building work at the Soviet Embassy?"

"Actually, Donald, I don't give a toss. I presume you work for Ealing?"

"Ealing? What are you on about? Can we just get on with what needs to be done?"

"Donald, you wouldn't be here if you didn't work for Ealing."

He took a packet of Pall Mall Menthols from his pocket. He fussed with a Zippo lighter, and Lucy caught the aromatic sharpness of the fuel. He was collecting his thoughts. Lucy's nerves screamed for a slug of nicotine, but she wasn't going to expose any lack of self-control to this man.

"I'm just a letterbox," he said, exhaling white streams from his nostrils. "I don't know anything else. It sounded quite puerile to me. I was to collect some papers from a book in the library and pass them up the line."

"Up the District Line to Ealing, I suppose you mean.

Then I imagine you were to wait for the 3.42 to Upminster to collect some more papers to put back in the library?"

"I haven't got a clue what all this tube station business is about. I'm a librarian."

"You've never heard of Siranoush?"

"A brand of washing powder?"

"Donald, what does the number 492 mean to you?"

"I couldn't care less. Perhaps it's the bus from Ealing to Upminster."

"You're a librarian who knows some Arabic, and 492 means nothing to you?"

"Can we cut the amateur spy stuff and talk about how we can get you out of here?"

"So you don't recognise the Dewey classification for Afro-Asiatic language? Never heard of 492? You're no librarian. Now listen. I want some shoes, and I want safe passage to the UK with my – " She fumbled for the word. "With my colleague Mark Bellamy."

"Never heard of him."

"And my involvement with this defection plan – and Mark's – is over."

"I'm lost."

"I've documented the whole mission, and mailed it to the UK."

Donald Waters sighed. He stubbed out the Pall Mall and gave her a long hard look.

"You tripped around the corner in bare feet and popped it in the pillar box by the village green? Bump into the vicar, did you?"

"I did it yesterday at Garden City Post Office. When I had shoes. I have a receipt."

"I see. I wouldn't put it past you."

"How would you know what you could or couldn't put past me, Donald?"

He smiled grimly. "I've read your file, and I'm amazed that they put you on this job. You're completely unreliable. If what you say is true—mailing information about your mission—then you've signed your death warrant and a lot of others. But that'd be bloody typical."

Lucy had seen bloodless chameleons like Donald Waters in her time with Ealing. She hadn't believed the hapless librarian persona, not that it had lasted long once she'd told him that she had mailed her story to the UK. The funny thing was that it was true; ever since Ealing had blackmailed her into ten years' servitude, she'd made a point of documenting each mission and mailing it to her brother. Six envelopes lay unopened in his safe at Smedley, Vickers and Reynard, Solicitors, of Lowestoft, Suffolk.

Donald Waters—if that was his real name—now sat poised and ready to do business.

"You realise that by abandoning your mission, Her Majesty's Government will lose an extremely valuable asset. I'll help you, if you help us. Otherwise you're on your own."

"My story goes public if I don't make it home."

"Never heard of a D-notice? We'll take that chance. Are you in or out?" Waters asked.

"Will *Le Monde* give a stuff about your D-notice? Anyway, is it as simple as 'in' or 'out'? You don't need me to complete this mission. You could just handle it yourself. Why am I here in Cairo? Why is Mark Bellamy here? Why this bit of silly theatre? Why not just take your asset to the airport and fly him home yourself?"

"I'll file all that under R for rhetorical. You know I

won't answer, so don't bother asking any more questions."

"File it up your backside, for all I care. Just get me some shoes and a temporary travel document, and put me on a plane to Heathrow with Mark Bellamy."

"What have you done with your passport?" Donald Waters asked.

"The Russian's got it. Your asset, he's got it."

"And who's got the Briggs passport?"

Lucy hesitated for a moment, computed the moves, calculated the risks.

"Mark Bellamy has it. And while we're on the subject, why does a defector need a passport? Surely MI6 can tell customs at Heathrow to look the other way? I can't imagine Burgess and Maclean had to queue up to get their passports stamped before they were let into the USSR."

"None of your business."

"I'm making it my business, you infuriating twerp. I've worked it out for myself," Lucy said.

"Worked what out?" Waters asked.

"Get lost. Just do what I've asked you. Get me and Mark Bellamy out of Egypt."

"Worked out what?" This time the voice was raised.

Lucy didn't exactly know what she'd worked out. It was more of a suspicion, an instinct about Ealing; that it followed in its own eccentric orbit, detached from the mainstream of the civil service, detached from government oversight. A defection would need to be cleared at Cabinet level. Was Ealing functioning independently from executive government? She held back; best to keep Waters guessing at her suspicions.

"It doesn't matter," she said. She watched him, trying

187

to decipher his intentions from his stony expression. She must continue to unsettle him, ensure that he could not predict her next move. Shoeless, grubby and abandoned, she had nothing to gain from playing safe. She rushed to the window, threw it open and yelled, "*gasus isra'ili.*" Waters took her down with a rugby tackle, whipped one arm behind her back and clapped a hand over her mouth. They lay on the floor in silence, waiting for a reaction from outside. There was none.

Lucy smiled to herself. She had Donald Waters in her grasp, despite the fact that he held her immobile.

She felt him relax. Waters removed the sweaty hand, and she wiped her lips on her sleeve to get rid of his salty taste.

"I'm not agreeing to anything, Donald. Get that into your head."

"You're a loose bloody cannon. I'm going to drive my car right up to the doorway. Come down in two minutes and get in. I'll take you to the Embassy and we'll sort it out there."

"What's my guarantee that I'll actually make it to the Embassy?"

"I can't give guarantees." He was right, she thought. Nobody could guarantee anything in this toxic scenario. And who the heck was Donald Waters anyway? Was he just another blackmail victim, carrying out disjointed orders? Or was he one of the cardigan clique who issued the instructions? Could she find out?

"What have they got on you, Donald? Gambling, booze, underage girls?"

"You don't give up, do you?"

Waters slipped out of the door of Apartment 421, and Lucy listened for his footsteps on the stairs. From the window she saw him stride fifty yards down the street and get into a blue Peugeot. The car slowly pulled away from the kerb and turned back towards the building. Lucy wrapped her short blonde hair in a towel and padded down to the entrance vestibule. There was no *bawwab*, just a man in a safari suit standing in the doorway looking out into the street. On the floor behind him was a black bundle from which protruded a patent leather court shoe.

It all happened in a blurred second. The man raised a pistol and aimed at Waters, Lucy grabbed the shoe and drove the heel into his ear, the gun discharged and blasted out the rear window of the car, Waters hit the accelerator and was gone.

The man—he wasn't young—turned and trained the gun on Lucy. He dabbed blood from his ear with a handkerchief and then adjusted his tinted glasses.

"Come with me and bring your property," he said in precisely accented English.

The car took her away from Zlotnik's building. She was squashed in the back between the man in the tinted glasses and a security police officer. When she had seen Donald Waters' car approach the building, it hadn't occurred to her that the street was empty. Cairo streets were hardly ever empty. Now she could see why. Traffic cops were waving people and vehicles back into the roadway; it must have been temporarily blocked off during Waters' visit to her.

She was stricken with hopelessness at her prospects. She knew—or was almost sure—that the man in tinted glasses was Mark's torturer. Donald Waters might have been fairly easy to knock off balance, but this safari-suited character was in a class they hadn't yet invented.

She watched a barefoot mendicant on a street corner.

At least she had her shoes.

And that wasn't all. Despite whacking the man with her patent leather heel, she stood no chance in a contest of strength with these burly police. But she knew about odds, about chance, about assessing how events might play out. She was Lucy Vickers, Arabic speaker, expert in mathematics in medieval Islam, proud owner of a master's thesis on Al-Khwarizmi. Lucy bloody Vickers, Britain's top specialist on the *hawala* system of underground money transfer in the modern Middle East—actually, make that former top specialist. Lucy Vickers, dropped by the smug bastards at Ealing into a plot that made no sense, except the bit where she ended up dead.

They were travelling fast, with a motorcycle escort clearing the streets before them. Suburbs flashed by. The glimpses she could catch across the big male shoulders were blurred. Then they were on a more open road, speeding for ten minutes and then slowing, pulling over to stop by a van. The security officer got out, leaving the seat next to Lucy empty. He rapped on the back door of the van. The doors were opened from the inside, and she saw Zlotnik bundled out in handcuffs. The officer prodded him into the seat next to Lucy, and banged the door closed. The Russian smelt rank. He peered into his lap and murmured something in Russian.

"What did you say?" Lucy asked.

"*Myortvye dushi.* We are dead souls," he groaned and then clamped his mouth shut.

"*Yalla,*" the man in tinted glasses said to the driver, covering his nose with a handkerchief.

"Yes, Mr Dimashqi." So he had a name.

The car turned into a security gate. It was quickly cleared through, and Lucy glimpsed the word *mustashfa* on an official-looking sign. A hospital?

While they parked, a cluster of security police

gathered under a covered walkway that seemed to connect a row of prefabricated buildings.

"Put his on, and then your own," Dimashqi said, handing Lucy two padded eyeshades with elasticated headbands. Lucy leaned across Zlotnik, flinching at his rancid smell. His clothes, she realised, were wet.

Strong arms pulled her from the car, and then grasped her on each side as she stumbled forward. There were steps, then a ramp of some kind, then long corridors that smelt of disinfectant. She heard low voices, the hum of equipment, hissing—oxygen cylinders? She was led left, right, straight, left, right again, deeper and deeper into a black warren.

A door clanged and the arms freed her. "Take the eyeshade off now."

It was a woman's voice, Egyptian-accented English. Lucy rubbed her eyes and blinked. A white coat, thick black hair, middle-aged. They were in what seemed to be a private hospital room.

The woman indicated a door. "Undress and take a shower, and leave the door open." There was a pile of clothing and a towel on the bed.

"Leave the towel here. And the clothes you're wearing."

"Where am I?"

"It doesn't matter. Do as I say."

Lucy turned away from the woman and began to undress, stooping in embarrassment. But she stopped, straightened up, and turned around. She boldly met the woman's eyes, and peeled off the fetid clothing and flung it to the floor. She would not be intimidated. The woman's eyes dropped to the scar on her abdomen.

"You have a child?" she asked. There was a trace of

concern in her voice.

"The child is dead."

"A boy or a girl?"

"A boy," Lucy said. She hesitated. Why was she telling this to a stranger? Why the urge to reveal this sad private history at such a time? But perhaps that was it—at such a time when her life might almost be at its end. When better to invoke the beloved child's memory?

"*Allah yarhamuh.*" The woman looked away, and then said, "I had a son too."

"He died?"

"Nineteen sixty-seven."

"*Allah yarhamuh*, God bless his memory," Lucy said. She stepped into the bathroom and showered, then came out and towelled herself by the bed. The woman in the white coat looked away, but said over her shoulder, "The clothes should fit."

The underwear was of an old-fashioned design and a little large, but seemed to be new. There was a conservative blouse and long skirt. Her own clothes had been stuffed into a plastic bag, which the woman had placed by the door.

The woman offered her a Cleopatra, and they both smoked without comment. Lucy gulped the sweet acrid smoke greedily. She became a little dizzy, and leaned on the bed. My last cigarette, she thought, whatever happens. If I get through this, every bloody fag I smoke will transport me back to this awful room. She stubbed out the butt in a tin ashtray. Farewell, it's over between us. I'm stronger than you.

"You may as well rest. We will come for you later," the woman said. Just before she banged the door closed, she stopped as if to add something, but seemed to change her mind. The lock clicked and Lucy was alone.

* * *

She woke from a doze and looked at her wrist, but her watch was missing. She remembered placing it on her clothes when she'd undressed. The plastic bag was gone. Her mind ran through the past hours. It had been late morning when Waters had been shot at, perhaps early afternoon when they had reached the hospital. Her bladder was full, and she was very hungry. Her body told her that it must be evening, Friday evening.

She wondered about Zlotnik. Remembering Mark's shocking description of his torture in the City of the Dead, she had a good idea that Zlotnik had suffered the same treatment. Had Dimashqi got what he wanted from him? Would she be next? But then, would they subject a woman to such an ordeal? What were the moral codes of a torturer? She pondered on her white-coated gaoler, on the bond they had ever so briefly shared.

Some food was delivered, the door opening and closing in a flash, showing a glimpse of khaki overalls, a tin tray placed on the floor. It was *fuul* with chopped boiled egg and parsley, a flatbread loaf, and a glass of water buffalo milk. She ate without enthusiasm. This was fuel; she needed it. After the meal, the old familiar nicotine craving sidled into her brain. She slapped it away.

Later, perhaps an hour or two, she thought, the woman returned and handed her a sheet of paper.

"Read this. We will come for you in ten minutes," she said, and left.

I am Lucy Vickers. I am a United Kingdom citizen. This is my confession. I make it freely and without duress.

193

*I conspired with Mark Bellamy, a United Kingdom citizen, and
with Ivan Maksimovich Zlotnik, a citizen of the USSR, in a plot
to assassinate President Anwar Sadat.*

*The assassination was to be carried out by an Egyptian citizen,
Pierre Farag, to whom we paid a sum of 10,000 US dollars. Mr
Farag was to shoot the President with a Beretta pistol supplied by
the State of Israel. The funds for the plot were also supplied by the
State of Israel.*

*Mr Bellamy and I entered Egypt using counterfeit passports
supplied by Mossad.*

We throw ourselves on the mercy of the Egyptian Government.

Lucy was incredulous. It looked like a joke but it
couldn't be. She read it again. Dimashqi had created a
crazy puzzle. But what was the solution? Four disparate
individuals condemned as assassins. To what end?

She was blindfolded again, led through corridors, and
then delivered to a small theatrette. Three security
police, the woman in the white coat, and Dimashqi
awaited her. Behind a desk at the front of the room was
Zlotnik, scrubbed up and wearing a boiler suit, but
lolling as if drugged. An officer led her behind the desk,
and then moved to the centre of the room where a
movie camera stood mounted on a tripod. Where was
Mark? Did they have him? Was he to be put on show
with her and Zlotnik?

"Where is he?" she shouted. "What have you done
with Mark Bellamy?"

Dimashqi spoke. "Mr Bellamy's welfare depends
entirely on your cooperation in the matter to hand."

"You're a liar. If you had him, he'd be sitting at this
desk."

"Can you be sure we don't have him? Can you be sure
that he isn't in such a condition that we would prefer

not to show him publicly?"

He stepped forward and placed two passports on the desk, opening them at the photo pages. Hers and Zlotnik's. What agonies had Zlotnik suffered to give them up?

A floodlight was turned on. Lucy squinted at the outlined figures at the back of the room. As the camera began to roll, one of the officers held up a copy of *Al-Ahram*. The operator removed the camera from the tripod and hefted it onto his shoulder. He focused on the front page of the newspaper, stepped forward and panned to the passports, then stepped back to take in Lucy and Zlotnik.

"Read the statement," Dimashqi said.

"I'm not reading this rubbish!"

"Stop!" Dimashqi commanded.

The camera operator switched off, and the floods were dimmed.

"Read it or he dies now in the next room. I only have to give the order!"

Lucy scanned the faces. The eyes behind the tinted glasses glowed red. The security police shuffled anxiously. But the woman in the white coat looked fixedly at her, until, locking eyes, she very slowly shook her head, just a millimetre or two.

"All right, I'll read it," she said. Like hell, she would.

She'd think of something in the next ten seconds.

The lights came up again, the camera was switched on, the newspaper was held up.

But from outside there came the muffled crack of gunshots and raised voices. The camera operator switched off and the lights were dimmed again. The door of the theatrette sprang open and a panting security officer ran in.

"*il-hikaya eh ya ibn kalb*?" Dimashqi snarled, 'what's the story, you son of a dog?'

"The *inglizi* was here!"

"Here? Where? Talk sense!"

"He was with Fawzi, here with Fawzi!"

Dimashqi grabbed the man's lapels. "Stop jabbering and give me some facts!"

"The *inglizi* escaped and Fawzi's dead."

The meaning of the Arabic words sank into Lucy's exhausted brain. The Englishman escaped, and Fawzi's dead? Mark Bellamy, here, and now gone? And who was Fawzi?

"Get the English bitch out of here. And that Russian idiot!" the torturer yelled before he ran into the corridor.

Lucy looked at the woman in the white coat. Was there the trace of a smile on her lips?

PART THREE: SIRANOUSH

Chapter 14: Solaris

Saturday 6 October 1973

Lucy and Zlotnik were swiftly handcuffed and led from the theatrette by the two security police, who remained after Dimashqi and his staff had rushed out. Lucy caught a glimpse of the white-coated woman slipping out of an exit at the back of the room.

There were no blindfolds this time. In fact, the security police seemed unsure about what they were expected to do with the two captives. They traded suggestions as the group moved through the corridors of what Lucy now confirmed was a hospital. She couldn't make much of what the men were saying; it seemed to be shorthand references to locations in and around the hospital. "D Wing, Department Q," and other indecipherable phrases. "Look straight, walk straight," shouted one of them.

Lucy realised she'd been caught staring at the warren of wards and nursing stations they were passing. Everywhere were military officers and staff in white coats, apparently busy preparing for a great influx of patients. Boxes of medical supplies were stacked in every spare corner. But for whom? What catastrophe were they preparing for? An epidemic? A war?

Zlotnik seemed to have recovered from his torpor. "The dead souls have been resurrected, for the time being," he whispered to Lucy with apparent cheerfulness.

"What happened to you? Weren't you drugged?"

"Hypoglycaemia," Zlotnik said.

"You're a diabetic?"

"No, but I am a good actor."

The security officers yelled at them to be silent. They were picking up a faster pace now, almost running the captives through more corridors and past yet more wards and medical supplies.

At last they stopped at a door. They were shoved inside without a word. It was the room where Lucy had showered under the supervision of the white-coated woman. The lock snapped shut.

Lucy leaned her back against the wall and slowly slid down until she was sitting with her head between her knees. She was hollowed out, her brain exhausted, emotions evaporated. She looked up at Zlotnik and said, "I was hoping I'd never see you again."

He laughed economically. After a little while he asked, "What next, then?"

As if in answer, a squad of boots marched past the door and slowed. Lucy flinched; fear overcame her exhaustion; she held her breath, expecting the door to be flung inwards. Then the boots carried on, the sound diminishing as they turned a corner until Lucy could hear only a soft rhythmic tapping. She unclenched her jaw, breathed again.

"We can't just do nothing," she said. She got up and

examined the doorframe and the bathroom fittings, then sat back on the floor. No way out. Stupid, stupid, stupid. Why hadn't she told the double-dealing swine at Ealing that she was finished, refused the assignment and taken the consequences for whatever they said she'd done?

"You have an alternative?" Zlotnik asked. "You think you can play one of your childish tricks and we'll discover a hidden trapdoor? Forget it. The souls might be temporarily resurrected, but we're still dead." He eased himself onto the bed and stretched full length, resting his hands on his chest as if awaiting embalmment. Then he abruptly sat up and said, "I'm so sorry. Please, you lie on the bed, Miss Patchett. My manners have departed me." He swung his legs to the floor.

Why not, she thought. The bastard owes me. They swapped places.

"Thanks, and you can forget Miss Patchett. She doesn't exist."

"I know. Shall it be Miss Vickers then? Or Lucy? We might be sharing a room for some time. I am quite happy to be called Ivan."

What was wrong with the man? Was this the time for gracious introductions? She had better, or worse, things to think about.

"Frankly I don't give a monkey's balls what we call one another."

"Monkey's balls? Oh, yes, I see. Nevertheless, what is your father's name?"

"Eric. Why do you want to know?" Why doesn't he shut up and do something useful?

"So that I can give you a patronymic. We will spend our remaining time together like civilised human beings.

I will call you Lucy Erikova. My patronymic is Maksimovich."

"Suit yourself, if it makes you feel better." But she suspected his intent, his desire to erase her disgust at the brutal body search. Nevertheless, it had happened, however he dressed things up with polite formalities. But why bother? Why was he so eager to polish his moral credentials when they may have hours—or just minutes—to live?

The prospect of her mortality loomed like a grey wall. She visualised its grainy nothingness, its cold futility, its infinite burden of regret and sorrow. She suppressed a welling sob, fudged a cough, wiped her eyes on her sleeve. This patronising Russian wouldn't get a chance to see her distress.

They remained silent for a few minutes. There was distant shouting far away in some corridor, and then the deep rumple of a large aircraft flying low.

Lucy said, "Ivan, do you know where we are?" Bugger the patronymic.

"Yes, of course. This is an air force hospital. We're not far from the city. I've been here on a number of occasions."

"Why didn't you say so before, for God's sake? And why were you here?"

"In a professional capacity," Zlotnik said.

"What professional capacity?"

The Russian sighed but said nothing.

"And why are there no patients?" Lucy asked. "Why all this activity? It's as if they are expecting a war to break out."

He chuckled.

"What is it? What's the joke?"

"What do you think the time might be, Lucy Erikova? I forgot to wind my watch."

"I lost mine. But early morning, I think. Saturday the sixth. I'm losing track."

"Yes, that is about right," Zlotnik said. "And a war is going to break out—today. I have no doubt whatsoever. Sometime in the next twelve hours or so, the Egyptians will cross the Suez Canal into Sinai and the Syrians will invade the Golan Heights. In forty-eight hours these wards will be awash with blood, and the Israelis will be at the gates of Cairo."

Lucy raised herself onto her elbows to stare at Zlotnik. He was looking at the floor, slowly shaking his head. Her skin prickled inside the ungainly polyester clothes. The Russian's solemn speech was an ugly shard of steel piercing her brain. She struggled to assemble her fragmented thoughts into some rational shape: the bogus defection, the implausible coincidence of she and Bellamy being deployed together, the ridiculous confession, Dimashqi's assault on Donald Waters. But war?

He went on. "And now we have played our petty parts in somebody else's tawdry drama. My defection, for example, it was never to be."

Lucy's despair turned to anger. "Why did you want to defect? Wasn't it all idyllic in the proletarian paradise? Surely a man in your position must have built a nice little nest of privilege."

"Why did you become a scholar of the orient? Wasn't Hampshire or Surrey sufficient to satisfy the whims of a middle class girl? Tennis, shopping at Harrods, stockbroker husband on the train to London each morning with *The Financial Times*?"

"You're very knowledgeable about me. Except you've

got it all wrong."

"Perhaps some of it wrong, Lucy Erikova. But you're quite transparent, you know."

"And you're an opinionated windbag with a rather simplistic view of England, and of women, for that matter," Lucy said.

"And your view of my life is so nuanced and profound? You couldn't possibly imagine . . . "

He was cut off by a low whining that rapidly increased in volume and frequency into the ear-scouring wail of a siren. Lucy pressed her head to the mattress and jammed her fingers into her ears. There must be a loudspeaker in the corridor, she reasoned. The wail subsided, but its echo jangled in her head.

"A test, surely," Zlotnik said. "Nothing to concern us."

"Will there be bombing – here in Cairo?" Lucy struggled to keep the anxiety from her voice.

"Bomb Cairo? Kissinger won't allow it."

"Henry's a friend of yours, is he? Anyway, we were talking about your defection. Didn't you suspect that something was fishy?"

"I am a Soviet diplomat. I am trained in scepticism. But on this occasion I dared to put my trust in others. And you, Lucy Erikova, did you suspect that your mission was a charade?"

"I don't want to talk about it."

She lay back and stared at the ceiling, disgusted at her own naivete.

"And us, Ivan? What happens to us? You seem to know an awful lot. Do you have an answer?"

He laughed. "We shall say our prayers."

"I gave up praying when I was ten. And aren't you

supposed to be an atheist?"

"You'd be surprised."

"Surprise me then."

Zlotnik began to hum a tune with a delicacy that defied his rumpled appearance. He stopped and said, "I'm sorry. I have a terrible voice."

"I know that piece," Lucy said. "It's a Schubert sonata, for the cello and piano. My mother loved it. But what's that got to do with praying?"

Then she remembered; he'd said before that he played the cello. Said that he wasn't a barbarian.

"I've played it hundreds of times," he said. "But why? Why do I persevere? Is it merely the technical achievement, fingers on string and wood, muscles, bone, nerves, brain—all working in unison? Like an exemplar of Soviet industrial production? Playing sonatas by the thousand to fill the five-year plan?"

"Tell me why you have to play it over and over," Lucy said. "Say it. Say it, Ivan Maksimovich."

The Russian made a curious noise between a grunt and a squeak. He dabbed his nose with the back of his hand.

"My words would be clumsy ciphers. Words like soul and spirit—they turn to ash on the tongue."

The siren started again, grinding out its discordant lower notes, and rising to mid-speed. Lucy dropped to the floor and curled up under the bed. She held her body rigid in anticipation of the ceiling collapsing under the dreadful impact of blasted steel and concrete and fire.

But the filthy whine slowed and faded away.

In the fragile silence a sombre melody came into Lucy's mind from nowhere. She hummed a few bars.

"It's Bach," Zlotnik said. "Hum some more."

Lucy hummed, more strongly as she caught the melody. She stopped.

Zlotnik said, "But you've sung it based on a curious arrangement. I know it, but I can't grasp where from."

She looked up at the ceiling, at the network of cracks in the plaster. Then she knew where the melody came from: *Solaris*, the long final scene when the psychologist Kris Kelvin finds his dead father's home on an island in a boundless ocean. She was suddenly overwhelmed by the memory of that wet afternoon in the cinema in Kensington when she had sat in desolation: desolate for those she had lost, her son, the man in the hotel on Queensway.

"Of course, Lucy Erikova," the Russian said with tenderness. "The poster in my apartment. It's Bach, Chorale Prelude in F-Minor. Artemiev wove it into Tarkovsky's score. It haunts me still."

They dozed for a while with the ceiling light blazing. When she got up to use the lavatory he woke, grimacing at his stiffness. He stood on the bed, reached up and unscrewed the light bulb sufficiently for the current to be cut.

"Get on the bed, Ivan. We can lie top to tail." But even in the dark, Lucy could not get back to sleep. The Russian snored like a lawnmower, but then woke choking for air.

"I disturbed you, I'm sorry."

"It's fine. I was already awake. You sounded as if you were drowning," she said.

"It was my dream. I dream it every night. I'm under the water and the weeds are pulling me down."

"You've been watching too many gloomy Russian movies," she said. He'd made his point; the cynical Soviet diplomat and his maudlin Russian soul. She felt gritty-eyed and sour-mouthed; she'd had enough of feeling sorry for herself. She kicked him.

"Oy. Put the light back on."

He screwed in the bulb and they winced at the glare. Lucy went into the bathroom and took off the long skirt. She used her teeth to make a rent above the hem and then carefully tore the bottom six inches off the skirt. The fabric was nastily shiny and tore easily, leaving long threads. The seams were tougher to cut, and she sheared the edge of her tongue with her eye tooth, bright blood smearing the strip of cloth when it finally parted. She put the skirt back on, now calf-length, tore the cloth into two and stuffed one piece into the sink waste.

"Ivan, come here. Use this to block the shower drain."

"Why?"

"We're going to flood the corridor."

With both taps gushing there was soon a shallow estuary of water lapping the door of the room. Zlotnik's boiler suit was drenched but he was laughing like a donkey as he held the cloth plug on the drain with his shoe.

"What's the point of this?" he yelled.

"There isn't one, but we can't sit here and do nothing." Lucy left the sink running and grabbed a pillow. She stuffed it in the toilet bowl and flushed the cistern. Putting one foot in the bowl to hold the pillow down, she reached over the sink to maintain the blockage, flushing the toilet each time the cistern refilled. She whooped along with Zlotnik.

Suddenly she felt chilled. An air current pressed the wet clothes to her skin. Somebody had opened the door from the corridor. They stepped out of the bathroom, braced for what might come. In the doorway stood the white-coated woman. A hospital trolley was visible in the corridor behind her. The woman looked exhausted. Lucy saw that she was older than she had first seemed— a senior military doctor? The lines in her face told a story of conflict, compassion, moral gravitas.

"I want you gone from my hospital, now!" Lucy opened her mouth to speak.

The white-coated woman, trembling with rage, pointed at the doorway. "Now!"

The body bag stank of cheap rubber. An inch of zipper had been left open above her neck, but the wet clothes and heat generated a nauseating fug. Lucy clenched her teeth, stifling vomit as the trolley raced and swerved through the corridors. Invisible arms lifted the stretcher and she was slammed onto a metal floor. The impact forced her teeth to clamp onto her sliced tongue with electrifying pain; at the same time her lower back cracked against a raised channel on the floor. There were more thumps. An engine started with the petrol smell of a badly tuned engine. She must be in a van. A mortuary van? God knows. Was Zlotnik in the van with her? What was that second thump after she'd been dropped? Dare she call out? Who were her deliverers? Where were they going?

She was, she realised, lying with her head just above the back axle of the van. The grinding of gears swamped any other noise. The van's suspension was hard, and the points of contact with the floor—her head, shoulders, elbows, buttocks, heels, absorbed the sickening shock of each bump.

She slipped into woozy half-consciousness where visions of Mark Bellamy danced before her. Sometimes he was alive, sometimes dead. She caressed his shoulders but they turned to vapour under her fingers.

He kissed her and her body turned to water, but then he was a corpse with dry film on his eyes and a black tongue. Then she was in a rubberised bag on a yawing metal floor. Arms pulled her off the floor, she was hoisted into a sitting position like a child, the zipper was undone, and she was looking into bright sunlight in a sinister landscape of miniature houses and narrow flag-stoned streets that looked like a city of tombs. A streak of graffiti on a crumbling wall said 'long live the 1923 constitution'. Two men in the tunics of medical orderlies helped her out of the body bag. She looked back into the van; it was empty. The men gently guided her to the entrance of a brick courtyard containing a Muslim shrine decorated in sweeping Kufic script. One man said in Arabic, "This is where our aunt told us to leave you."

"Where am I?"

"*il-'arafa*," he said. He beckoned to his brother and they got into the van and drove away.

Lucy sat on the shrine, shielding her eyes from the sun with her hand; she guessed it was midday. The City of the Dead—*il-'arafa*. This was to be her end: tortured as Mark had been by a man so banal in his malevolence that he turned up each day for work in a polyester safari suit. But she wouldn't let him torture her; she'd make a run and force him to shoot her dead. She checked her rambling thoughts. A safari suit? Shouldn't she be beset by profound feelings? Crushing regret, ugly terror? Last thoughts of the man she loved and would never see again? A silly voice in her head repeated *safari suit, safari suit*.

There was the sound of an approaching car. She wanted to exorcise the foul Dimashqi, to think her own thoughts, face her death lucidly, like Lucy; *lucid like Lucy*, the foolish voice snapped back. Shut up, let me think, let me get that bastard out of my head.

She jumped up, clamped her hands over her eyes and yelled, "Damn your safari suit, damn your stinking safari suit!"

A car door slammed shut. She uncovered her eyes, picked up a lump of broken stone, and faced the entrance to the narrow flag-stoned street.

It was Donald Waters.

"Well," he said. "We are in a bit of a tiz."

* * *

She stumbled across the threshold of another stuffy flat after Donald Waters: more faded velvet curtains, the Cairo smell of exhausted sofas and ancient dust. She glimpsed another lethal Vesuvius geyser through the bathroom door, another pancake bed, another array of door locks and bolts encrusted with ossified layers of cream paint. In the gloomy salon, a gap in the drapes sheared a plane of dust-flecked silver light.

"Keep them closed, especially after nightfall," Waters said.

"Where are we?" Lucy asked.

"A few minutes from the Embassy. It's just for a night or two. We're getting you out through Libya."

"Libya? Why? Where's Mark Bellamy? For God's sake, tell me what's going on."

"Mark Bellamy will be here tonight. You'll be taking a ship to Cyprus."

"With Mark?"

"With Mark."

She stared at him, struggling against fatigue to make sense of what he said.

"He'll never come here. He'll think it's a trap."

Waters looked at her for what seemed a whole minute. "Help me, then," he said.

"How?"

"A word, a phrase, something he'll know comes just from you."

"Tell him *Allons-y Alonso*. He'll know what it means."

She became conscious of her own body. Looking down she saw the ripped skirt, her scratched and bruised legs. Somehow she was still wearing the stupid patent leather shoes. Her heel hurt, her tongue was lumpily sore, there was a metallic pain stretching from her hip to her ankle.

"I need a shower. And aspirin."

He nodded and stared at her. "By the way, what's that dangling round your neck?" he asked.

It was a piece of stout cord attached to a clear plastic bag which contained something dark blue. She took it out and examined it. A UK passport. The name in the window of the pasteboard cover was Miss Victoria Patchett.

Donald Waters eased it from her fingers. "Safer if I hang on to it for now." He took her arm and guided her to the bathroom.

"There we are, plenty of hot water and towels. You'll be right as rain. There's food in the kitchen and some odd clothes in the bedroom. I'm going out now."

The apartment door closed. She stripped naked. The Vesuvius exploded and hot water spluttered down. Layer by layer she washed away the last forty-eight hours until she found herself in that brief hour of ecstasy with Mark in Champollion Street.

Chapter 15: Allons-y Alonso

Sunday 7 October 1973

"Relax, make yourself at home," Pierre had said when he left Bellamy and Zouzou in the villa the previous night. No introductions had been made other than, "This is Zouzou, this is Mark Bellamy," but then, when a woman is confronted with a blood-soaked man in a strange house in the middle of the night, it wasn't exactly an occasion for social chitchat. He assumed that Zouzou was a relative of Pierre's, but was mystified by the social status of a young—or at least youngish—Egyptian woman being left alone with a foreigner. Perhaps not a relative, then; a courtesan, a woman used to being alone with strange men? But she seemed demure and quite plain in her black robe. The candy-striped hatbox added to the mystery. And there was her sole remark, like a viper, when Dimashqi's name had been mentioned.

He made camp in a big dusty bedroom with a mattress on the floor. Pierre's clothes—grey trousers and a white short-sleeved shirt—were a size too small, but the shoes fit without too much of a pinch. His own outfit was bloody and ruined, and he hadn't located his holdall in the villa. Worse still, he couldn't find his

211

passport—or at least Clive Rogers' fake passport. The only room he hadn't searched in Pierre's absence was Zouzou's, but the door was closed and there was no sound from within. It would wait till Pierre returned; he'd be back late, he'd said.

With a few hours to spare before he learned the next step in Pierre's byzantine plans, Bellamy had little choice but to roam among his jangled thoughts. At the forefront was Lucy—her whereabouts, whether she was alive or dead, or worse. He marshalled all the mental tricks he could find to cool his thoughts, to think with reason rather than emotion. He visualised a long corridor with custardy paint and dozens of doors, each containing a fact or a scenario: Room 62, Lucy's part in the defection; Room 73, Fawzi's rescue mission; Room 91, the bandaged Briggs. On and on the rooms stretched along the corridor, disconnected, isolated scenes, no key or cipher to sort them into a comprehensible map. Then reason broke down, the corridor dissolved, and he was left with the sole, afflicting notion that somehow he must be reunited with Lucy.

At midnight Pierre's motorbike growled up out of the darkness. The Egyptian carried a shopping bag of prepared food: flatbread, cold aubergines, white cheese, tomatoes and bananas.

"My aunt prepared it," he said. "How is the lady?"

"I haven't seen her. I presume she's in her room," Bellamy said.

Pierre prepared a plate of food, knocked on Zouzou's door, and slipped inside. There was a little flurry of conversation and he closed the door behind him. Bellamy heard a raised voice—surprise, relief? Then Pierre came out and joined him in the salon.

"Please eat, my friend."

"Where is Lucy, Pierre? Does Dimashqi have her?" Bellamy waved away the food.

"There have been some developments," the Egyptian said.

"Developments?" Damn his coyness. "Spit it out, man, where is she?"

"She is in good hands. You will see her tomorrow morning."

"Who's hands? Why should I believe you?"

"Because she passed on a message."

"What message?"

"She said *Allons-y Alonso*." "When was this?"

"An hour ago."

It was their private joke at the school for spies at Shemlan. He'd taken her to see *Breathless* at a cinema in Beirut, and Jean-Paul Belmondo had said it to Jean Seberg. As they left the cinema Lucy had said, "*Allons-y Alonso*," and they'd laughed like idiots. "What does it mean? Who's Alonso?" she said.

"Same as Daddy-o," Bellamy had said. "Gotta go, Daddy-o."

She'd locked arms with him and said, "Who's more beautiful, me or Jean Seberg?"

So she was alive, for now. Bellamy stared at the Egyptian private detective. Despite his relief and euphoria at hearing the message, Bellamy's face was neutral; this was no time to expose any weakness that could be exploited. He wondered what price Pierre would demand to deliver him to Lucy; and what part he and Lucy would play in his endgame.

"You haven't told me who she's with," Bellamy said.

"A British man. An official."

Bellamy sat, stunned. It wasn't possible. He'd been

dumped by the Embassy; he didn't exist. And he was convinced that Lucy was in the same position. He needed to know more.

As if anticipating Bellamy's question, Pierre said, "There's something else. A rather big something else."

She'd been injured; she'd been tortured; she was with an Embassy doctor. He fought back the vile scenes playing in his mind. "Tell me!"

"War," Pierre said. "War has broken out, my friend. Eight hours ago."

In its contorted logic, it made a kind of sense. Bellamy slumped, resigned to the fact that he'd been played like a puppet: the charade in Dimashqi's car about the attack scheduled for a month hence; the bungled rescue mission; the defection that was never to be; the curious coincidence of his being partnered with Lucy. The core of the matter was not a defection, it was a war.

"Where's the fighting?" Bellamy asked.

"In Sinai. We've crossed the canal."

"And who's this official with Lucy?"

"He calls himself Donald Waters."

A distasteful memory flashed through Bellamy's mind; the name was familiar. "What does he want with us?"

Pierre held his palms out and shrugged his shoulders.

"How do you know this man, Pierre?"

"My dear friend, you're questioning is becoming more like an interrogation. Sometimes, it is more profitable . . ."

"Shut it, Pierre. If you don't intend to tell me, then just say so. I'm tired of your evasive waffling."

The Egyptian folded his arms and looked at the ceiling.

"When can you take me to them?" Bellamy asked.

Pierre unfolded his arms and made a charade of bruised dignity.

"Can you take me there now?" Bellamy asked again, louder this time. It was dark outside, just past midnight—the time for furtive journeys.

Zouzou came into the room, barefoot and wrapped in her robe. "I was sleeping. What are you arguing about? Pierre, who is this *khawaga*?"

"*Habibti*, go back to bed. I am taking my friend to El-Duqqi."

* * *

Donald Waters, Bellamy thought, bouncing on the metal pillion seat with his arms around Pierre's waist. Surely not. The motorcycle ground through an infinity of dark lanes and alleys. Few people were about in the early hours—odd men in *galabiyyas* ambling through the gloom, a *bawaab* nodding over a few coals in a brazier, a boy leading an animal—a goat or a sheep perhaps. Pierre kept the headlight switched off so that they seemed to be plunging into formless murk. Once they skidded in unseen muck so that the bike wobbled and Bellamy's knee was scraped on some projection. He reached down and felt warm blood on ripped cloth. When they emerged onto a roundabout, Bellamy looked up at a familiar billboard: the boy with the black splodge and the bottle of Sinacola.

"One minute," Pierre shouted. He drew the bike up beside an apartment block that could have been one of thousands.

"The entrance door is unlocked. Take the stairs to apartment 105." He twisted the throttle and was gone.

Bellamy stood for a moment, savouring the sensation of solid pavement beneath his feet. The night hum of traffic—always present in Cairo—was barely audible. Eighty kilometres away, he thought, men must be dying on sand and rock. The city was quiet, watchful, waiting for what fate might bring with daylight. He entered the building and pulled the heavy door behind him, then took the darkened stairs two at a time. He tapped at door 105. No answer. He tapped again and a tap answered him. Lucy and he had learned Morse Code at Shemlan from a couple of ex-Signals types who'd sit in class signalling to one another with their fingers. "You'll never know when it'll be useful," they'd said.

He tapped ALLONSY.

She tapped back ALONSO.

He had a thousand questions to ask her, but they embraced each other urgently and half-walked, half-fell along the dark vestibule with mouths locked together. They made love like condemned prisoners, devouring each other as if this was to be their last night on earth.

Afterwards Lucy turned on a dim bedside lamp. She gasped. "My love, you've scraped half your hip away!"

Bellamy sat up and examined the deep graze. God knew what filth had got into it. Lucy went to the bathroom and came with a wad of cotton and a bottle of alcohol. He closed his eyes and winced as she dabbed. When she walked back to the bathroom, he noticed the deep scratches on her legs and the purple bruises across her back.

"Who did this to you?" he asked.

Lucy lay down and kissed him. She held a hand over the scar on her abdomen.

"Mere scratches, my delicious barrow boy. I've only been abducted, imprisoned with a smelly Russian, forced to watch someone being shot at, given a fake confession to read, abducted again, dumped in the City of the Dead . . ."

"The City of the Dead? For God's sake, they didn't .
. . ?"

"No, my darling, I wasn't tortured. I think I was
rescued actually, by an Egyptian woman, a doctor. But
you, where did you lose this chunk of flesh? And why
were you dressed liked a ventriloquist's dummy when
you arrived?"

Bellamy's heart was seized by regret. Regret that he'd
lost her for so many years, that they might have so little
time together.

She seemed to sense his mood and said, "Let's enjoy
every second. We're together here and now. We're in
horrible danger, but it doesn't matter. Nothing matters
but the next minute, and then the next, and then the
next."

The blanket of regret was cast off. He looked into her
face, so animated, so optimistic.

"Come on," she said. "What happened to you?"
Bellamy held up a hand and enumerated the events,
finger by finger.

"Shot at near the Pyramids, kicked out of my hotel,
abducted, holed up in a villa with an Egyptian wise-guy,
raided a military hospital, drove a getaway car while the
bloke next to me got his head blown off."

"Anything else?"

"Hmm. Yep. Dumped a big Mercedes in the Nile,"
he said.

"It was you! You went to the hospital to rescue me?
My God, we were just yards apart yesterday evening—
when I was stuck in front of the movie camera and
Dimashqi's people ran in and yelled that the *inglizi* had
got away."

"Zaki said you weren't there. I've been crazy with worry," he said.

"Who's Zaki?"

"The guy whose head was blown off."

Bellamy lay back, his mind crammed with clashing images. He was exhausted, but a thousand years beyond sleep.

"We need to have a serious talk," Lucy said. "About all this. I'm feeling overwhelmed."

"We'll talk in a little while." He slid his hand down to her abdomen and passed his index finger along the scar. "Tell me about it."

"It's my business. Oh dear, that sounds very blunt."

"I want to make it my business too."

"You will, my love, when I'm ready."

The lovemaking was more deliberate and more tender this time.

"Hmm," she said afterwards. "That was very sweet. Like dessert"

"So how was the time before?"

"Deliciously primitive," she said.

Then, "It's 3am, Mark. We have to get serious. Put some clothes on and we'll pretend to be professional intelligence agents. Let's work out where we've both been for the last few days so that we might get an idea of where all this is going."

They sat across the kitchen table with a sheet of paper between them. Bellamy drew a line down the centre of the sheet and wrote L at the top of one column and M at the top of the other. Lucy turned the paper towards her and jotted down everything that had happened to her in the last two days, the most recent at the top, coolly summarising the events as she wrote. The oldest entry was when she slipped Briggs's passport into Bellamy's hand at the traffic intersection. Bellamy turned the paper round and wrote his entries, drawing connecting lines between the two columns and, like Lucy, summarising the events.

Lucy interrupted him.

"Wait, what's this about a war?"

"It started yesterday evening. Didn't you know?"

"The Russian said it would," Lucy said. "He thought Kissinger would keep Cairo safe."

"*In shaa' Allah*," Bellamy said. "And this Donald Waters. What do you make of him?"

"Up to his neck in God knows what. Ealing through and through."

"Therefore not to be trusted in any respect," Bellamy said. "Look, I think I might know him."

"Your age, slightly camp perhaps. Speaks Arabic like Vera Lynn."

"Could be him. He was in Aden very briefly, perhaps a day or two. I couldn't work out what his business was, but I got the idea that he was there to check up on people. You know, like the political commissars in the Red Army."

"So let's try and make one big picture out of all this," Lucy said in businesslike fashion.

"One more thing," Bellamy said, and he told her about the conversation he'd heard in the car after he'd been tortured by Dimashqi.

"OK, that clicks in nicely. Let me sum it all up as I see it, Mark."

"Go on."

Lucy sat up and began her account.

"There's a war brewing between Egypt and Israel.

Sadat's been making aggressive noises for months, keeping the whole world in a state of suspense. Has he got the nerve? Could he win? Will the Soviets back him? Is he just a vainglorious Oriental windbag? But he has chosen a date—yesterday, in fact, but somehow or other it has been kept secret. Otherwise the Israelis would have made a pre-emptive strike. Have I got it right so far?"

Bellamy nodded.

She went on, "There's been a deception campaign—really clever, and run by some brilliant people. This Dimashqi, for example—OK, he's a cruel bastard, but he's brilliant. The word is slipped out, probably to a few select people, that the war will begin a month from yesterday. Now this Zlotnik has been sitting in Cairo stewing about his future, and how he'd like to go to the West where he spent his golden school days. He learns the bogus date and thinks he can use it to trade with the British."

"So who has conned him?" Bellamy asked.

"Dimashqi," they said in unison.

Bellamy said, "OK, let me take over. The cardigan crew at Ealing have decided that you and I are dispensable, for whatever reason."

"Just stop for a moment," Lucy said. "There's something I didn't tell you. I was supposed to denounce you to the Egyptians as an Israeli spy."

Bellamy's jaw dropped. "Denounce me? Grass me up?"

"Grass me up? That's a funny expression, but yes. Then once I saw that you were Clive Rogers, well . . . "

Bellamy looked her squarely in the eyes. "If it hadn't been me, would you have denounced whoever it was?"

"That's completely theoretical, Mark."

"It's not, it's important. It's something important that I need to know about you."

"I can't tell you, Mark."

They said nothing for a moment or two, Bellamy absorbing the moment as if it was distasteful medicine.

"Mark, we hardly know each other. Remember that. We've got a lot of finding out to do."

"Tell me about the baby."

She looked at her hands.

"Tell me."

"Don't bully me," she said.

"I'm not bullying you. You know what I want to know."

"It was yours."

"Was?"

"He didn't survive the birth."

"A boy?" he said. She nodded.

Somehow Bellamy had known the first time he had seen the scar. But her confirmation tipped him into a gulf of grief and confusion. He placed his head in his hands, felt the wetness in his eyes. She stood behind him and embraced him.

"There's time for this later. Do you think I haven't cried a thousand times?"

He wiped his eyes on his sleeve. The flood of emotion had charged him with a clarity and freshness of mind. She was right. There was time later.

"Ealing," he said. "They want to get rid of us. Perhaps we're an embarrassment. Perhaps they sense that we've had enough and we might blow the whole thing apart. So they send us here to manage this defection."

"A defection that was never to be," she said. "Because

a war was to start on the same day."

Bellamy nodded. "But how did Ealing know that the war was going to start? The British Government couldn't have known."

Lucy drew two more connecting lines between the two columns.

"There's only one explanation. Ealing was in on the deception campaign."

"In with the Egyptians? And nobody else was? Not MI6? Not the Foreign Office?"

"QED," Lucy said.

He remembered the old expression from school; you wrote it at the end of solving equations.

"Darling, you might be an accomplished mathematician but the *quod* isn't quite *demonstrandum*. Why did Dimashqi go to so much trouble to convince me that the war would start a month later?"

"Hmm. To persuade you that you were clear to go ahead with the defection."

"There's more to it, I'm sure," Bellamy said. Something niggled. A piece was missing, and it had to do with Dimashqi.

They sat and absorbed the imperfect conclusion they'd reached. After a while Lucy said, "You smell like a camel, my darling. There's a shower down the hall."

"It's a manly smell, I rather thought. Do you know that when I was a kid we didn't have a bathroom? When I was thirteen the council gave us a grant to put one in."

"I'm not at all surprised. And I expect you had chip butties for tea. Just go!"

As he was showering he reflected on the fact that they knew almost nothing of one another's upbringing and origins. There was time later.

When he had dressed he said, "Donald Waters will make an appearance today, I suppose."

"Yes."

"So what do I do? Listen politely or smash his teeth in?"

"Smash his teeth in and then listen politely," Lucy said.

"I'm serious. We could ambush him and get the truth out of him."

This time Lucy was the one with a distasteful expression. "You can't mean that you'd torture him."

"For you I would."

"I wouldn't want you to. I forbid it."

Bellamy suppressed his irritation. It was illogical: risk their lives to spare this shit Waters a bit of pain?

"Let's agree to differ on this," he said. "We'll play it minute by minute. If I get the slightest hint that his intentions are anything but honourable, I'll beat it out of him."

"What happened to you when you were growing up, Mark? Where did this come from?"

"It's the barrow boy in me," he said. "Right now our priority is to save ourselves."

Outside, the ragged tide of the dawn prayer washed across the city. They crouched below a window sill and opened the curtains an inch wide to observe a city at war.

"There's a radio," Lucy said. She tuned it to Voice of the Arabs and returned to the vantage point from which they could observe the wakening street. The Egyptians had crossed the canal, the radio said.

"Look," Lucy said. A curious performance was being

played out in the street below, where groups of men were gathering. In the centre of each cluster of men there was one person reading aloud from a newspaper. "They're translating the news into dialect," she said. "I'm going down there to buy a newspaper."

"The hell you are! I'll go," Bellamy said.

He took the stairs to the street. As Lucy had guessed, the readers were switching back and forth from formal Arabic to dialect to make sure the listeners understood. He hung around on the edge of one group until somebody turned to glare at him. "Hey, *khawaga*. Mind your own business!" He bought a newspaper from a strolling vendor and went back to the flat.

"Let me see," Lucy said.

The headline in *Al-Ahram* said, 'Our forces have crossed the canal and broken through the Bar-Lev line.' An inside page showed captured Israeli soldiers, some of them with long hair and moustaches; like exhausted and bloodstained hippies with wrists bound.

They spent the next two hours switching between Cairo Radio, Voice of the Arabs and the BBC World Service. The picture emerged of a stupendously successful operation to land tanks and infantry in occupied Sinai under a blanket of air power. Against any expectation, the Israeli Defence Force seemed to have been caught sleeping in on the Yom Kippur holiday.

From their vantage point behind the drapes they could see the streets beginning to fill with animated groups of people. The mood seemed relaxed, jovial, almost like a holiday. When an enormous transport plane lumbered above, hands waved to the sky.

At 9.30am a blue Peugeot drew up outside. The nearside rear window was boarded up with stiff card and what looked like a mile of sticky tape.

"He's here," Lucy said.

* * *

Bellamy immediately recognised Waters when he let himself into the apartment.

"Keep your distance, Waters. Yes, there, by the sideboard. Do you have a weapon?"

"Don't be ridiculous."

"Take your jacket off and throw it to Lucy. Then turn all your pockets inside out."

There was no weapon.

"What's your offer?" Bellamy asked.

"What's my offer? This isn't some kind of transaction. Who do you think you are? You're a couple of amateurs out of your depth and you should be bloody grateful that I'm going to get you home."

"OK. We'll hear you out," Lucy said.

Waters lit up a menthol. "Let me get one thing straight right away. I don't work for Ealing. It doesn't matter to you who I work for, but my people are under instructions from Cabinet."

"Can you prove that?" Lucy asked.

"Not right now. You'll have to take me on trust. Just hear me out." His eyes swivelled from Bellamy to Lucy and back to Bellamy, as if he were waiting for their agreement.

He continued, "If you'll cast your minds back, you were both briefed by a woman at Ealing. She is now being detained under a special Cabinet provision."

Bellamy locked his eyes on Waters'. The story was too bizarre to be believable. But then, wasn't Bellamy's very presence in this room beyond credibility?

"Detained? You mean arrested?" he asked.

"Along with a senior civil servant from the Foreign

Office." Waters' reply was slick, well-rehearsed. He'd planned this encounter meticulously.

Bellamy said, "Crusty old bloke in a pin-striped suit in an office in Whitehall? The one who blackmailed me?"

"I met him too," Lucy said. "Foul old bastard. Why are they under arrest?"

Waters tossed the menthol to the parquet and ground it with his shoe. He flicked open the pack for a fresh cigarette, but changed his mind. "It's a rather complicated story. It started coming through last night and I'm only now getting the details from the Embassy. You two are bloody lucky it broke now—luckier than you deserve."

He reached for a chair.

"Don't move!" Bellamy said. "You can say your piece standing."

Waters puckered his lips and said, "If that's what you want. Can I go on?"

Bellamy and Lucy nodded.

He explained that Ealing had been raided two nights ago, with its senior staff detained. A clandestine line of Foreign Office funding had been uncovered by a persistent journalist with an inside contact; the reporter had been arrested and had spilt what he knew to the Joint Intelligence Committee. More digging had turned up an intelligence operation off Ealing Broadway, operating quite independently of government.

"And JIC had never heard of it?" Lucy asked, flashing Bellamy a 'he's got to be kidding' look.

"Your crusty old bloke, his name doesn't matter, was funding a kind of private MI6, with the woman we've detained in control of day-to-day operations," Waters said.

"I've never heard such rubbish," Lucy said. "Clandestine funding? There are plenty of government operations whose budgets never see daylight; you're talking to an expert. And why were you playing librarian yesterday, all keen and eager to get this ridiculous defection over and done with?"

Waters sighed. "We had to let it run, not alert the people that Ealing had put in place."

Bellamy laughed grimly. "So you bumped off the real librarian? Whacked him with the *Encyclopaedia Britannica*? Laced the handle of his date stamp with cyanide? This is a bloody comedy, my friend."

"I wish it was a comedy. But how's this for a joke? You two are released from your blackmail contract. You're free."

"I'll believe that when I'm back in the UK," Lucy said in a voice heavy with scepticism.

"Let me go on. You've heard of the Arab Mafia, of course?"

This time it was Bellamy who flashed a look of incredulity at Lucy, but she seemed unfazed.

"I've heard of it," she said. "That was the Foreign Office, wasn't it? Eton and Cambridge characters with a penchant for Bedouin boys?"

Waters smoothed the creases in his trouser legs, lit another menthol, and explained. The Foreign Office had been influenced for decades by a group of Arabic experts trained at Shemlan. Arabists headed numerous specific sections or, lower down the scale, acted as gatekeepers to senior staff. Successive prime ministers had been peeved at the frankly lukewarm stance towards Israel in the Foreign Office, but had been unable to tip the balance against these 'Lawrence of Arabia types'.

"I suppose we were on the fringe of it. I remember

some of them at Shemlan," Lucy said.

"You were very much on the fringe," Waters said. "But it was a thing to behold when you were in the thick of it. You sometimes wondered whether the loyalty of some of these types was to the British Crown or the Sheikh of Shithouse Mountain."

Bellamy felt a nudge of unease. So far he hadn't been able to get the measure of Waters. The casual 'shithouse mountain' remark jarred. There was a phoney edge, a jangling note. He glanced at Lucy, who was frowning.

Waters seemed to pick up on the whiff of disapproval, and continued in a more considered tone. His 'team', he said, had swooped the previous night, quarantining the Ealing building and scouring its files. The Prime Minister had been 'tickled pink' to be given an opportunity to take a swipe at the Arab Mafia, and the Joint Intelligence Committee of Cabinet had monitored the situation into the early hours. Instructions had been issued to get Bellamy and Lucy safely back to England. There would be an extensive inquiry into what Ealing had been up to, and the pair would be important informants.

"You'll both be debriefed, and it may not be very pretty."

"You think we've had a pretty time of it here in Cairo? It'll be a tea party," Bellamy said. "But before we agree to anything, can you offer a single shred of evidence to support this story? Believe me, I'd be doing cartwheels if Ealing was closed down. But put yourself in our shoes."

"In fact," Lucy broke in, "we're not going anywhere unless you've got some proof."

Waters sighed and looked at the ceiling. Was he really considering the request, Bellamy wondered, or was it just a charade? Waters finally spoke.

"You've got a bloody cheek demanding anything at all. But if it makes you happy I'll try to get a photograph from the UK that might convince you."

"That'll take a week. There's a war on," Bellamy said.

"The Embassy's just got a telecopier. I'll see what I can do overnight."

"We'll be depending on you," Bellamy said. "And how are we to travel—if we travel?"

"There's a ship from Benghazi and I've got you places on it. It's due to leave the day after tomorrow. You'll go to Libya by service taxi in the morning."

Bellamy remained silent. Lucy could take the lead. "Donald," she said. "I'm prepared to gamble on the fact that what you've explained may not be a complete heap of rubbish. But we still want to see your pictures."

Waters cocked his brow in a little gesture of acknowledgement. They both looked at Bellamy.

"I'm with Lucy," he said.

"Splendid."

"And Pierre Farag. Where does he stand in all this?" Bellamy asked.

"Him? Just a local asset with ideas bigger than his ability. Nothing in the larger scheme of things."

"And the Russian?" Lucy asked.

"A dupe. Expendable."

"And what about passports?" Bellamy asked.

"I've got temporary documents organised. You'll be travelling under your own names. Be ready at seven in the morning," Waters said.

"Just one thing, a matter of curiosity," Lucy said. "What's *Siranoush*?

Waters hesitated and then shrugged. "The code name

for the defection operation—one of Ealing's obscure Orientalist conceits. Apparently Siranoush was a famous opera singer who performed here in Cairo. At any rate, forget it. It's history."

The front door slammed shut and Waters' shoes clattered down the stairs. Bellamy sank into a sofa. Despite the tempest he had endured since landing in Cairo, his mind was in a condition of perfect clarity. The world was reduced to this small room, a man and a woman, disconnected from the city outside, from the war, from their future. What had Lucy said about the next moment, and the next, and the next? The room held him in an existential equilibrium; only the present moment had validity.

Lucy opened the drapes a few inches and sat on the opposite sofa in a bar of honey coloured light. She was, he reflected, a woman he hardly knew and yet knew profoundly. Only this moment—he and she in the timeless dust-specked cube of fractured sunlight—only this mattered.

"What are you thinking, my love?" she asked.

"About this moment, nothing else."

"Me too. I don't care if what Waters said was true or not." She got up and came to the sofa. "Move up. We've got a lot of talking to do."

"You start. Tell me who you are," Bellamy said. She laughed gently and began her story. Like Scheherazade, he thought.

* * *

After Pierre had dropped Bellamy at the apartment in El-Duqqi, he rode the darkened streets to his office at Ramses Square. Among the few buildings with their lights on, some had windows that glowed coolly with the faint blue of air-raid paint. Sandbags spilled from around the concrete blast-walls into the gutters, making shady mounds that might throw a cycle rider to the cobbles.

The Englishman who Pierre knew as Donald Waters was in the office where he had left him an hour ago. The little room was thick with cigarette smoke. The man lounged in the leather office chair with his feet on Pierre's desk.

"Please place your feet on the floor where they belong."

"You've delivered him to the woman? Nothing went wrong?"

"It was done." That was all the man was getting. Pierre was not here to be interrogated on his efficiency, especially by a man with such an unpleasantly insincere manner. This was a deal, an arrangement.

"You have his passport?" Pierre nodded.

"Then show it to me."

Pierre took Clive Rogers' passport from a slim pouch around his neck and handed it to the man. He fingered through the pages, raised the dark blue booklet, and flicked his eye from the photograph to Pierre's face.

"It's not much of a match," he said.

"I will dye my hair, get it cut in a similar way, wear a little make-up when I need to."

Donald took another British passport from his jacket pocket along with two sheets of paper. He made a little stack with Rogers' passport and handed it to Pierre like a travel agent. Pierre flicked open the other passport: a woman, short blonde hair, Victoria Patchett. The papers were orders written on US Embassy paper, entitling the bearer to a berth on the *Cynthia*, departing Alexandria on October 11.

"And what of Bellamy and his lady?" Pierre might be a man used to getting his own way by unorthodox means, but he had a dark suspicion about the fate of the Englishman he had so briefly known.

"That's an operational detail that I'm not supposed to reveal, but I'll stretch a point and tell you that they are travelling under their real names with temporary documents. These passports are of no use to them whatsoever."

This man, Pierre thought, is loose with his words. Or is he trying to reassure me of Bellamy's safety?

"And you said ten years."

"Ten years," Waters said. "We may call on you at any time. You'll be paid well when it happens. Once you get to Britain, just forget about us. We'll find you when we need to."

"That is all?" Pierre asked.

"Just one detail. You must travel to the UK on the Calais-Dover ferry on November 4. You and the lady will get off last."

Waters departed. Pierre had no interest how or whither. The stink of treachery hung in his tiny office. He sat at his desk and cradled his head in his hands. The words of *Ecclesiastes 3* crept into his consciousness. *Il y a un temps pour naître, et un temps pour mourir; un temps pour planter, et un temps pour arracher ce qui est planté.* This was indeed the time to harvest what had been planted, to harvest a lifetime of tiny acts of concealment and compromise and duplicity, to gather it all in to find himself at last an exile with another man's name and an invisible leash around his ankle.

He pictured Zouzou waiting for him in the villa, then raised his head to stare at the swirls of the multi-religious calendar on the wall; Coptic, Muslim, Western, the events of their respective years woven through the year like a skein of coloured yarns. No, he thought, I will give a decade of my life to no man. Zouzou and I will not be hostage to that odious person and his foul masters. I am a man who lives in the niches and the shadows. I will take Zouzou to England, but we will slowly disappear.

* * *

Bellamy woke as dawn broke on Monday. He looked down on Lucy's sleeping form and imagined always waking with her. Her eyes opened and she pulled him close. "They'll come for us soon, Mark. We haven't very much time."

After they'd made love they untwined their limbs and fired up the Vesuvius. The spluttering bursts of cold and scalding hot water jolted Bellamy into a state of urgency. They rinsed off the antiseptic smelling soap and towelled themselves dry. Bellamy put back on Pierre's borrowed clothes while Lucy rummaged among some garments in a cupboard.

"Look, Mark. Sexy or what?" she said, pulling up a pair of baggy Levi's. She ripped another ten inches off the polyester dress and tucked the frayed ends into the waistband of the jeans. The battered patent leather shoes finished the picture.

"You look like a square dancer from Alabama!"

"And you look like an organ grinder from Naples!"

The apartment door opened. Waters stood at the threshold with two bulky Egyptian men.

"Who are they?" Bellamy asked.

"Shut up and hold your wrists out. You too, Lucy." Walters trained a pistol with a silencer on Lucy. One of the Egyptians advanced on Bellamy, peeling a strip off a roll of thick electrical tape.

"So what about that big performance yesterday?"

Lucy said. "We knew it was a load of rubbish. Pull the bloody trigger and see where it gets you. Don't forget—I've got insurance."

Waters flicked off the safety and held a steady aim on Lucy's heart. "Your brother, do you mean, you silly bitch? We've paid him a visit and he's shitting himself."

"You're a gutless cunt, Waters. You won't shoot her. I remember you from Aden, sniffing around in your brothel creepers. You're a pen pusher. Fuck you."

Bellamy switched to Arabic and shouted at the man with the electrical tape. "The *khawaga*, it's a trick, he's aiming the gun at you, watch out!"

As the Egyptian wheeled round to face Waters, Bellamy leapt sideways and yelled to Lucy, "Get behind me!"

"OK, enough!" Waters said, and calmly shot Bellamy in the foot.

The ensuing moments may have been minutes, may have been hours, or perhaps seconds. He remembered flashes of crunching fists, flaming pain in his foot, Lucy's screams, flailing arms, his good foot kicking Waters' nose into a pulp, the sweat smell of the big Egyptians, a needle, sticky tape, and then nothing.

* * *

"Where am I?" His vision was fuzzy, and only one eye seemed to work. Lucy's sweet face came into view, a massive purplish bruise down one side of it. Remote outposts of his body began to come alive. He was aware of a great woolliness somewhere along his right leg. The sense of sight was reinstated and he saw webbing and canvas. Sound was switched on—deafening aircraft engines. It was cold, bitterly cold. His arms were pinned by some kind of strap under a layer of grey blankets. Turning his head, he saw his bruised Lucy similarly pinned into an aluminium jump seat fixed against the curved fuselage wall. A swaying figure loomed towards them, picking a path through crates and machinery lashed to the floor. A woman, broad-faced, stern, and wearing military fatigues. She knelt beside him, wrapped a blood pressure cuff around his arm and put the stethoscope in her ears. She pumped, listened, nodded, brought her mouth to his ear and shouted, "Moscow, two hours."

Chapter 16: Pluck up what is planted

Monday 8 October 1973

On the Monday morning, there wasn't exactly a holiday feel in Cairo, but it didn't feel like a war. There was an air of optimism and confidence that you could almost touch. How long would it last, Pierre wondered? How long till mothers learned that their boys had been maimed or blown to bits? How long till the casualties dulled the shine on Sadat's brass buttons? The Fiat edged through the crowds on the way out of the city. Pierre wore dark glasses under his newly tousled brown hair. Zouzou's headscarf slipped momentarily to reveal the blonde crop beneath. Surprisingly, the roads to Alexandria were open. Even the trains were running, they'd heard.

"Delta or desert, cousin?" the Bulgar asked.

"Delta, I think."

They slowed where a crowd spilled into the street. Here the faces were grimmer. A loudspeaker fixed to a shopfront blared a woman's voice, plaintive, almost hysterical. "Citizens, your sons and brothers are falling at the front. Your blood is needed for our heroes . . .

glory to the fallen . . ." The recording repeated, and patriotic citizens rolled up their sleeves to shove into the queue.

So this, Pierre glumly thought, is how we understand the true meaning of these vile wars. Soon there will be men on the streets with bandaged arms and heads, then those on crutches with their feet missing. Then we will harvest what has been planted in our fertile Egyptian soil. Men in muddy *galabiyyas* will cry tears in their trachoma-blighted eyes when their neighbour reads them the death announcement, "In the name of God the Compassionate the Merciful, we belong to him and to him we shall return. We beg to inform of the passing of . . . "

* * *

"You have never left Egypt?" Zouzou had said with disbelief in the villa.

"On national service I spotted the Libyan border –"

"*Habibi,* you will buy me high tea at Claridges, and snails in Rue Montorgueil."

He glanced across at her: Zouzou, who had lived a whole life of excess and excitement in just a few years. He, a man 'turned in on himself', fleeing the city whose cracked concrete his roots spread and burrowed in. He forced back a wave of panic, the like of which he had never experienced before, gripping the baggy fabric of the car seat. The moving panorama outside the car windows took on the form of a stream of snapshots that Pierre must memorise, that he must lodge in his memory to mark this, his last view of Cairo: a turbanned man in a *galabiyya*, a squat shrine to a local saint, a *kushari* stall, a child selling strings of jasmine flowers, a snub-nosed traffic cop with semaphore arms, three laughing women in summer dresses and white sandals.

And what was Zouzou thinking at this moment? He couldn't imagine. Indeed, he wondered at the folly of their flight from Egypt. What did she want from an insignificant man like himself? She possessed an almost frightening dualism: tough and cynical in one moment, demure and sweet the next. How would these contradictory spirits meld? And then she—the national bitch—had resisted his proposal to make love to her in the villa.

The Delta road opened and the Fiat coughed into top gear, gobbling up the yellow dusty miles, slowing for robed children with great burdens on their heads, for swaying trucks piled high with sugar cane, chassis girders sagging onto bald tyres. They stopped for convoys of army trucks, flatbed trailers loaded with missile launchers, gigantic earthmovers. Car drivers waved and smiled at the soldiers. The war was a street party.

The Fiat barrelled through Benha, then Tanta; the big Delta towns were like islands in the green ocean of sugar cane and palms and brown ponds. They hit big traffic queues at Kafr El-Zayat where two main routes merged, then sped on towards Damanhour.

"Look behind, Pierre. The Mercedes with the broken aerial," the Bulgar said when they were ten miles from Damanhour.

"It's been behind us since Tanta," Pierre said. "Probably nothing."

They slowed down as if to stop, and craned to see the passengers in the Mercedes as it overtook: six men packed in and laughing like donkeys, spitting peanut shells and swigging Sinacola.

Zouzou spoke for the first time since they had left Cairo, "There will be eyes on us, but we will not know

238

where they conceal themselves."

They slid quietly into Alexandria as the sun was sinking. The Fiat stopped outside a beachside hotel in Gleem. The couple quickly stepped out of the car and entered the tiny reception area. The Fiat chugged away and the Bulgar was gone.

The owner of the hotel, a friend of Pierre's father, embraced him and then turned to Zouzou, offering his hand.

"We are honoured, *sitti hanim.*" The archaic title sounded gracious in the speech of the old man, who was in an ancient but immaculately pressed three-piece suit. Zouzou took his hand in her fingertips, cast her eyes down, and replied, "We are honoured by you." Then a middle-aged woman was at her side, ushering up the stairs to her room.

"My niece will take good care of her. Is it really Aziza?" He gave Pierre a room key and invited him to join him for dinner in an hour.

Pierre's heart was always freshened by Alexandria's sea coast, by the salty air, by palm trees that were not begrimed with grey dust. The hotel room looked out over a dark sea striped with the luminescent reflections of car headlights, the odd street lamp and blued windows. The blackout was apparently being complied with to some extent. The walls of the room were hung with large monochrome photographic prints. Pierre stared at the one above the bed, attempting to unravel the fluid shapes of human limbs and, surely not . . . but the composition resolved itself as a lemon pip nestled in the crook of two extended fingers.

He'd had no time for art, no time for anything beyond the practical. Sure, he'd studied glossy plates of famous paintings in art books, but these images had never reached inside his heart. The lemon pip photograph disturbed him in a way that was strange to him; the subtle eroticism and the *trompe l'œil* effect belonged to an unfamiliar and exotic dimension. His apprehension about leaving Egypt was amplified; firm ground was dissolving under his feet.

* * *

Zlotnik was wearing a boiler suit when he woke up in his apartment. He tottered from the bed—grubby, sticky, his face itchy. There was stubble on his jaw—how many days? His stomach was empty and his mouth was dry and foul tasting. It was faint daylight outside the blinds, but what time? Dawn or dusk? What day? He had a faint memory of a stopped watch; the English woman, Lucy Erikova, she had lost her watch. Fragmented memories of the last day—or perhaps two days—jumped around his consciousness. He went to the kitchen and felt behind the cleaning materials under the sink. Yes, it was there—a brandy bottle with a stale inch remaining in the bottom, hidden after some long past blinder.

The mouthful of spirit sparked his brain. He had to know what the time it was, work out how long it had been since they'd dumped him in the street. Recent events were clear now: the white-coated woman, the hospital trolley, the sack over his head, the boot of a car.

An electric alarm clock in the bedroom said it was Monday morning. Zlotnik calculated rapidly: Irina's bed was Thursday; sometime after that a massive binge, yelling something stupid into the night, noises in the apartment, men hauling him into a car, cobblestones, water. Then a clearer recollection of being incarcerated with the blonde Englishwoman, and Dimashqi's attempt to have her read the ludicrous confession.

Seventy-two hours at least. Seventy-two hours of absence from the Embassy. Yes, he'd intended to call in sick on the day of the defection. He laughed out loud, although his voice mustered barely a croak. His defection! And there was Irina; he'd all but confided his plans to her.

He tossed the empty brandy bottle into a corner, lit a cigarette and considered the situation.

First was his position at the Embassy. His department head was the *rezident*. Nobody asked tricky questions of the KGB First Chief Directorate's man in the Embassy, let alone his staff.

Second, Zlotnik's work lent itself to a measure of flexibility not available to most of his colleagues. Long lunches, odd contacts and unexplained absences were the tools of his slippery trade.

Third, his drinking was no secret. This wouldn't be the first time he'd locked himself away for a couple of days after a bender.

The splinter in his toe was Dimashqi. For God's sake, he thought. I was incarcerated by a colonel in the General Intelligence Directorate who knows that I planned to defect.

But, turning the dilemma this way and that in his mind, Zlotnik began to contemplate a possible solution, a balancing of the negatives and positives that might lead to a scheme in which he and Dimashqi could resume their symbiotic coexistence. The priority, though, was to discover whether Dimashqi had already denounced him to the *rezident*.

He took the key to the telephone dial lock from where it was hidden among his socks, safe from the cleaner. He wouldn't try to call Dimashqi directly yet; better to creep up on him.

The man he dialled was a medium-ranked staffer in Dimashqi's office who Zlotnik knew had some connections with a student communist group he'd prefer not to have bandied around.

"Good morning. I have been calling Colonel Dimashqi's number, but I cannot find him." Zlotnik spoke in careful English; his contact knew a bit of Russian but it wasn't up to this particular job.

"Please, one moment." There was muffled talk. A hand over the mouthpiece?

Then, "I cannot speak about this."

"What do you mean? What can you not speak about?"

"I cannot speak. Sorry, Sir." The man's voice had an edge of panic.

"Has something happened to the Colonel?" A worm of hope turned in Zlotnik's chest; had Dimashqi been sent to the front? Killed? Or perhaps denounced and detained by his own people?

"Sorry," the man said stupidly.

Zlotnik guessed there were people in earshot. "Tell me in Russian."

The man made some *umms* and *aaahs*, then said, "*Izchez.*"

Izchez? Disappeared? Is that what he had said?

"*Ushol.*"

Gone away? What was he talking about?

"Where has he gone? Tell me in Russian."

"*Nye znayu, nikto nye znayet.*"

"Thank you, comrade." Zlotnik cut the connection. Nobody knew where Dimashqi had gone. There was hope.

He tuned the radio to the BBC World Service and opened the drapes. Apparently, the war had begun with stunning success, and he had slept through what looked to be the Arabs' finest moment. The strolling citizens and insouciant street vendors defied any impression of a country in mortal combat.

A shower restored Zlotnik to a state approaching normality. He guessed that some kind of sedative had been administered to him in the last twenty-four hours; there was a suspicious bruise on his arm. Better go easy on the liquor, he thought. He called the Embassy, but there were no cars available. A taxi, then. There was a cleanish suit in the wardrobe, and he fished out the least offensive of the shirts in the laundry basket. *Bozhe moi*, to be strolling across Red Square on a crisp October morning, or better still Greenwich Village. How he loathed this sewer of a city.

* * *

The Embassy hummed with quiet industry; the war was going Egypt's way for now, and the USSR's leadership and diplomats were shifting into the next stages of the conflict: managing the massive arms lift from the USSR to counter the stream of US aircraft rushing materiel to Israel; and anticipating the end of hostilities and negotiation of a settlement of what must be a short war.

Zlotnik walked with slow deliberation through the corridors, grimacing and massaging his abdomen. Irina came up behind him and fell into step.

"Over your sickness, Ivan Maksimovich?"

"A little better. Thank you for your concern, Irina Andreyevna."

"And no other problems, I hope?"

"All perfectly well, Irina Andreyevna."

"And I think you have a meeting with the *rezident* at midday?" she said, and strode quickly away.

The *rezident*? He made a note to thank her for the

warning, and indeed for not denouncing him. Surely he was right about Irina, that she was like him, her loyalty to the party a flimsy fiction.

He catalogued the reasons that the *rezident* might want to see him: his defection attempt had been exposed, and he was to face censure, or worse; they knew about the defection attempt and would demand that he try again with the aim of becoming a mole in the West. The ashtray on his desk piled up and he made a feeble show of working, as the clock crawled towards noon.

The phone jangled. It was the Egyptian intelligence functionary he had spoken to earlier.

"Can we please meet?"

"When?" Zlotnik asked. It was 11am.

"In fifteen minutes. Groppi. I have motorbike."

* * *

Zlotnik got out of the taxi just as the Egyptian entered Groppi. For all the carnage under way just eighty kilometres away, the elegant coffee house seemed unruffled. Plump dames in silk dresses picked at impossibly dainty pastries, suave men read *Al-Ahram* and drank tiny *tasses de café*.

Zlotnik and the Egyptian ordered *citron pressé* from a waitress with a milky eye, and waited for their drinks with apparent nonchalance; two officials having a casual meeting. When the tall glasses arrived, the intelligence functionary stirred four or five spoonfuls of sugar into the scarifyingly tart drink.

"Well?" Zlotnik said.

"I could not tell through telephone. The man we talk about has left Egypt."

Zlotnik's heart galloped. He sipped the acid drink and swallowed more then he intended, choking into his napkin. A bitter mess of bile and sweetened lime sat in his throat.

"Where has he gone?"

"We think he go to Libya. In a service taxi on Sunday."

"Was he authorised to leave?" Dear God, please let Dimashqi have absconded.

The Egyptian looked puzzled. He hadn't understood the question.

"Did he have permission to leave Egypt?"

"No, Sir. He has gone absent *ya'ni* without leave. With his daughter and her children and her husband. Somebody think he is an Israeli agent."

Angels, thought Zlotnik, are singing songs of joy and bliss in the blue sky above the smog of Qasr El-Nil Street. Harps are gushing with sweet melodies. Massed choirs are belting out the *Hallelujah Chorus* and Handel is frolicking in his grave. He could have kissed the scrawny, nervous man in front of him.

"I am in your debt," he said. "Go quickly."

The man lingered. Zlotnik took from his pocket the roll of banknotes and passed them under the table.

* * *

At midday Zlotnik knocked on the door of the *rezident*. A dark-haired woman he thought he recognised invited him in. She indicated a chair at the conference table and sat opposite him.

"The *rezident* apologises. He had to confer with the Ambassador. I am Varvara Manoukian. I came in on Sunday."

"Came in?"

"From Russia. On a military transport."

Another Armenian. He remembered her now from

his time in Yerevan. Russian first name. No patronymic. What is it about these people, quietly carving out their state within a state wherever they go?

"And?" Zlotnik asked.

"I am your replacement. This is for you." She passed him a letter signed by the Ambassador. It was bald and brief. Zlotnik was to return home in one month for medical rehabilitation. Before his departure he was to brief his replacement on his work so as to effect a trouble-free handover.

"Medical rehabilitation?" he asked. As if it was any of her fuck-your-mother business anyway.

"We work to the highest standards of behaviour, Ivan Maksimovich. You are a MGIMO graduate, a gifted and dignified man, but . . . "

"But?" he asked. But he knew the answer. He was a boozer, a drunk, a soak. Perhaps he was also a traitor, destined for the *gulag*.

"Thank you for informing me. It will be a pleasure to brief you. Now I will excuse myself. I am feeling slightly unwell."

"No, stay please." The woman slid two photographs from a folder across the desk: Lucy and a man Zlotnik knew to be her British companion.

"Do you know these people?"

His mind momentarily turned to fuzz. He focused and looked up at her. "The woman looks familiar, but I meet a lot of people. The man, I don't think I know him. Who are they?"

"They are British intelligence agents. We recruited them five years ago. They were sent here on a mission, but something went badly wrong and they believed they were about to be exposed. They defected to Moscow on

Saturday."

Zlotnik stifled a giggle as a wave of something akin to hysteria swept his mind. He buried his face in a handkerchief and blew his nose so hard that his eardrums almost burst. The notion was too ridiculous, the fiction too absurd. But then, wasn't that how it worked? Tell a big enough lie with straight-faced conviction, and truth bends to fit untruth. What did Orwell call it? *Doublethink*!

He adjusted his expression to one of professional concern. "A very serious business. How are we placed at this end, given that they are no doubt being debriefed in Moscow?"

"That's really why I asked you to wait, comrade. The *rezident* wants a full report on their activities in Cairo since they arrived last Thursday or Friday. Frankly, that's a problem for me; I don't know a soul in this city, so I'm relying on you. We'll work together, talk to your contacts. There's this fellow called Dimashqi, for example, an informant of yours, I believe. We'll put together a report and the people in Moscow can compare notes to see who these two are really working for."

She ended this speech with a bright smile, like a youngster donning the red scarf after taking the solemn oath of the Vladimir Ilyich Lenin All-Union Pioneer Organisation.

But it was shit; she knew it, he knew it. Varvara Manoukian was First Chief Directorate and for people like her, smiles had nothing to do with happiness.

"Oh, I forgot, one more," she said through the clamped teeth. Zlotnik felt the blood drain from his face as she slid the photograph across the desk top. It was the British man who, three months previously, had sought him out and proposed the defection.

"You won't see me again," he'd said in a cloud of menthol cigarette smoke. "There's a local who will look after you, Pierre Farag. You can trust him," he'd added.

Zlotnik looked steadily into Varvara Manoukian's eyes. They were, he realised, expressionless.

"Never seen him in my life."

Chapter 17: This Love Business

Tuesday 9 October 1973

The next day passed in an atmosphere of serenity. Pierre and Zouzou spent the daylight hours on Pierre's terrace in demure fashion, each in a deck chair. The hotel staff had been told that they were brother and sister, so that the moral standards of the establishment would be preserved. Zouzou alternately flicked through French magazines and browsed a *Livre de Poche* detective novel, while Pierre tried his hand at sketching.

"An artist, *habibi*?"

Pierre hadn't drawn a line since his schooldays, but the lemon pip picture had awakened in him some deep lode of creative sensitivity. He began by copying photographs from Paris Match—the hotel had an ample stock of artist materials and magazines—and he soon found himself frowning in concentration with his tongue stuck out sideways.

Zouzou giggled and broke his concentration. "I remember that look from the Agami days when you played pocket chess with my father."

And I usually let him win, Pierre thought. He had

been a precociously intelligent child with a remarkable memory for facts and the ability to attend to multiple mental tasks simultaneously. His parents loved to show off Pierre's party tricks, like counting alternately up to a hundred in Arabic and down from a hundred in French: *Wahid, cent, itneen, quatre vingt dix neuf, talata*—he could still do it. But to draw? His school efforts were poor stuff, displaying no trace of imagination or emotion.

That evening, Zouzou dined with the owner's niece while Pierre took his dinner in the old man's private quarters. The furnishings were heavy and the meal was bland, served by a boy in a blue silk livery. The old man spilt a drop of gravy on his tie, and the boy was at his side instantly with a tiny shaker of talc.

At the end of the meal the owner said, "I want to intro-duce you to some friends." He steered Pierre towards a door behind a tapestry curtain in the vestibule. Closing the door behind them, the old man led Pierre down a flight of stairs into a wide, low-ceilinged room—a cellar converted into a kind of salon. Half a dozen men sat in armchairs, and at a heavy dining table with a glass top, beneath which were trapped black-and-white family photographs that seemed to date back to the forties. The BBC World Service was playing softly on a radio. Three of the men were in heated but apparently genial conversation. All were smoking and drinking coffee. Pierre noticed that one man wore a silk cravat and another smoked a pipe. All were characterised by one affectation or another that marked them as out of the mainstream.

The old man introduced each friend to Pierre. As hands were shaken and cordialities exchanged, Pierre recognised some of the names as those of journalists from intellectual magazines that you didn't browse at the news-stand without checking who might be watching.

"They meet here out of the view of—well, out of view, let's say," the owner said obliquely.

"You honour us," one of the men—an economics professor—said to Pierre. "I knew your father quite well, God bless his memory."

Pierre sat in an armchair and absorbed the conversation, all of it concerning the war, and all of it frank to the point of rashness. The President, a donkey? The editor of *Al-Ahram*, a propagandist? And Zouzou's General, the big zucchini, an Israeli double agent? Pierre was sweating with nervousness when one of the men glanced over and said, "Don't worry, brother, there are no *mukhabarat* here. We're just a bunch of big-mouths exercising our jaw bones."

* * *

That night Pierre knocked on Zouzou's door to wish her goodnight after checking the staircases and corridors to be sure that no servants were abroad.

"Hello, brother." She was sitting at a dressing table in a silk gown, brushing her hair. "How was your evening?"

"A little disturbing," he said, and told her about what he'd heard in the salon.

"Ouf!" Zouzou said. "I've heard things about these high-ups that would make your hair go white."

She looked at him with obvious fondness. "I think I will fall in love with you, Pierre. I've spent most of my adult life with men whose hearts are hard and bitter, and I've never known the real love of a man."

Pierre pondered her words. He'd thought perhaps that she was already in love with him, although they'd barely had time to discuss such matters. And of course, there was her refusal of him in her bed in the villa. These were difficult topics for a man 'turned in on himself'. Nevertheless the discussion must be had.

"Zouzou, *habibti*, we've hardly spoken about our future, our life, what we will . . . " The sentence sputtered out.

"Do you love me, Pierre?"

He wrapped his arms around his chest and rocked back and forth in his chair. No woman had asked him this question before. He thought about the woman in Shoubra; no love there, just commerce. Then it hit him hard in his stomach. Yes, he loved her beyond reason.

"I love you, Zouzou."

"Then I will love you and I will share your bed." He raised an eyebrow. Dare he ask when?

In answer to his unspoken question she said, "We must marry first, *habibi*, and it will be in France."

"Marry—yes, of course." In France? Marry? He was out of his depth with this love business.

"There is a reason, Pierre, and you will learn of it after our marriage. Now kiss me and go back to your room."

* * *

Lucy's rudimentary Russian studies were a small consolation for the shocking realisation that she and Mark Bellamy had been abducted to the USSR. When the military plane touched down, a medical team entered the aircraft, bringing with them a waft of cold fog and aircraft fuel fumes.

The leader of the team glanced from her to Bellamy and back again. "Are you injured?" he asked Lucy in Russian.

"*Nyet, ya khorosho*." Lousy Russian, she thought, but at

least the medico was now on his knees, unstrapping Bellamy and preparing to check his vital signs. The man put a line into Bellamy's arm, and the other team members hoisted him onto a stretcher.

"You come with us," the medico said. One of the team unstrapped her and handed her a thick anorak with a fur-trimmed hood. It smelt of perfume and sweat, but Lucy was instantly warmed as the garment trapped her body heat. Bellamy was groaning. His foot stuck out from the blankets, a brown-stained giant sausage of bandages.

It was night on the tarmac. They slid Bellamy into an ambulance in which a uniformed and armed man already sat. The medico jumped aboard and extended a hand to help Lucy into the vehicle. They sat on the bench next to the stretcher, and the man said something about legs, and rubbed his calves vigorously.

"*Da*," Lucy said, lost for a reply. Yes, her legs were stiff from the cramped flight. Feeling was returning to her feet. She took off the battered patent leather court shoes and rubbed her toes until they hurt, all the time watching Bellamy's face.

His eyes opened. "Lucy!"

"Stay still, darling, we're on the way to hospital." She looked up to the tinted window. They were moving across a dark expanse of concrete dotted with military planes and helicopters. The lights of a long, low building were visible in the distance.

The doctor adjusted the drip, and Bellamy half sat up. "Where the bloody hell are we?"

Lucy knelt on the floor and hugged him. "Australia, my beautiful man. Or perhaps Brazil. Or perhaps Ceylon. We'll be at the beach soon."

"If only! We're in bloody Russia. What's that out

there?" The lights were resolving into a civilian terminal building topped with a sign saying *Sheremetyevo*.

"Moscow airport. Sorry, it's a bit of a way to Bondi Beach."

Lucy slid back onto the bench and they watched in silence as the terminal building receded and the ambulance approached a guardhouse complex manned by troops in fur hats. The ambulance door was opened from the outside and flashlights penetrated the interior, blinding Lucy. She could make out silhouettes of two people in fur hats. A clipboard was thrust into the ambulance. The armed guard and the medico signed something, the clipboard was taken back, the doors closed. They were off again, gliding onto a wide motorway bounded by forest.

"One hour," the medico said, holding up a finger. Lucy nodded and sat back on the bench. Bellamy seemed to be dozing and she thought it best to leave him; she shuddered at the thought of what was beneath the bandage. The dark landscape glided by, lulling her into a state of calm and contemplation. Her shoulders slumped, her jaw unclamped. For the first time in days her thoughts were her own, uninterrupted.

Her father had always praised her resourcefulness and independence. It was a standing family joke that if she was dropped by parachute into Outer Mongolia, Lucy would have the nomads serving her tea and scones in ten minutes. There were variations: Eskimos would be playing cricket; Australian stockmen would be putting on a Gilbert and Sullivan. She bore these corny jokes with equanimity, but she knew that they served to cover her vulnerabilities. This was the English way. Keep a stiff upper lip, roll out the eccentric humour and shut down weakness. Once she'd struck out at her father during a family meal attended by some old friends of her parents.

"Dad, I'm not a bloody paragon of virtue. Stop it please."

There had been a flurry of harrumphing and refilling of glasses as her mother smoothed the ruffles. Of course, there was an invisible and dangerous wreck beneath the calm waters that the family contrived to cruise on. The deceased child—the lost grandson. If Lucy mentioned the boy or even hinted at the topic, her mother would retire to a corner with a library book, and her father would set his jaw and stare into the garden. She visited them rarely in the years after the boy's death, but how she ached to shout out loud—something, anything to shake them out of their reluctance to face the thing that loaded her heart like a tonne of black stone.

And then came Mark Bellamy, lost in the past but not lost in her soul. She was certain now that he was the missing fragment in her broken life. And she didn't give a damn whether her new, complete life was to be lived in Outer Mongolia, the Australian outback, or even bloody Moscow.

Signs of urban life were appearing outside. She guessed that they were travelling on one of the outer ring roads around Moscow. There were bulky apartment blocks separated from the road by parkland. She watched a couple under a street lamp, kissing, fat bundles in thick jackets and hats. It seemed incongruous; people kissed beyond the Iron Curtain? A lifetime of indoctrination, she supposed. I'd never thought of it. The streetscape was austere, unmarked by advertising hoardings. She read a slogan in red lights that topped a building. *Communism is Soviet Power +*

Electrification. The words made sense, but not the purpose. Did people thrill to this sentiment each time they passed the sign? Or did it slip unnoticed into a mental rubbish bin, like the big *Yes* on the Benson & Hedges advertisements on the London Tube?

The guard in the ambulance was eyeing her. She smiled back and tried to say that the view outside was beautiful: *"Krasivy."* The man looked away, and she turned her mind to their fate. She was certain that they were not in physical danger; their deaths could have been easily and quietly arranged in Cairo. There was another purpose; they were valuable commodities in the abstruse game of point scoring played by rival intelligence agencies. They had been for years.

"I think we're here, Mark." The ambulance had pulled into a parking lot next to a massive concrete building. The stretcher was swiftly lifted onto a trolley, and Lucy gripped Bellamy's hand. Inside the hospital building a bustle of female nurses in curious old-fashioned uniforms swept Lucy and the trolley down a gleaming corridor to a treatment room. Lucy was ordered to sit outside, but she refused. She dredged up some fragments of Russian, *"Eto moi muzh"*—'that's my husband'. Well, not quite, but it did the job; they pointed at a chair.

They gave Bellamy a shot of something strong and his head lolled. The brown-stained bandage was unwound and the remains of the shoe cut away. Lucy stood up and watched through a gap between the shoulders of the medical staff. The foot was blue and horribly swollen, and she could clearly see the mess where the middle toes should have been. She felt consciousness slipping from her and strong arms preventing her from falling from the chair.

* * *

Bellamy woke to a sunny morning. A tiny bird hopped from bare branch to bare branch outside the window. Sitting up he saw an alien cityscape outside: Moscow's broad boulevards and immense squat buildings. A huge hoarding bore the face of Lenin, but he could not read the slogan below.

Lucy was in the other hospital bed, asleep. She stirred and her eyes opened. She looked across at him and then out the window. They both laughed.

Bellamy became aware of a sharp, spicy smell. Pipe tobacco. A man was sitting on a steel chair by the door, tapping a pipe into a saucer.

"Who are you?"

"I'm Derek."

"Derek who?" Lucy asked.

"I'm afraid I don't have a punchline for that. I'm out of practice with English jokes."

"You're from the North—Manchester—aren't you?" Lucy asked.

"Leeds, actually."

"So, who are you?" Bellamy asked. Derek was in his fifties, dressed in a saggy tweed jacket and grey twill trousers.

"I'll be looking after you during your stay here."

"Looking after us?"

"Yes. Flat, clothes, job, all that."

"And how long will we be here?" Lucy said.

Derek fussed with the pipe and turned to Lucy. Bellamy noticed that he had that odd habit of angling his face upwards and closing his eyes when he began to speak.

"I can't tell you, my dear. I don't get mixed up with

that side of things. But the main thing is that you'll be leaving here tomorrow to stay in another place so that they can ask you a few questions."

"What other place, and who's 'they'?" Bellamy was disturbed by the sinister undertow.

Derek got up. "I'll be with you at every turn. You can trust me." He tapped his nose and made a stage whisper, "I know all the lurks around here. Back tomorrow. Toodle pip!"

When he had gone Bellamy asked Lucy, "Does that door lock from the inside?"

She got up and checked. There was a turn bolt, which she clicked into place. She took a towel and hung it over the glass square in the door.

"This might hurt," Lucy said, as she pulled off the hospital gown and straddled him on the steel cot.

Chapter 18: The Cynthia

Wednesday 10 October 1973

By breakfast time on Wednesday, Pierre had made a respectable representation of Zouzou. She giggled with delight. "You have flattered me, *habibi*. My nose is much bigger, but you've caught me."

They spent the rest of the morning on the terrace, he sketching and she reading, until the owner's niece rapped on the door. "Please come with me, to the salon, quickly."

Without asking the reason, Pierre and Zouzou followed the woman down the stairs and passed behind the thick curtain in the vestibule. The room where Pierre had spent a congenial hour with the loose-talking writers was dark and stale. A constellation of coffee rings arced across the glass table top. The empty ashtrays were wiped clean but the stink of cold ash clung to the furnishings.

"A police officer has taken a room for the night. You must stay hidden now," the owner's niece whispered.

It could be something, it could be nothing. Pierre thought it inconceivable that the goings on in the salon were invisible from the *mukhabarat*. Indeed, any one of the intellectuals could be a spy. While he was almost nauseous with worry outside the well-trodden grounds of his Cairo, Zouzou was completely relaxed. He had become fascinated with her unpredictability, and watched her scanning yesterday's *Al-Ahram* under a desk light in the dark salon. What would she say next? he wondered. Would she look up and intone one of her fatalistic, resigned pronouncements, or would she whimsically express her desire for a thatched cottage in the English countryside? She threw the newspaper to the ground and shrugged, "What can we do, my love?"

When the police officer had gone out, the niece installed them in Pierre's room with instructions not to leave. Blinds were to be closed. Meals would be delivered. They were not to speak. The servants were to be told that they were both very ill with a contagious condition.

Zouzou yawned and stretched, and declared that she would take a siesta. She lay on the bed, covered herself with a black robe, and was asleep almost immediately. Enthralled by her insouciance, Pierre sat in an armchair watching the slow rise and fall of her chest, imagining his caresses on the little patch of bare ankle that peeped from below the black cloth, mentally disrobing the delectably contradictory woman they called the national bitch, forcing from his mind grotesque images of the old General—the big zucchini—advancing on her naked body. His fascination with Zouzou turned to disgust at his own tormented thoughts. He dragged his gaze away, lit a Cleopatra and picked up his sketchbook.

Flicking through his clumsy scratching, the notion slowly took shape that his ties to Egypt were dissolving, that the clinging constraints of family and his unsavoury professional network were fading. A door had opened into his heart, or out of his heart, perhaps. The man who was 'turned in on himself' had glimpsed the same man turned outwards. He looked again at Zouzou, trying to visualise himself in her eyes, trying to imagine what she saw in his soul. It occurred to him that he was at a moment of epiphany; the centre of his life had shifted to one side, and Zouzou now stood beside him. His past was his past, not a part of now or tomorrow.

Evening was heralded by the Ramadan prayer. Zouzou stirred at the first ripple of the call to worship and was awake by the time that every mosque in the city was signalling the end of the day's fast. She opened her eyes in puzzlement, then smiled when she saw Pierre.

There was a tap at the door. The owner's niece discreetly peeped inside. "The police officer is back," she said. "Sir, be prepared to flee. We will give you a signal. I will look after your sister. Make your way to the tram stop at 11pm, and she will be waiting for you in a car."

The signal came within the hour. The owner's niece explained in a rapid whisper that the old man was trying to delay the police officer's demand to examine the guest register. He had asked to use the telephone at the reception desk and had been heard making some obscure remarks about 'birds' and 'cages'. Someone at the end of the telephone line had been asked to 'bring a net'. In the meantime, a ladder had been placed against the terrace of Pierre's room.

Zouzou robed herself, covering her face. She picked up her luggage and followed the owner's niece to some hidden women's quarter. Pierre took his holdall out to the terrace, where he could see the top of a ladder against the balustrade at the side of the building. It was now night time and the blackout left the bottom of the ladder in almost complete darkness. He clambered down and found himself in a walled garden of cacti. He scanned the path that led to the corniche. A few passers-by ambled along the road, evidently walking off their big sunset meals. There was a gap, and Pierre skipped across the corniche and onto the beach. Looking back at the hotel, he saw no signs of alarm.

The onshore breeze ruffled his hair. He tried to imagine the scents of Europe in the zephyrs on which the last gulls of the day swooped and glided. A party of young people were chatting and smoking in a circle on the dark sand, and he walked away from them. They called out, "Sleep well!" He waved an acknowledgment.

Somebody called out from the darkness.

"Who are you?" An old man's voice.

A good question, Pierre thought.

"I do not know," he replied. He could make out a shape on the sand, a person sitting cross-legged.

"Why are you here?" An even more difficult question.

"Can you tell me?" Pierre asked.

"You are here because of God's love."

"How do you know that?" Pierre asked.

There was a dry laugh and a belch from the shape in the sand, then the clink of bottles. A drunk.

But the questions remained. Who was he, and why was he here? He carried the false British passport of Clive Rogers; he sensed that he would never again call himself Pierre Farag. He was nameless, stateless.

With no conscious understanding of his actions, Pierre slipped his late father's Rolex from his wrist, kissed it, and hurled it in a high arc above the black mass of the sea.

The tram-stop was a kilometre away. He hoisted the

holdall onto his shoulder and set out along the sand.

Thursday 11 October 1973

As dawn broke Pierre and Zouzou woke in the back seat of the car, which had been parked in an alley behind a shop. The driver—another relative of the hotel owner, Pierre guessed—had promised to return at 6am. Here he was, tapping on the windscreen.

He drove them to the passenger dock, where the couple made their way to a customs shed. A dented tub bearing the name *Cynthia* leaned against the dockside in the sickly light.

"Take off the robe, Zouzou. We are English people now."

Zouzou sat self-consciously, smoothing her short blonde hair. A uniformed man—some kind of port official—sidled up to the doorway, smoking and eyeing them.

"English now," Pierre whispered.

The man approached and barked, "*gawaz is-safar!*" He wanted to see their passports.

Pierre made a blank expression.

"*Bassbort!*"

"By Jove, so that is what you require!"

"Jolly good," Zouzou chimed in. They both handed the dark blue passports over. Pierre breathed slowly to calm his pounding heart. Zouzou smiled brightly at the man, who flicked Pierre's passport back to him. The document fell into a puddle of greasy water.

"Come wiz me," the official said to Zouzou, fingering her passport, his eyes locked onto her breasts. Pierre got up, but the man said, "Stay!"

"Where do you take me?" Zouzou asked.

"You come. Official business!"

A group of people wandered into the shed. Americans, Pierre thought. Zouzou ran up to the eldest of the party, a dignified silver-haired gentleman in a white suit.

"Ambassador!" she cried. "How lovely to greet you in this place."

Pierre glanced at the uniformed man; a look of panic flashed across his face, and he flicked Zouzou's passport into the same puddle where the other lay. When Pierre looked up he was gone, and Zouzou was making an elaborate show with the old gentleman,

"Jolly sorry, Sir. I mistook you for His Excellency!"

"Who was he?" Pierre asked when the Americans had passed on.

"I'm not certain, but I'm sure I met him at a kind of party once," she said darkly.

* * *

By 9am, the shed was beginning to fill with people and luggage. A restive crowd of sweating foreigners ringed the counter where confused Egyptian officials were making a show of checking documents for the *Cynthia*. Porters hung around the mountains of suitcases and cardboard boxes bound with sticky tape and marked with addresses in Washington DC, Portland, Charleston, Little Rock. Pierre and Zouzou lingered on the periphery. By late morning the Americans had whipped themselves into a mutinous state. Red-faced women yelled at the Egyptians that their senator would be hearing about this. Big men in sweat-soaked suits banged their fists on the counter. The officials began a half-hearted effort at checking passports, but the Americans broke through the lines and ran onto the dock where the *Cynthia* was tied up. Some of the foreigners hefted their own luggage, and the porters lugged the rest. The passengers fought their way up the gangplank. A suitcase burst open and a shower of socks and paperback books fluttered into the filthy water. A pink corset nudged a soccer ball in an oil-slicked eddy by a waste pipe at the waterline. The porters, despairing of their gratuities, began trying to hurl luggage up onto the deck, but most of the cases hit the rusted hull and slid into the water.

Pierre and Zouzou slipped through a gap in the ragged stream of Americans and scuttled up the gang-plank. Inside the steel doorway at the top there was an American who seemed to be in charge, surrounded by passengers bawling "I want a fucking first-class cabin" and "Who organised this fucking mess?" The phrase "my fucking senator" seemed to end every demand. The man glanced at Pierre, who handed him the US Embassy dockets through the forest of waving arms. The man quickly glanced at the papers, nodded to Pierre and turned his attention back to the barrage of curses.

The couple found their way to an outside deck and leaned on the rail overlooking the dockside. The ship was a reeking heap, surely not long for the scrap yard. The last passengers straggled up the gangplank and the device was cranked away from the *Cynthia*. A big crowd was forming on the rear deck. Shouts of anger and incredulity filled the air. Pierre forced his way to the stern. A Soviet navy ship was moored behind the *Cynthia* and a shaky crane was hoisting grey tubular objects onto the dock. One of the tubes slipped in its harness and bumped the concrete with a clang. As the *Cynthia*'s engines groaned rheumatically into life, an American in a suit and a baseball cap pointed at the Soviet ship and shouted, "Look, they're unloading fucking missiles!"

* * *

The Cynthia struggled out of Alexandria harbour in the early afternoon, with the Americans arguing over the cabins. Braying like donkeys, they complained that they "only ever sailed in fucking first-class" or "wouldn't stand for a fucking starboard cabin." The very air was thick with the ugly English word. It was as if a race of civilised beings had reverted to savagery. The women, Pierre thought, were even more vulgar than the men.

Zouzou had quietly solved the problem of their accommodation. Amazingly—no, nothing amazed Pierre about Zouzou by now—she spoke Turkish. An enraptured steward from Northern Cyprus secreted the pair in a double cabin that was apparently unavailable to the wailing Americans.

"*Teşekkür ederim*," she breathily thanked him. The tongue-tied steward bowed and scraped his way into the rust-streaked corridor. Zouzou clanged the door shut. "Top or bottom bunk, brother?"

* * *

The Americans had settled down by nightfall, but more trouble erupted in the dining room. While Pierre and Zouzou quietly picked over an unedifying dish of macaroni and pinkish meat sauce, the Americans gestured angrily at their plates and demanded to see the chef. The fat, sweating man emerged from the kitchen, wiping his hands on his string vest and coughing over the last puffs of a cigarette. He spoke no English and left after a brief pantomime of apology, but not before flashing a look of resignation at Pierre; one middle-easterner to another. So much for the English gentleman!

The next morning it was hot and breezeless. The

toilets had overflowed during the night, and there was listless mopping in play. The Turkish steward escorted Zouzou to some private facilities and stood guard outside while she performed her ablutions; Pierre made do in the reeking public bathroom, where American men in sodden hotel slippers cursed the *Cynthia*. By midmorning the Americans demanded that the swimming pool be filled. Pierre and Zouzou knew enough Greek to understand that the crew thought the idea mad. But the State Department had hired the "fucking ship" and if they couldn't use the "fucking pool", their senators would know about it. As the tiny tank filled, the ship slowed and began to list to port. Within two hours it was struggling through the smooth sea like a duck with a broken leg. The Americans demanded speed. The pool was emptied.

* * *

The couple disembarked at Piraeus two days later with three weeks to fill before catching the Calais-Dover ferry on November 4. They bought tickets on a ship to Toulon via Genoa, leaving in two days.

"In France I will be free," Zouzou said, sipping a thick Greek coffee in a café among the bone-white buildings around Piraeus Harbour.

"Free from what, *habibti*?"

"Free from the thousand years resting on my shoulders."

Pierre looked at her intently. He thought he understood.

* * *

They meandered northwards through the early French winter, staying at pensions in separate rooms. They both spoke French with ease, but were often asked where they had acquired it. Zouzou's acting skills weren't as bad as she'd made out, Pierre thought, as Miss Patchett explained in English how she'd had a wonderful teacher at school in Suffolk. "Madame Clothilde from Annecy—she was our absolute favourite!"

Their hazy identities suited their purpose of melting into the background. They didn't quite look French, but they could pass as something like it. In the rural villages they sometimes pretended to be *pied noir* from Algeria, or planters from French Indochina. Zouzou bleached her roots as the glossy black appeared close to her scalp; Pierre touched up his fluffed-up brown quiff, untouched by pomade for weeks now.

Pierre read the war news in *Le Monde*, but it conveyed the impression of events on a different planet. He tried to evoke pride in Egypt's initial victory, sorrow over the thousands of dead, admiration at Sadat's surviving the dreadful setbacks of the encirclement of the Third Army and Israel's incursion into Egypt, satisfaction at a ceasefire that had preserved his country's honour. His country? But he had no country.

He frequently thought of Bellamy, imagining that they might meet one another by chance in England. "Let us slope off for a half of bitter," he'd say, slapping his old acquaintance on the back. In darker times it was Dimashqi who filled his thoughts.

By the end of November, they arrived in Paris, disembarking at Gare du Nord.

"We will be married here," Zouzou declared when they struck out from their hotel in Rue D'Aboukir, strolling through the rag-trade district. She frowned at the middle-aged prostitutes showing the tops of their pushed-up breasts in the nippy air.

"Somewhere   nicer   perhaps.   What   about

Montmartre?"

But it wasn't so easy. Enquiring at the *mairie* they found the French legal impediments impossible to overcome. The list of required *certificats* seemed endless, and they certainly were not willing to request documents at the British Embassy on the basis of their phoney passports. And besides anything else, they were required to reside in France for thirty days.

"It is hopeless, my love," Pierre told her.

"But could we not marry in a religious way?"

"In a church? But who would do this for us?" Pierre asked her.

"We will find a priest. I am determined."

She had used this phrase more frequently in recent times. Pierre knew by now that her determination was unshakeable.

The next day, a Thursday, they took a local train out of Paris and got off at a village some two hours away. The trees were stripped of their summer verdure and the hedgerows were soggy with dying weeds. The village's main street was empty, the houses shuttered up against the stiff wind. The couple wound their scarves more tightly. The only sign of life was a café, where a girl with chapped legs and rubber boots swept dead leaves from the cobbles. When the girl brought coffee and brioche, they asked directions to the church.

The flinty exterior of the Eglise St. Bernard glowered at them as they plodded through the puddles, but the door was open. The austere interior was even more discouraging. Pierre had lukewarm notions of religious faith, but had grown up with the luxurious iconography of his two denominations, and a deep feeling that God and gold ornaments were inextricably connected. This French greyness and simplicity would surely shrivel an eager soul.

"*Bonjour*," Zouzou called. Silence. She called again and there was a shuffling from the side of the church. A very old man in an archaic *curé* costume of dusty black peered at them.

"Such a beautiful church," Zouzou said.

"And rich in history," declared the robed ancient, waving vaguely at the barren roof beams.

"Sir," Zouzou said, clearly not sure how one addressed a French priest. "Will you marry us right now?"

The priest's jaw dropped. Pierre guessed he was shocked at this blatant kick in the *derrière* to the secular laws of *La République Française*.

"We have a shocking story to tell, Monsieur." Zouzou was in the finest form.

"*J'écoute.*" The look of surprise had dissolved. The priest now seemed intrigued, perhaps at the thought of some entertainment to fill his day in this dull town.

The funny thing was that Zouzou told him the truth. She sat next to the old priest in the pews and recounted their tale: the days of Agami, her years in Beirut, the men who had 'looked after' her. Then, Pierre's story: his parents' deaths, his work in Cairo, the dangers forcing him into exile. And then her devotion to Pierre: "The only man I ever loved, and ever will."

The priest sat back. "I cannot marry you, my dears. I am afraid that Bonaparte placed the laws of France above those of the church. You must obtain your *certificats*."

Zouzou looked at him with tragic eyes. This was real, not drama, Pierre thought. What next?

"But I can perform a blessing. Will that suffice?"

"That will suffice. Thank you, Sir."

The couple knelt before the altar while the priest intoned formulae in old-fashioned French. Zouzou kissed his hand. They crossed themselves and walked back to the station.

"Did you find it?" the girl with chapped legs asked.

"We'll stop for a cognac," Pierre said.

* * *

They arrived at their Metro stop in the evening and took a light dinner at a restaurant in Boulevard Montmartre. At bedtime they took turns to wash in the minuscule bathroom. Zouzou was naked on the narrow bed when Pierre came into the room, her face to the opposite wall.

"Pierre," she said. "I have something to tell you."

"What is it, *habibti?*"

She waited as if gathering the right words, her face still turned away from him.

"Have you heard of those tricks that women— generally bad women—are taught to play?"

"What on earth do you mean?" Pierre could barely keep his hands off her, but she was evidently not ready.

"They learn to trick a man, using their hands, their thighs, the darkness."

"What are these tricks?"

"To trick a man into believing he has—entered her."

What on earth was she talking about? Yes, of course he had heard whispers of it. Then, he guessed, or half guessed, the reason for the marriage, or at least the blessing. He looked at her with wonder.

She said so quietly that he could hardly hear her, "I am a virgin."

PART FOUR: EXILE

Chapter 19: For the New Year

December 1973, Moscow

A daily routine set in after they left the hospital and moved into the tiny flat. They went to Russian classes in the morning and interrogation in the afternoon. Bellamy was walking with a stick now. He hobbled on Lucy's arm to the tram stop from which they clanked through the slush into the city centre. The flat was in the Ostankino District, rather than in one of the distant suburbs. "They've done you proud," Derek said. "Quite the celebrities."

The Russian language school was in the bleak concrete annexe of a science institute. The students seemed to be strays from around the communist bloc and the non-aligned world: Laotians, Cubans, Angolans, Algerians, never more than two or three of each. Lucy was quickly promoted to the intermediate class, and Bellamy was left bumping along the bottom with a dozen dullards who seemed to be repeating the last term's class before they could enrol in their degrees in engineering or chemistry.

He took a dislike to the language almost straight away;

the alphabet looked like a line of radiators, each letter distinguished by meaningless bars and curves. The words sounded like susurrous slurring. The blandest utterance was delivered with a tone of high indignation. His foot throbbed and his hip ached from walking with the stick. The old-fashioned clothes he'd been provided with were lumpy and tight.

At the morning break, the students smoked and filled their tea glasses from a samovar, the various nationalities joining their comrades for a chat in Spanish or Laotian, or whatever tongue united them. Lucy would come in smiling and chattering with two or three classmates in what sounded like reasonable Russian. She would break away from her friends and join Bellamy to moon around in the corner until the break ended.

After lunch in the institute canteen—most often fatty soup and potatoes—Derek would meet them for the tram journey to Dzerzhinsky Square. The KGB Headquarters was next to *Detskii Mir*—the Children's World department store. Derek would shepherd them through the security point and leave them for the afternoon. Bellamy's questioning took place in a bare room with a steel table and two steel chairs. Lucy reported that her room was identical.

Bellamy's interrogator was a genial forty year-old who spoke impeccable English and conducted himself with courtesy and patience. The sessions lasted three hours, during which the interrogator—"You can call me Peter"—took pages of detailed notes in exercise books.

Lucy reported that her sessions were identical, except that her interrogator was 'Irina'.

"What's she like?" Bellamy asked.

"Dark, skinny, efficient. She doesn't look Russian." At 5pm Bellamy and Lucy would meet outside *Detskii*

Mir and take the tram home.

Around the ninth or tenth day they let themselves into the flat after navigating the washing hanging in the common hallway. The radiators in the tiny room throbbed with the steam that overheated every corner of the building. Bellamy threw the walking stick down and stripped off his coat and jacket.

"I need a bloody drink."

"You're on half a bottle a day," Lucy said. "Just make it the one glass."

Bellamy grasped the vodka bottle and swigged a mouthful. "I'll drink what I bloody like."

He slammed the bottle down and looked at Lucy. Her face was stricken, tears brimming. He cursed his feeble cruelty.

"Sit here and stew yourself in vodka, Mark. I'm going out. You know what I hate about this? I'll tell you. You're not even bloody trying!"

He watched, loathing himself as she wound her neck with a scarf and put on a fur hat.

"Sorry," he said, hating the word; an impotent, stupid token of his weakness. The door banged.

He prepared a simple meal for her return: macaroni, some sausage, pickled cucumber. They had learned only the rudiments of Soviet shopping, with Lucy negotiating the dockets, the cashiers, the wrapping, the queues.

Derek had said, "If you see a line of people, get on the end because there might be something to buy when you get to the front."

After an hour he heard her working the key in the lock.

"You're back."

"What does it look like?"

She stripped off and piled her clothes on the radiator, hopping around in what looked like military-issue pants and bra. She wouldn't meet his eye.

"Lucy, look at me."

"Leave me alone."

"Please, it's important." She looked up and he emptied the vodka bottle down the sink.

"I've been a prick."

"How could you, Mark? After what has happened to us? I thought better of you."

Bellamy turned to the tiny aluminium counter where they prepared food. He sliced the sausages and stirred them through the macaroni. The phrase came back from down the years, 'I thought better of you'. The scholarship boy at the private school on the hill. He'd been caught fighting in the copse at the far boundary. A prefect had dragged him to the headmaster. Trousers had been dropped. A cane had been laid across his arse. He broke away from the beak and pulled up his trousers, yelling, "You fucking old cunt!" The prefect sniggered in the corner.

But the beak locked eyes with him, replaced the cane behind the desk without releasing Bellamy from his gaze, and stood before him for a full minute.

Then in a voice weary with resignation, the voice of a man now certain that the lines of class were inviolable, a man whose vain hopes had been dragged down too many times, the beak said, "I thought better of you, Mr Bellamy."

She wrapped herself in a towel and sat opposite him. They ate the sausage and macaroni without enthusiasm. When they had finished, she said, "That hurt you badly, what I said."

How had she known? He thought he'd hidden his distress.

"You're a barrow boy at heart. You're proud, and you can't stand being patronised."

She was right, well, almost right.

"That's the end of it, Lucy. I won't insult you by saying sorry again."

"Thank God for that. I couldn't stand it. Christ, what's in this sausage?"

* * *

They assumed that the flat was bugged. Bellamy had searched the gaunt concrete walls and ugly furniture for an electronic device. In the end, the ceiling light-fitting was the only place unsearched, but they had no means of disassembling it without causing alarm or getting a shock. For the first few days they turned on the taps and the radio when they spoke. They developed the habit of talking about mundane matters as they moved around the flat, but had long whispered conversations in bed.

Each night they pooled the experience of their separate interrogations. Day by day, they tried to divine from the questioning why they had been brought to Moscow. The interrogators first worked like minesweepers through their early lives and their university years, checking and rechecking events as if traversing an invisible grid. Then it was their careers, including the years in Ealing's grip.

"How much should we tell them?" Lucy whispered after the first day of questions about their work.

"Everything, nothing, some of it? I don't know."

"Those missions we did for Ealing, for example. Did you know why you were sent to the Middle East, Mark?"

"Never. I went to Morocco, Syria, Yemen, Iraq.

Usually I delivered some documents. Sometimes I passed on some cryptic sounding message. But I never knew the purpose of any of it."

"Same for me."

"So we just tell them, I suppose," Mark whispered.

Lucy was quiet for a moment. "Later they are going to ask about what happened in Cairo."

"So? Tell them. Maybe we're here to pass on disinformation. It'll be their hard luck."

"That's if we're here because of some rational plan rather than a foul-up."

"Let's go to sleep, Lucy. I'm knackered."

She turned over but he knew that she was awake, thinking. After ten minutes her breathing hadn't slowed.

"It's Zlotnik you're worried about, isn't it?"

"If I tell them about him, it'll be his death sentence," Lucy said.

"He made his choice."

"It's not that simple, Mark. I got to know him. He behaved like a shit, but there's a decent human underneath. I'm not sure I can be his executioner."

But Lucy did tell. It was on a day when they were both feeling seedy and enervated. When Lucy brushed her teeth in the morning her gums were bleeding.

"Mine are bleeding too. We need Vitamin C," Bellamy said. "Let's ask Derek."

* * *

Their interrogators refused to answer any questions about why they had been brought to Moscow other than repeating, "You are guests of the USSR. We will inform you in due course of your future activities."

"We'll go on hunger strike," Lucy said, and they ate no food for three days. Derek met them in Dzerzhinsky

Square on the fourth day. They had each swayed with glazed eyes during the morning language classes.

"I'm taking you for a decent meal," Derek said.

"Not until you tell us why we're here and when we're going home," Lucy hissed.

Derek nodded and signalled to a black limousine that was idling in the snow.

They ate lunch in the private room of a plush hotel for foreigners under crystal chandeliers. The dishes were choice and dainty. There was wine from Georgia.

"Eat very slowly," Derek said. He drank a full glass of wine, took out his pipe and pushed his plate away.

"Well?" Bellamy asked. His mind was beginning to sharpen after the first mouthfuls of food.

Derek sat back and toyed with the pipe, scouring out the dottle with a little penknife. He took out a flat yellow tin of Erinmore Flake. "Diplomatic pouch," he said, raising his index finger to his lips.

"Derek, we're waiting." Lucy put her knife and fork down. A cloud of sweet smoke rose above the table.

"I'll tell you what I can. Firstly, we saw an opportunity in your dilemma in Cairo. We knew all about you, and we knew what Comrade Zlotnik was trying to set up. We also knew that your charming employer intended to have you eliminated."

"Eliminated?" Bellamy asked through a mouthful of veal.

"I won't go into the details, but just accept that you owe your lives to the KGB. Now, I said that we saw an opportunity. I'll be blunt. You are commodities that we intend to exchange for other commodities."

"A spy swap?" Lucy asked.

"That's what the *Daily Mirror* will call it. I think it's a vulgar term, but, essentially, yes. This may not happen for a year or two. You can imagine that such an arrangement depends on many delicate factors coming into perfect alignment."

"Do we take it, then," Bellamy asked, "that the British Government is in on this? Waters was the go-between, is that right?"

"I think I've said enough about those particular matters. I expect you want to know what happens next."

Derek performed his trick of tilting his head up and closing his eyes. He held the pose for a few seconds.

"You're going to work," he said.

"Work?"

"Yes, work, honest toil. No shirkers here in the USSR. Didn't Marx say 'from each according to his ability, to each according to his needs'? Now have some dessert, but don't gulp it too quickly or you'll be sick."

"What kind of work, Derek?" Bellamy asked. He had a chill vision of them cracking rocks in a *gulag* in Siberia. "You start next week in a publishing house—editing, translating, rewriting."

When Bellamy and Lucy had finished the meal they sat back and considered their bellies. Derek poured a final glass of wine for each of them.

"All clear, then?"

"Just one question," Lucy asked. "Who are you, Derek?"

"I wondered if you'd recognised me, my dear, but you didn't; you were a little girl when I last saw you. I was a friend of your father. We were at Cambridge together, and at Bletchley Park later. I often think of him."

* * *

As Christmas approached, Lucy gathered a few treats to

celebrate the season: Armenian brandy, sweet biscuits, ham and pickled mushrooms. She bought some New Year cards to brighten the flat: Faux-Christmas items of cheesy design in attenuated greens and reds, depicting Santa on a cartoon space rocket. The caption grimly read *snovym godom*, 'for New Year'.

Lucy had seen Mark regain the strength that had propelled him through the trials of Cairo. But even after his recovery from the episode of drink-sodden self-pity, she sensed a new brittleness in him. She worried that she might yet have to buttress him against whatever storms bore down on them. But for now he was becoming more comfortable with the language, and he seemed prepared to make a fist of the job at the publishing house.

December 25 fell on the second Tuesday of their careers as editors. In the evening they prepared a meagre festive meal. Mark poured them both a small brandy and they lay top to tail on the small sofa to read. This was Lucy's favourite time of day: no noise except the hissing of the radiator, her lover's legs intertwined with hers, the banalities of Soviet life shut out until tomorrow.

Christmas Day was also seven weeks since her last period. She wasn't sure, but her body seemed to be sending faintly familiar messages. A notebook contained the Russian vocabulary she'd need when she sought out a doctor. Mark didn't need to know until she was certain. There was a knock at the door: *God Save Our Gracious Queen* played on one knuckle.

"It's Derek. What does he want?" Lucy said. She wanted the evening to Mark and herself.

"To wish us Merry Christmas? Stay there. I'll go."

Derek stood on the threshold against a backdrop of washing.

"Quick visit. Won't take my boots off. I've got one or two things for you."

"Have a quick snifter before you go. It's Christmas," Mark said.

Why couldn't Mark just take whatever Derek had brought, and get back onto the sofa? Lucy's patience with Derek was wearing thin. She had grown particularly irritated by the way his presence in the USSR was supposed to be some kind of private joke among the three of them. She was in no doubt that this pipe-smoking Yorkshireman was a powerful and sinister player in Soviet intelligence.

"No, really, I won't linger. It's just these." Derek handed over a bag of oranges. Lucy's mouth filled with saliva. She hadn't tasted fresh fruit since Cairo.

"I get them from an Armenian. He flies up from Yerevan with a couple of boxes every month. Very enterprising chap."

Lucy held an orange to her nose. "Sunshine—it's the smell of sunshine."

Derek hung around by the door. Why didn't he just leave, Lucy wondered. He has a look of conflict, a man torn between fleeing and holding his ground.

"There's this too," he said, thrusting an envelope into Lucy's hand. He turned, muttered something that might have been "Merry Christmas", and slammed the door behind him.

She tore the envelope open. Inside was another envelope marked with the British Royal Crest and 'Her Majesty's Service'.

The letter was on expensive notepaper, bearing the address of her brother's house in Lowestoft.

My Dear Lucy,

I have terrible news, all the more terrible because I haven't been able to let you know immediately. I don't know where you are, but I've been assured by the Foreign Office that the best efforts will be made to convey this letter to you.

I'm so sorry to tell you that our father passed away on December 2. The circumstances of his death aren't clear, but there will be a coroner's inquest. I do know that he left a note. I can tell you no more. Mother is with us in Lowestoft for now. I'd like to tell you that she is bearing up, but I have grave fears for her health.

Wherever you are, please come home when you can. The FO says that you are doing important work for Britain, but in the present circumstances surely our mother's life is more important.

Your loving brother, Alan

Chapter 20: A City of Little Cards

December 1973, London

"Mrs Scullion left another card, Zouzou."

"The third this week. The same thing?"

"Yes, there hasn't been an escalation of hostilities at least."

"Ouf, Pierre, can't we just speak Arabic? You talk like the Oxford Dictionary."

"When in Shepherds Bush, do as the shepherds do," Pierre said. It was something Tony Hancock might have said. He insisted that Zouzou watched comedy shows on their rented TV to 'improve her British idiom'.

The little square of card read, *To Mr and Mrs Rogers. To obviate inconvenience to other tenants, please limit ablutions to thirty minutes daily per individual. Kind regards, J.D. Scullion.*

"That woman knows no kindness. But Pierre, *je t'en prie*, when can I stop bleaching my hair? I look like a shorn lamb."

They had been lucky to find a bedsit at Mrs Scullion's. Pierre's translator cousin had virtually slammed the door in his face when he turned up from the airport with Zouzou.

"You can ask at the pub—the Ham and Blackbird, just turn left past the bus stop. It's still half an hour till closing time," he said, not a trace of Armenian hospitality evident in his cold eyes and set lips.

"But we are family, Rafi."

"It doesn't work like that here."

A fine drizzle had gently soaked them by the time they reached the pub. Zouzou was a pitiful sight; her cropped blonde hair stuck to her scalp, her panda eyes smeared down her cheeks. Pierre pushed the door marked 'Public Bar' and they were met by a wall of cigarette smoke, shouting, and a yeasty aroma so thick you could slice it like *bastourma*. Pierre glimpsed a large red-faced woman on a bar stool with her tight skirt rucked up to her thighs, and a laddered stocking. She caught his eye momentarily and made a lascivious expression.

"I cannot enter such a place, my sweet love," Zouzou declared. "It is below my station."

They stepped back onto the pavement. Pierre searched his mind; he had read about the protocols of public houses in books by Graham Greene and Somerset Maugham. Yes, there would a saloon bar. And there was its door.

Inside, the noise was at a murmur, as if all the drinkers were competing to be unobtrusive. A wood fire burned in a grate. The walls were papered in pastel green and hung with prints of horses and dogs. Pierre marvelled at the prospect, and whispered to Zouzou in Arabic, "You see, the saloon bar, the epitome of English social intercourse."

Somebody at a nearby table said, "Oy, English in here, mate," and Pierre heard another drinker mutter, "Fucking Paki."

They approached the bar and the landlord raised an

enquiring eyebrow.

"We seek a room for the night."

"Seek? Ah, yes, I see, seek, is it? And would it be a double room ye're seeking?"

"Yes please."

"I have to have a name to write down," the landlord said.

"I am Mr Rogers and this is Miss Patchett."

"I'll write down Mr and Mrs Rogers then."

"Thank you," Pierre said. Was this the England of loose morals that he'd read about? Free love? Swinging London?

"And ye'll be English folk, then?"

"Recently arrived from South Africa."

The landlord gave Zouzou an up-and-down look, then said to Pierre,

"That'll be tirty quid for the night." 'Night' sounded like 'noit'.

"Tirty?"

"Tirty—tree-oh."

"I see. Will you take US dollars, Sir?"

The man opened a newspaper—the *Evening Standard*—and scanned a page of figures with a game eye.

"Fifty dollars to ye, Mr and Mrs Rogers from—where was it?—Sout' Africa."

Pierre gulped and said, "For one night?"

"Ah, it's terrible expensive in these times of decimal currency. Will ye be taking a drink?"

He pulled a handle over a tall glass and a black liquid oozed from the spigot. Meanwhile, he took a tiny bottle from a shelf, emptied the contents into a shallow glass and popped a gelatinous red cherry into it. Pierre watched in fascination as the landlord completed the oozing process and handed him a glass of black beer with a head like water buffalo cream.

"A point of Guinness and a Babycham, on the house." Zouzou sipped her drink and glared at Pierre. But Pierre was soon lost in malty reverie. The texture of this Guinness—he was familiar with the name from James Joyce—was like liquid black silk, almost erotic in its sensuality, a taste that was repulsively seductive, a taste that shouldn't be, but was. The alcohol crept into his veins like a crafty mistress.

"Do you know where we can find a flat?" he woozily asked the landlord, who wrote an address on the back of a beermat.

"Troi Mrs Scullion. Tell her O'Keefe sent ye. She's an old bat but she's not too fussy about her tenants. Married tenants, of course," he said with a histrionic wink.

Pierre drank more of the Guinness. Halfway through the glass, the character of the stout changed as his palate recognised its black caress; the first sips had seduced him, and now he and Guinness were lovers.

* * *

A month after their arrival on the Calais-Dover ferry, Victoria Patchett and Clive Rogers had burrowed into the dowdy fabric of Shepherds Bush, making their nest at Mrs Scullion's. They filled the flat with English exotica: a cambric eiderdown, Bovril, Green Shield stamps, pork luncheon meat and fat library books with polythene dust jackets.

The terraced house next door was shared by a loose tribe of young people who played grinding, repetitive music all night; the sound penetrated the damp brick walls like a construction site. The inhabitants often loomed through the overgrown privet hedge in the tiny front garden: the smell of marijuana clung to the young men with shaggy hair and army greatcoats; there were young women there too, who wore skirts, either so long that they swept the floor or so short that they showed their underwear. One night Zouzou answered a knock at the door of their bedsit, and a girl with saucer eyes said, "Have you seen my shit?" Zouzou looked stunned, and then said, "Look up your arse, Miss," slammed the door and went back to watching *The Two Ronnies*. Pierre tapped her shoulder with approval; Zouzou was improving her idiom.

Pierre and Zouzou cast off their own names. At first it was exciting being Victoria and Clive, then hard work. Pierre remembered the first and only time they used their new names making love.

"Ouf, *habibi*," Zouzou said. "I can only imagine Queen Victoria being mounted by Clive of India. It's quite revolting. I'm sure he looked like a goat."

Pierre was sometimes shocked by Zouzou's forthrightness, especially in matters of love. But he came to understand that past experiences had laid a protective patina of brashness over the tender girl he'd fallen in love with at Agami. Slowly, the patina rubbed off until there were moments of almost tragic rawness.

One day he came home to find her wearing her great glossy black wig and weeping deeply at the dining table. Three fish fingers were congealing on a plate.

"What is it, *habibti*? Was Mrs Scullion being a pest?"

"I want," she wept, "a glass of *karkady*, that's all."

"*Ayy khidma ya habibti*," he said tenderly, 'at your service, darling,' and set off by bus to a shop on the Edgware Road where dried hibiscus leaves were sold. For himself, he'd lost the taste for the old life of Cairo.

Indeed, he'd lost the taste for anything at all in the oppressive murk of a December London.

It was on the Edgware Road that he met men like himself: Middle Eastern exiles of every variety; swart Sabeans, Assyrians, Maronites, pinch-faced Yemenis, Iraqi communists. They haunted the Arab cafés, attended public lectures by other Middle Eastern exiles, published short-lived newssheets. They resembled a wartime army, hastily assembled from the remnants of defeated battalions, each man—there were no women—fighting his private war while they moved in ragged unison towards an ill-defined utopia.

On a bus he overheard some Armenians chatting in their mother tongue, but the topic was so depressing— an unedifying surgical procedure—that he let go of the opportunity to make their acquaintance.

* * *

Pierre had written 'Poste Restante Shepherds Bush, London, UK' in Aunt Serpouhi's address book the night the war started. "I might just go abroad," he'd told her. Once a week he visited the Post Office, which doubled up as a newsagent. These places fascinated him. The array of glossy magazine covers spoke of a nation of avid hobbyists. He imagined them behind their net curtains, building radio sets, breeding small dogs, cooking elaborate cakes, studying the stars, knitting bobble hats (a new word for Pierre). And on the top shelf were the men's magazines, the covers displaying huge-breasted women wearing elaborate underwear and louche expressions; there was always a man bashfully browsing one, slipped in between the pages of Vintage Motorcycle or Home Brewer Monthly.

"What name?"

"Clive Rogers."

"Nuffink for that name." He'd worked our *nuffink* and *sumfink* early on.

But on a bitter December Tuesday afternoon when the last smudge of daylight had retreated into the charcoal sky, the man behind the counter held out a small package covered in familiar cross-hatched tape. 'Opened with the knowledge of the censor,' it read in Arabic.

Pierre stepped into a pub and ordered half a pint of Guinness. "And a pickled onion, please," he added, and then smiled grimly to himself at the irony: the English gentleman, eager for news from home. He unwrapped the parcel. It was a cassette tape from Aunt Serpouhi. She had written 'Farid El-Atrache' on the label.

Zouzou was out when he got home. She had bought a cassette player to record English pop songs from the television—mostly ballads, which she learnt by heart and sang mournfully when she tidied the flat or ironed her clothes. 'Killing me softly,' she sang over and over with deep tragedy, despite the wistfully sentimental lyrics. When Pierre asked her to sing something more cheerful, she said, "This London, it is killing me softly with its drizzle and its cups of tea and its pavements."

Pierre started the cassette. It was *Yaritni Tir*—'If I could fly'. He closed his eyes to shut out the frowsy flat and let himself be transported back to Cairo by the *'oud*, the words of hopeless yearning, until he could almost touch and smell the old city—cumin and coffee, honeyed *shisha* tobacco and lamb brochettes smoking over charcoal.

The song ended. There was a click. Pierre opened his eyes. And then, in Armenian, "Bedros, my boy, I have some news for you." He instinctively got up and closed the curtains. A thin drizzle streaked the windows.

His aunt haltingly explained that she had almost all the papers she needed to leave Cairo for California. The tape kept stopping and starting as the old lady gathered her thoughts. Kebabjian would look after the boarding house—bring in a manager. He'd paid her the key money, but she didn't say how much. Pierre could imagine how much his aunt had been scalped; he wouldn't trouble her for his own stake in the place.

There was a long account of the health and illness of various relatives, and some careful comments on how difficult life was in Cairo. The news began to peter out, and she said, "Well, my boy, that's about all I have to say." A pause and a click and then, "But there is one other thing that I shouldn't mention if it is going to worry you." Another click and the tape resumed; she had evidently decided to risk worrying him.

"A week after you left, I had a visit from the police, well, the secret police I suppose. They asked me a lot of questions about a man called Dimashqi. If you knew him, if he had been to Pension Serpouhi, if I had seen him, if my gentlemen had ever mentioned him. I thought this Dimashqi must be a big shot who had gone missing. And, well, this was the frightening thing, they searched your room. I was terrified. They asked if you had a gun, and if you had gone to Israel." The old lady faltered and stopped. There was another click, and she said, "Come to California, Bedros, in the New Year. I miss you. I know you're a good man."

* * *

One day, Pierre said to Zouzou, "We must find work." The US dollars he'd accumulated before they fled from Cairo were diminishing, despite economies. Zouzou thought she had money in an account in Beirut, but the risks of trying to access it were great.

"The General will have his spies," she warned.

Pierre reflected that the General—or at least his wife—had been very generous when she had learned, in Cairo, that Zouzou had disappeared. On the first morning of the war she had met Pierre briefly in Ma'adi and slipped him a firm package.

"You are certain that we will never see her again?"

"Certain."

"God rest her soul," the wife of the big zucchini said, pulling the gauze veil over her face.

* * *

Pierre visited his friends in Edgware Road and learned that no work could be obtained without a P45 certificate; and a P45 could not be obtained unless one had worked previously. The friends explained how a man in a pub in Kilburn could provide the document and thus close the bureaucratic loop. Money was passed over in Kilburn, and Pierre and Zouzou found themselves fiscally qualified for employment.

They visited the Labour Exchange, where they studied the little job cards on the wall: butcher, Harrow; warehouse assistant, Wembley; dentist receptionist, Harmondsworth. They picked some cards, and Zouzou found a position behind the perfume counter at a department store in Watford, while Pierre got a clerical job in a travel agency in Acton.

On the Sunday before they began work, they took the train to Hampstead for a walk on the Heath. There were blowy showers, and Zouzou stung her legs on wet nettles.

"I have never seen anywhere so green," she said. "Or so poisonous. They don't like us here. You can feel it everywhere."

"Us?" asked Pierre. "Who is 'us'? This is a city of strangers. Look at him!"

They had turned off the Heath onto a residential street of grand houses. A robed Arab man was stepping out of a Rolls Royce. The gown was so gleamingly white that he seemed to carry his own aura against the soggy dark green hedges in front of the house.

"They will hate him too. They only respect his money. Pierre, I am drowning in this wet country. I want to go somewhere else."

She's right, Pierre thought. This place was hard-bitten, ungenerous, its soul perished. It was time for them to think of disappearing, out of reach of Donald Waters and his masters.

"What about California?" he asked. She squeezed his arm and smiled radiantly.

"San Francisco, Los Angeles," Zouzou said, as if tasting grapes grown on sun-baked slopes.

"We'll need papers. And new names," Pierre said. "It'll take time."

Each morning the two exiles with false names and hidden origins took their separate ways, one to the north and one to the west, swept under the city in soot-smelling tube trains packed with London's hotchpotch of people from somewhere else.

In early December, Zouzou asked Pierre to go to Ealing Broadway in his lunch hour to buy some small item in a certain shop. After buying the item he was about to plunge down into the tube station when a figure walking in front of him raised goose bumps on his skin. He followed, keeping back, sure of his intuition. The set of the shoulders and the tilt of the head belonged to only one man. Dimashqi stopped to buy a newspaper from a stand, stooping to check the foreign titles. Pierre drew nearer, and saw that he had chosen an Arabic newspaper. Pierre's old foe adjusted the tinted glasses and walked on.

Dimashqi turned into Uxbridge Road and stopped by an anonymous-looking four-storey office block. Pierre hung back, watched him enter the front door, waited another minute, then strolled casually past the building. The sign on the door said, 'Invalid Pensions Review Section'.

There was a telephone box on the corner, smelling of cold dog-ends and pasted with the usual little cards: 'Call Rita for French Polishing', 'Special lessons for gentlemen'. A city of little cards.

He dialled his employer. "Hello, this is Clive Rogers. Terribly sorry, sore tum. Just came on—food poisoning, I think. Could I be excused for the afternoon?"

He felt a dart of anger, the delayed shock of seeing Dimashqi, perhaps. The array of grubby cards on the smeared glass faded to a vision of Fawzi and of his father's grave. A large pink face filled one of the panes of the telephone kiosk, and a sausagey finger tapped the glass in impatience. Somebody on the end of the phone line was saying something about a sick certificate. Pierre said, "Absolutely, thank you very much," put down the phone and lit a cigarette. The angry finger tapped again and Pierre caught the words "bleedin' liberty." He gave the pink face a two-fingered salute, shoved the door open and walked quickly away, scanning the area for a spot from where he could observe the Invalid Pensions Review Section.

At five-thirty, Dimashqi exited the building and strode to Ealing Broadway Station. Pierre, stiff and damp from staking out the narrow street, pursued Dimashqi at a distance. He almost lost him, but spotted him heading, not for the tube, but for the overground trains. Pierre insinuated himself through the commuters in their gabardine macs and trench coats, finding himself two rows behind Dimashqi at the crowded edge of the Paddington platform. He grasped his umbrella, calculating the force and angle needed to shove Dimashqi into the path of a train. But, being a man of caution, he waited, he considered, he calculated the odds.

A through-train screamed past the platform, followed by a stopping train that pulled up in front of the damp, heaving crowd. Dimashqi took the door to the left, Pierre the one to the right. An hour later, Pierre watched him enter a semi-detached house in a respectable tree-lined street in a place called Finchley.

* * *

Over the next week, Pierre left work every day just in time to stand behind Dimashqi on the Paddington platform. He moved unseen through the sooty weft and weave of the city, another anonymous immigrant, a man with an unmemorable face, a man who had memorised the times of the through-trains to Paddington.

On the Friday before Christmas—British Christmas, of course—Pierre took his place behind Dimashqi, two minutes before the through-train was due. The crowds smelt of wet raincoats and cigarettes. Office girls struggled gamely with handbags and Christmas shopping. There was a spirited mood, quite unlike other afternoons. People bore their coughs and sneezes affably. Some clutched each other with tipsy affection. There were outbreaks of courtesy, "No, you first", "No, please, you're loaded down". It was an afternoon when nobody in the jovial crush would notice an unmemorable immigrant prod a man in tinted glasses and a plastic mac.

He grasped the handle of the umbrella with his right hand, slid his left hand past the ring that held the ends of the spokes in place, braced his muscles, and whispered the little speech he had rehearsed a hundred times, "You will die for Fawzi, for my father, for Egypt."

Heads turned towards the roar of the approaching through-train, and the soggy chorus line leaned away from the platform edge. Dimashqi's face was caught in profile: the sagging neck, the scrappy grey curls on the temple, the striated brow, the expression of dejection, a caterpillar of mucus below one nostril.

And there was a hand on Pierre's shoulder, light fingers on his neck. He wheeled around, and it was Zouzou, smiling her California smile.

When he turned back, Dimashqi was gone.

THE END

I love to get feedback on my novels. Readers' comments motivate me to keep writing, and help me to spread the word about my work. If you enjoyed *Cairo Mon Amour*, scan the QR code below to tell me what you liked. You can write an essay or just a few words! Thank you very much – Stuart.

You can find out about Books Two and Three of the trilogy *Bury me in Valletta* and *The Sunset Assassin* at my website.

www.stuartcampbellauthor.com

Background to *Cairo Mon Amour*

In 1973, the world was in the midst of the Cold War. The Soviet Union and its allies were locked in an ideological struggle with the West, a struggle that was enacted through proxy wars. Egypt found itself at the epicentre of the Cold War in October 1973 when it launched an attack on Sinai to regain land occupied in 1967 by Israel. For a few weeks the world stood on the brink of a direct conflict between the USSR and the US, the respective patrons of Egypt and Israel. The wartime atmosphere of Cairo, where I happened to be a student at the time, provided a rich setting for my story.

At the same time, the Cold War was being fought by way of elaborate espionage tactics, unseen by the public except when spy swaps and defections broke through into the press. The fictional Cold War spy exploits of my Soviet diplomat Zlotnik are as plausible as anything that might have happened in real life.

I have connected the settings of Egypt and the USSR with a third thread: the Armenian genocide and diaspora. I was lucky enough—in retrospect—to observe the mood of a city at war in 1973 through the eyes of Egyptian Armenian relatives I had acquired through marriage. Their community lived a sometimes uneasy existence in Cairo, and many had already left for safe havens in the West. Some Armenian families had been 'repatriated' to the USSR in the fifties at Stalin's invitation. At the same time, many Soviet citizens of Armenian origin attained senior positions in science, administration, industry and the arts. Perhaps the quintessential symbol of this link is Artem Mikoyan, the Soviet Armenian aircraft designer; the MiG aircraft that led Egypt's air attack on Sinai are named for Mikoyan and his co-designer Gurevich. Coincidentally, *Cairo Mon Amour* was written in the years before and after 24 April 2015, the centenary of the Armenian genocide.

The following notes explain some of the background to the novel, with references to some of the many sources I consulted—some scholarly, some propagandistic, and some whimsical.

Chapter 1

I had Pierre affix a fiscal stamp to the translation under the assumption that there would be a fee for lodging the document with a government office of some kind. Fiscal stamps were widely used in Egypt since Ottoman times. Such is the complexity of the field that the American philatelist Peter Feltus published a *Catalogue of Egyptian Revenue Stamps* in 1982.

As a fighter pilot, Pierre's father would have learned Russian during his military training in the USSR. He may even have spoken it quite well, as did ex-President Hosni Mubarak. According to an article in *Kommersant*, Mubarak spoke Russian with Vladimir Putin. See http://

www.kommersant.com/p720969/r_1/Reelection_of_
Muhammad_Hosni_Said_Mubarak/ (downloaded 27
April 2016)

Chapter 2

The Giles cartoon that Bellamy looks at in the *Daily
Express* can be found at
http://www.gilescartoons.co.uk/
cartoon.asp?cartoon=202 (downloaded 23 April 2016).

Bellamy's record as a signals intelligence operative in
Aden is informed by Richard Aldrich's *GCHQ*
(HarperCollins, 2011) and James Bamford's *Body of
Secrets* (Anchor Books, 2002). Of course Bellamy works
for 'Ealing' rather than GCHQ.

The mention of 'raucous Australians' at the Rocky
Horror Show is a doffing of my cap to my Australian
compatriot Jim Sharman, producer and director of the
Royal Court production that Bellamy takes his London
girlfriend to.

Chapter 3

As part of Egypt's deception plan, hospital wards were
emptied to prepare for war casualties under the pretext
of a tetanus outbreak. (*The A to Z of Middle Eastern
intelligence* by Ephraim Kahana and Muhammad Suwaed,
Scarecrow Press, 2009, p.76). See also Jim Garrett's
summary of the broader deception plan at
https://www. linkedin.com/pulse/operation-badrs-
bad-surprise-arab-deception-yom-kippur-jim-garrett
(downloaded 23 April 2016).

The Middle East Centre for Arabic Studies at
Shemlan, Lebanon, is now no longer in existence. I
loosely based the MECAS setting on Alexander

McNabb's novel *Shemlan, a Deadly Tragedy.*

Fawzi's "Perhaps, but it's a big perhaps," was a favourite saying of my late and fondly remembered Arabic teacher, Dr Ezzat Abou-Hindia at the Polytechnic of Central London, 1971-1975. He had a little stock of these sayings, which we students found hilarious. A favourite was "a housewife's name", as in "Nasser is so well known that he is a housewife's name these days."

Chapter 4

In 1973 the automatic teller machine was in its infancy. Bellamy would have had to find a Lloyds Bank branch and ask the teller to phone his own branch to authorise a cash cheque.

The Soviet personnel were expelled in July 1972. However, the topic is mired in historiographic controversy, about which there is a good overview at http://historynewsnetwork.org/article/41409 (downloaded 27 April 2016). A retrospective Russian account covering similar ground can be found at http://russiapedia.rt.com/on-this-day/july-18/ (downloaded 23 April 2016).

Zlotnik's background was pasted together from fragments of the excellent biographies of USSR diplomats to be found at https://en.wikipedia.org/wiki/Category:Soviet_diplomats (downloaded 6 May 2016).

In 1973 I visited the Soviet Cultural Centre where Pierre and Zlotnik would have met. It appeared not to be functioning. There was only an Egyptian caretaker on the premises and I left when he became suspicious of me.

Chapter 5

My main source for the story of Siranoush is http://
thisweekinarmenianhistory.blogspot.com.au/2013/05/
birth-of-siranoush-may-25-1857.html (downloaded 23
April 2016).

The '1923 Constitution' in the graffiti aimed to
establish representative government in Egypt for the
first time. An English translation can be found at
http://www.   constitutionnet.org/files/1923_-
_egyptian_constitution_ english_1.pdf (downloaded 23
April 2016).

The 'breeze around their turbans' remark is my
modification of an Egyptian proverb in J.L.
Burckhardt's *Arabic Proverbs*, Curzon Press, 1994, p.3.
The translation of the original reads, 'If the turbans
complain of a slight wind, what must be the state of the
inner drawers?' In his note on the proverb, Burckhardt,
who died in 1817, delicately translates the Egyptian
word *fassa* into Latin as *flatus*.

Chapter 6

The 'repatriation' of Armenians is dealt with in this well-
referenced Wikipedia article: http://en.wikipedia.
org/wiki/User:Yerevantsi/Repatriation_of_Armenians
(downloaded 25 July 2016). There is a story among my
Armenian relatives that they would have ended up in the
USSR if they hadn't missed the last ship leaving
Alexandria in 1952.

Lucy's perfume was probably *Maja*.

The female members of my writers group in Sydney
chided me for the position of Lucy's caesarian-section
scar, telling me that in 1973 it would have been higher.

Fayrouz's song *Al-Quds zahrat al-madaa'in* (Jerusalem Flower of Cities) can be heard here: https://www.youtube.com/watch?v=lYKnQ9814T8 (downloaded 23
April 2016).

Chapter 7

The standard morning greeting in Egypt is 'morning of goodness' with the response 'morning of light'. The response can be varied, e.g. *sabah il-full*, 'morning of jasmine'.

Zouzou is an affectionate form of the name Aziza. At around the time Bellamy was in Cairo, the smash hit in the cinema was *khalli balak min Zouzou*, 'watch out for Zouzou'. IMDB has a post on the film at http://www.imdb.com/title/tt0784146/ (downloaded 23 April 2016).

'The owl became an actress' is my modification of another of Burckhardt's proverbs. In the original (p. 114), 'The owl has become a poetess'.

Chapter 8

Kushari is the epitome of Egyptian street food, but the web abounds with trendy versions.

'Operation Full Moon' (*badr* in Arabic) was the code word for the October War.

SIGINT designates 'signal intelligence' and has such siblings at HUMINT 'human intelligence' and ELINT 'electronic intelligence'.

The question "Are you with us?" was asked of me by a taxi driver a day or two before the war began. I replied, "Yes", but the import of the question was not clear to me.

Chapter 9

Ovens were uncommon in Cairo houses. A dish in need of roasting would be sent to the local baker to be cooked.

Kebabjian is a genuine but uncommon Armenian family name, that translates as 'son of the kebab maker'. I have a rent receipt made out by my Armenian landlord in Cairo in 1973, written with a spidery hand in Arabic and French.

This Wikipedia link leads to an image of the Ottoman document ordering the detention of Armenian intellectuals: https://en.wikipedia.org/wiki/Deportation_of_Armenian_intellectuals_on_24_April_1915#/media/File:Instruction_of_the_Ministery_of_the_Interior_on_april_24.png (downloaded 6 May 2016).

Chapter 10

It is not at all unlikely that Zaki would have been involved in 'amateur dramatics', perhaps at university. In recent years the Egyptian Society for Amateur Theatre has sponsored the Arab Theatre Festival in Cairo.

Bob Azzam's delightfully cheesy *Ya Mustafa* can be found at https://www.youtube.com/watch?v=zNbrEPWnYCg (downloaded 5 May 2016).

An English translation of Umm Kulthoum's *The Ruins* can be found here: http://www.arabicmusictranslation.com/2007/11/oum-kalthoum-ruins-el-atlal-les-ruines.html (downloaded 5 May 2016).

The scene in Pension Serpouhi when the fragments

of the Israeli ammunition box were passed around is based on my personal experience.

Chapter 11
Belisha beacons were pole-mounted orange electric lamps installed near pedestrian crossings in Britain, named for Lord Belisha, who can be seen talking about traffic problems in the 1930s at https://www.youtube.com/ watch?v=bOBb3lYhG0Q (downloaded 5 May 2016).

The failure to recognise the abrupt evacuation of the families of Soviet advisers as a sign of imminent war has been discussed at length by historians, but this cable places us on the spot as US diplomats struggle to understand events: https://search.wikileaks.org/plusd/ cables/1973CAIRO03054_b.html (downloaded 5 May 2016).

Chapter 12
I found the TV images of Egyptian soldiers operating Malyutka wire-guided missiles tragically ironic; most of the operators would have owned no electronic device more sophisticated than a cheap transistor radio. A web search today will reveal deactivated Malyutkas on sale for 1,250 UK pounds by mail order.

Zlotnik's detention in the museum is based on reality: My wife and I were detained at a closed-up museum by the 'green goons', as we called the security police.

MGIMO is the Russian abbreviation for the prestigious Moscow State Institute of International Relations. See https://en.wikipedia.org/wiki/Moscow_State_Institut e_ of_International_Relations (downloaded 6 May

2016).

Although my account of the inner workings of the Soviet Embassy is entirely fictional, I did gain indirect insight from Viktor Israelyan's *Inside the Kremlin During the Yom Kippur War*, Penn State University Press, 1995.

Irina may have known the term *Homo sovieticus* in 1973 through underground publications, although it was not until the eighties that Aleksandr Zinovyev's satirical term appeared in open print, e.g. *Homo sovieticus*, Grove/Atlantic, 1986.

A 1981 thesis by Robert V. Badolato describes the aloofness of the Soviet advisers living in Cairo. They are said to have bought up expensive real estate in the city for their own use. The document is accessible from the Naval War College at Newport, Rhode Island at http://oai.dtic.mil/oai/oai?verb=getRecord&metadata Prefix=html&identifier=ADA160865 (downloaded 23 April 2016).

The little-known Mother Armenia statue was graced by visits of Western celebrities around the time of the genocide centenary. See https://en.wikipedia.org/wiki/Mother_Armenia (downloaded 6 May 2016).

Chapter 13

I own a framed manuscript like the one that Lucy examined in her father's shop. Stuck to the back of the frame is a letter from the Oriental and India Office Collections of The British Library that says much the same as Lucy did.

Under the D-notice system, the UK Government made official requests to news services not to report on matters of national security.

Dead Souls is a novel by Nikolai Gogol, published in

1842, in which a confidence trickster travels the countryside buying up serfs who have died, but are still registered with their owners. Perhaps Zlotnik feels an affinity with the duplicitous protagonist Chichikov.

Cairo was not bombed, but air-raid sirens were frequent. Egyptian TV showed public service advertisements with families calmly trotting off to an air-raid shelter, but in my part of Cairo we just crawled under the kitchen table.

Edward Artemiev's *Solaris Theme* can be heard at https://www.youtube.com/watch?v=M_vi67SHU4E (downloaded 5 May 2016).

Chapter 15

A grainy facsimile of the October 7 edition of *Al-Ahram* can be viewed at http://english.ahram.org.eg/ NewsContent/1/0/83317/Egypt/-October--Ahrams-frontpage.aspx%20Ahram%20front%20page%207%20 oct%20 1973 (downloaded 6 May 2016).

The Arab Mafia issue is discussed in this article: http:// www.jta.org/1977/06/02/archive/behind-the-headlines-pro-arab-bias-in-british-foreign-office (downloaded 6 May 2016). As a student at the School of Oriental and African Studies, I certainly sensed the strength of pro-Arab sentiment in intellectual circles in mid-seventies London.

The telecopier that Waters referred to might have been a Magnafax, Xerox's first commercial fax machine, introduced in 1966. See https://faxauthority.com/fax-history/ (downloaded 6 May 2016).

Chapter 16

My recollection of the bright mood in the Cairo streets in the first days of the war is confirmed by this and other US Embassy situation reports: https://wikileaks.org/plusd/ cables/1973CAIRO03094_b.html (downloaded 6 May 2016).

The First Chief Directorate was the KGB department for foreign intelligence matters. Varvara Manoukian is entirely fictitious.

Chapter 17

'*Communism is Soviet Power + Electrification*' was probably my favourite of the propaganda signs that adorned many buildings when I studied in Moscow in 1974. On the other side of the ledger, one of my Arabic teachers in London was said to have made a fortune from translating the Benson & Hedges slogan '*Yes*' into Arabic.

Chapter 18

The evacuation ship was actually the *Syria*. A colourful first-hand account of the events can be found at http://adst.org/2015/09/the-yom-kippur-war-and-an-evacuation-of-ungrateful/ (downloaded 6 May 2016). I changed the ship to the *Cynthia*, the tub I had arrived in from Piraeus a few weeks earlier. In fact, the *Cynthia* was originally considered for the evacuation, as this cable shows: https://search.wikileaks.org/plusd/ cables/1973CAIRO02997_b.html (downloaded 6 May 2016).

Chapter 19

Dzerzhinsky Square was named for Feliks Dzerzhinsky, who founded the Russian secret service. It was renamed Lubyanka Square in 1991.

Farid El-Atrache's *Yaritni Tir* can be heard at https://www.youtube.com/watch?v=oVEnmugjAEg (downloaded 6 May 2016).

Note on Arabic terms

I have rendered the Arabic terms in an English spelling that roughly represents the original pronunciation without being too visually complicated. The alternative was to use a scientifically correct representation, which would be largely incomprehensible to a lay reader.

About the author

Stuart Campbell was a university Pro-Vice Chancellor and a Professor of Linguistics before he took up writing fiction in 2011. His other books include the novels *An Englishman's Guide to Infidelity*, *Bury me in Valletta*, *The Sunset Assassin* and *The True History of Jude*, as well as the novella *Ash on the Tongue*. He is also the author of numerous academic works on Arabic-English translation, and on the Arabic component in Malay and Indonesian. Stuart lives at Manly Beach in Australia.